Cibou

A Novel

Susan Young de Biagi

Cape Breton University Press
Sydney, Nova Scotia

This book is a work of fiction which contains deliberate or accidental historical inaccuracies. The characters, places and events depicted are either products of the author's imagination or are used in a fictional context.

Cape Breton University Press recognizes the support of the Province of Nova Scotia, through the Department of Tourism, Culture and Heritage and the support received for it publishing program from the Canada Council's Block Grants Program. We are pleased to work in partnership with these bodies to develop and promote our cultural resources.

NOVA SCOTIA
Tourism, Culture and Heritage

Canada Council   Conseil des Arts
for the Arts   du Canada

Cover design by Cathy MacLean Design, Glace Bay, NS.

Printed in Canada by Transcontinental Gagné, on 100% recycled post-consumer fibre, Certified EcoLogo and processed chlorine free, manufactured using biogas energy.

Library and Archives Canada Cataloguing in Publication

Young de Biagi, Susan, 1957-
    Cibou / Susan Young de Biagi.

ISBN 978-1-897009-29-1

    I. Title.

PS8647.O89C52 2008   C813'.6   C2008-904248-4

Cape Breton University Press
PO Box 5300
1250 Grand Lake Road
Sydney, NS B1P 6L2 CA
www.cbu.ca/press

For Mark, who never stopped asking,
"When are you going to write about Captain Daniel?"

Mi'kmaq Pronunciations

Editor's notes: The following are phonetic approximations of Mi'kmaw words used in the novel; they should not be considered the definitive pronunciations. At the end of the novel, there is a glossary of terms and characters.

Cibou: from sibu – see-boo

Apukji'j: a-book-jeej
Apjelmit: up-jel-mitt
Apli'kmuj: up-lee-km-ooj
Beothuk: bee-oth-ick
Elmniket: ell-man-ee-get
E'se'ket: ay-say-get
Eune'k: ew-neg
Huronia: yer-own-ia
Jakej: jug-edge
Jijiwikate'j: jij-ee-wee-ga-tedge
Jipjawej: jip-jah-wedge
Kalkunawey: gull-koon-a-way
Ka'qaquj: gahg-a-guj
Kawi: ga-wee
Keknu'teluatl: geg-new-dell-oo-a-tl
Keptin: gep-tin
Kesasek: guess-a-sek
Kisu'lk: giz-oolg
Kitpu: geet-poo
Kloqntiej: glock-n-dee-edge
Kluskap: glue-s-cap
Ko'komin: goe-go-min
Ku'ku'kwes: goo-goo-gwess
Lentuk: len-tug
Maskwi: muss-gwee
Matues: mud-oo-ess

Me'situkwiek: may-see-dook-wee-eg
Mimikej: mim-ee-gej
Muine'j: moo-in-eyj
Najiktanteket: nah-jeek-done-tech-et
Niskam: niss-gam
Nukumi: no-go-mi
Sespewo'kwet: sess-bew-oh-gwet
Siklati: sig-la-dee
sismoqn: sis-moq-n
Siwkwewiku's: soo-gwe-ee-goose
snaweyey: snah-a-way
su'nl: soon-l
Taqtaloq: dahk-da-lock
waltes: wall-dez
Wikewiku's: wee-go-ee-goose
Wikumkewiku's: wee-goom-gew-ee-goose
Wikuom: wig-wam

Spellings of Aboriginal characters, places, etc., conform to the Smith
Francis orthography, which has been adopted officially by Mi'kmaw
Kina'matnewey, the Mi'kmaq education authority for Nova Scotia.

Cibou

Susan Young de Biagi

*I*nto the land of Kluskap came two brothers. One was saintly, the other worldly. One coveted men's souls; the other their fortunes. One I knew as completely as a woman can know a man. The other? I have not touched even the hem of his garment.

Bright Eyes once said that all good tales begin in the Long Ago, when Kluskap still walked among these mountains. Even today, the land bears the imprint of his hand. The rocks just offshore are all that remain of his canoe, smashed in a rage. Those broken islands are the maidens who dared to laugh.

Father Antoine laughed as I trembled for his safety, for our people whisper that Kluskap will one day awake to help them in their time of need. At night, I look out from my bed, to where he lies asleep under the mountains. I picture him stretching his great thighs, and throwing back the blanket of snow. Then I pray to Antoine's god, to protect our land from the coming wrath. Sometimes it is not until dawn that I feel it is safe to sleep.

My name is Marie-Ange and I have lived here below the sacred mountain since my birth. Until they came, I was named Apukji'j, in the way of our people, for the small mouse that trembles beneath the fallen leaves. Later, Antoine named me for the mother of his god, and the bright angels who attend her. There are times when I wish I had kept the name of the mouse. A little mouse does not have so far to fall.

After so many changes, it is difficult to remember that other life, before they came and changed my world forever. Of the days before I was born, I know only what my mother told me. She was a widow who lived in one of the humblest wikuoms, on the very edge of the village. In her youth, she had lost two sons and no one wanted to take a chance on her, even as a second wife. But sometimes one of the young hunters would bring her his quarry to dress. And that is how she lived, preparing the skin to make into fine clothing and receiving a little meat in return.

My father was French. Each spring, for almost a hundred years the French had arrived on our beaches, where they stretched out the fish to dry. Always I smell the faint odour of fish on the wind when I think of them.

He, my father, came only once to our land. He did not speak my mother's language, and so she could not tell him about the lost sons. She said it was good to have a man again, even one who was covered in hair and who could not speak as a civilized person. He came to her late at night, after the fish were cleaned and left just as the boats were leaving the shore. My mother was happy he came after the sun had set. She felt uneasy when he looked at her with the blue eyes of a young cougar. She wondered if, in his land, the people had completely transformed into humans. In the Long Ago, said Bright Eyes, humans and animals formed a single people, with a single language. Even today, it is whispered, some of us remain more animal than human.

My mother worried when I was born with the eyes of my father. I often felt her own eyes upon me, watching, for signs.

"You're too greedy," she would say, as I reached one too many times into the kettle, for another piece of meat. "You know that in the Long Ago, Kluskap changed the people into animals, for rushing to drink the sacred water."

That was not exactly how it happened, I knew, but I pulled back from the pot just the same.

We remained on the fringe of the village, my mother and I. With my birth, her chances of finding a husband had shrunk even further. Other women had borne a fisherman's child, but none with eyes like mine. People suddenly remembered that no one had known my mother's family. She herself had been born on the larger island, that ancient place the fishermen call Terre Neuve, meaning new. Perhaps there too, people whispered, the transformation from animal to human had not been entirely complete. To be safe, they warned their children, it was best not to get too close.

Only old Bright Eyes ignored the danger, sometimes bringing us a rabbit or a marten he had snared and staying to talk with my mother, sometimes far into the night. His real name was Kesasek but I had called him Bright Eyes since my childhood, when he would twinkle at me from across the fire. I sat at his feet as he told us about the world of Kluskap and his evil twin, Wolf. It was from these stories I learned the difference between good and evil. I listened, relieved, to hear how Kluskap had long ago banished the cannibal giants to the very edges of the world. All these things I learned from Bright Eyes. I did not, however, learn what young girls talked about as they sat round the fire, braiding each other's hair. I did not learn to recognize the secret signs that young men gave to the choice of their heart. These things were not revealed to me, the outcast. Yet, it was time. I had welcomed my monthly courses that summer.

On the morning the two brothers arrived, the entire village was asleep. All week, our men had been spearing the salmon that leaped up the river. The feasting and courting went on far into the night. As the favoured storyteller, Bright Eyes had been in great demand and so even he was yet abed that morning. I had wandered alone among the smoking fires, here and there picking up a piece of fish, flavoured with the spirit of the trees that grew in our land; here was half a cake, sprinkled with plump berries. Hair ornaments and embroidered belts also lay scattered, but these I did not touch. Much later, after they awoke and remembered the night before, their owners would come looking for them.

I did not know they were brothers. Yet, each in his own way, they stood out from the fishermen around them. One was dressed in blues and greens and yellows, as bright as a bird I had once seen perched on the rail of a French ship. Not even the shells in our wampum necklaces were as brightly coloured as this man's clothing, or glittered so brilliantly in the sun. He had black, laughing eyes, this one. It was, perhaps, best not to get too close to those eyes. Dazed, I turned to the second figure.

He was dressed all in black, in a large, heavy robe that reached to his feet. He seemed younger than the other, with blue eyes that looked carefully out at the world. Those eyes caught me kindly and steadily in their grip, quenching the desire to shrink from him. I chose instead to hunker down on the beach, watching as the fishermen pulled the boat up onto the shore. I already knew, as we all did, a few words of French. Although I listened as carefully as I could, I understood but little of the newcomers' speech, only common words like "boat" and "box." Still, I learned that the black-eyed one was named "Charles" – the black-robed one was "Antoine." Both were names I had heard before.

By this time, a crowd of children had gathered on the beach, followed by sleepy-eyed parents. Charles plunged into the crowd, letting the children stroke his clothing and finger the bright metal tools that hung from his belt. He strode up the beach, surrounded by the flock of children. Together, they formed a single large bird, with a brightly plumed head and sombre brown, chattering feathers.

The solemn brother held back. From time to time, the blue eyes turned to me, the outcast on the edge of the crowd. As he gathered up the boxes and bags from the boat, he beckoned, holding out a light bag for me to carry.

"Take the bag, Mouse," a voice beside me said. "He will need someone to guide him past the village dogs."

I turned to see our chief, standing just beyond the reach of the morning tide. It was the first time I had heard my name pass his lips. In my haste to obey, I slipped on the seaweed on the beach. The stranger was at my side at once, his hand on my elbow.

"Kwe," he said, his eyes smiling into mine.

"L'nui'sin?" I croaked in my surprise.

His look of confusion told me that, no, he did not fully understand the language of our people.

"Kwe," I said in response to his greeting, stretching my free arm out for the bag.

Later, as I stripped the feathers from the bird Bright Eyes had left us, I wondered why our chief had chosen that moment to speak to me – he who did nothing without intent. I wondered too why Antoine had chosen me out of all the people on the beach. I did not know then, that he had chosen me for the same reason I had once been rejected: my blue eyes.

k

*e*ach brother carved out his own realm among us. Charles slept on his ship, emerging each day to admiring crowds, all waiting to see what he would do next. Sometimes, he let the smallest children put on his great, black boots, laughing as they toppled over onto the sand. The large white cloths he kept in his pocket became gulls and butterflies in his clever hands. I myself saw him pull a gold coin out of our chief's ear, then laugh in admiration when the chief signalled that he would like a wooden chest full of such coins. They understood each other, those two.

The people of our village believed that Charles had powerful magic. Somehow, I sensed that Antoine's magic was stronger, and waited to see how it would manifest. I would sit and work on my skins, watching as he began to learn our ways. He was the first to try and live as we did. Unlike the fishermen, who slept in square dwellings of poles, Antoine slept in a small wikuom he built himself. To be sure, it was not like any wikuom we had ever seen. Its frame was shaky and it was covered with sheets of bark simply thrown on top, not sewn neatly together with sinew as ours were. The women of the village would have been happy to help him, but there was something about him that kept people from offering.

The most surprising thing about this house was the bed. As we did, Antoine had cut spruce boughs, then entwined them together to form a cushion. But where our cushions were soft and yielding, his retained the branches' hard spines. Early the next morning, everyone in the village found a reason to be near his wikuom, to see how he had fared on this strange bed. Yet he showed no signs of fatigue as he performed his morning chants. Up and down in front of his house he walked, a small black book in his hand.

That book! Bright Eyes and I tried to ascertain its magic. And magic it certainly was, for it was Antoine's most precious possession. Bright Eyes said he used the book to call on the spirit world for help. Its markings, he said, were like the sacred symbols used by the shamans to encode their chants and rituals.

"Once," said Bright Eyes, "I even heard him whisper the name, 'Kisu'lk'."

Susan Young de Biagi

It was our name for the Creator.

I thought Bright Eyes was mistaken. I had seen Antoine's face when the people spoke of our gods. It was the look our chief made when he spoke of the people to the south, they of the bristling war feathers and the harsh tongue that grated on our ears.

Bright Eyes and I always spent our mornings together, he arriving with a special treat gathered along the way: a handful of the nuts I liked so well; a cluster of tiny, sour grapes; a sack full of winkles to cook in the ashes. Bright Eyes was a resolute visitor and I a small shadow at his side as he made his rounds through the village.

These days, we stopped first at Antoine's fireside. Bright Eyes would catch Antoine's gaze, then roll his eyes towards me, as if humouring a child who begged to see a whale jump. I, in turn, hovered at Bright Eyes's elbow as though the old man could not manage a step without me. The truth was, each of us came for our own sake. Antoine was entertaining.

Our first visit began awkwardly. Unable to speak each other's language, both men pulled out the contents of their pockets, for the other to examine. Bright Eyes displayed his shark's tooth embedded with a small human bone, a stone in which waves of the sea had been forever frozen and a piece of black rock with white stars, that had fallen from the sky. Antoine carried a small metal knife that leapt out of a handle of bone, a small pot of horrid yellow paste that he smeared on his meat and a piece of crystal that made an ant look as big as a beetle. Bright Eyes and I spent much of the morning holding the crystal over blades of grass, grains of sand and the tiny lines of our own palms.

We did not like everything we saw. One morning, Antoine pulled a large white cloth out of his pocket and forcefully blew the contents of his nose into it. Then carefully folding the cloth into a tiny package, he put it into his pocket. We made our escape as politely as we could. Once alone, it was some time before we could speak.

"Do they all do that?" I asked.

"I think not. I have seen the fishermen expel the contents of their nose in this way, but they usually blow it onto the sand. Even they do not carry it on their person."

"What do you think he does with it?"

I did not wait for an answer, for by then an even more frightening thought had occurred to me. "Do you ... do you think he saves all his body wastes in this way?"

Bright Eyes considered for a moment, then shook his head. "No, for we would surely smell them on him. He must have a special purpose for the wastes of his nose."

If so, I hoped I would never discover what it was. My mind kept returning to the little pot of yellow paste, until I learned it contained no more than seeds ground to a powder and mixed with acid.

Though distressed by his habits, I kept going to Antoine's fireside. More and more I went alone, for Bright Eyes often waved me off, claiming his were old bones. I suspected there were other reasons.

By now, Antoine was used to me following him throughout the village. Sometimes, he would share his food with me, giving me a hard cake to gnaw. It had no fat, as ours did, but I was hungry and ate it anyway. Antoine seemed to prefer it to our own cakes, redolent with moose fat and sweet with berries. "Biscuit," he called it. "Kalkunawey," I responded in my own language, knowing he would nod and scratch a symbol onto a piece of birchbark. I did not understand the magic of symbols, but I carved the strange word into my mind, pressing down deeply so it would stay there – "biscuit, biscuit." In this way, we began to learn each other's language. My way seemed to work better than his. I could reach into my mind for the word more quickly than he could find the symbol in his book. More and more, we two spoke in his language, though he continued to practise our words with the other children who spent part of every day with us.

Slowly, as I grew to know Antoine, I learned a frightening truth about the newcomers and their language. In their world, "He Who Travels by Night" was simply "moon," a strange, flat word. The idea slowly grew in my mind that, to them, the being that strode so brilliantly and confidently across the sky was nothing more than a shiny flat disk, with no more power to charm or inspire than the mirror that hung from Charles's belt.

I understood more than they, I who had just come into my monthly courses. The waters that flowed in me responded to the call of He Who Travels by Night in the same way as the waters of the channel beyond our village. But Antoine knew nothing of these things. Unlike his brother, he turned his eyes away from our women. I, his shadow, was the only one who could get close to him. And I felt not even the lightest of touches on my arm.

Charles often watched us, black eyes thoughtful. Yet he never joined us. Each brother had claimed a part of Cibou for himself. Antoine lived in the village, slowly learning the language and getting to know the people. Charles stayed on the beach, supervising the cleaning of one of the smaller boats, used for coasting round the island. The boat had been hauled up past the water line, where it lay tipped on its side like a dead whale. Bright yellow strips of new wood stood out sharply against the deep gray of the old. Then it all disappeared under a layer of thick, sticky tar that the fishermen boiled in vast kettles.

Charles asked some of our men to help repair the boat. Skilled in the ways of watercraft, they ran their hands over the smooth planks, testing the strength of the keel and the delicacy of the lines. The fishermen, happy for once to have someone else to fetch and carry, saw them only as labourers, but Charles recognized them for what they were: serious students who wished to learn the secrets of these new craft. In his eyes, I saw an idea take hold and grow.

From then on, Charles began working more closely with our men. Some of the youngest and strongest were allowed onto his big ship anchored in the bay. Later, around the large fire, they boasted about climbing to the very top of the vessel.

"The sails are attached to a large tree that is stripped of its branches and polished to a fine smoothness. Every morning, we compete to see who will scale it the fastest," said Taqtaloq. I had known him since childhood. A member of a chiefly family, he was also a bully who had pinned me to the ground and sat on me because he was strong enough to do so, and because I had no brother to challenge him. Now, as a fine young warrior laden with trophies, he simply ignored me as one too lowly to notice. That night, he sat in all his slim strength, absently stroking his hair, sleek with fragrant oil and decorated with shells and feathers. Underneath the smooth self-assured exterior, I could see the same gross spirit I had feared as a child.

"You should see it, Uncles," cried another young man, not waiting for the customary nod to speak. "From so far above, we feel like giants, peering over you just as you would peer into an anthill. Not since Kluskap strode over these hills have any of our people received such a view of the world!"

The older men shifted uneasily. Things were changing. Before the brothers' arrival, the young men had passed their time studying the old ways. Some sat with the hunters, chipping fine stone into deadly points and crafting light feathers onto lethal missiles. Young men of the chiefly line had spent their time with the shaman, learning the discreet art of governing with a light hand. Now all were drawn to the shore, where Charles Daniel was teaching them to fire the bright muskets he kept locked in his ship.

Charles was striding among them, laughing every time one of them fired awry and clapping them fondly on the shoulders every time the bullet hit its mark. The young men were beginning to look upon him as they looked upon the shaman, seeking his approval for every action.

Like the Elders, the fishermen were also uneasy as they watched the small group on the shore.

"I don't see as it's a good idea to teach them boys how to shoot," grumbled Johann, the shore master. Antoine had withdrawn to his wikuom, and I returned to another favourite activity: helping the fishermen shred old rope to stuff between the planks of the boats. Johann's fingers were too twisted for the task, but he sat and smoked his pipe as he watched the other men. No one paid any attention to me. They would not have thought I could penetrate the quickness of their speech.

"They'll turn those guns on us one day," Johann nodded grimly. He turned and shot a long black stream of tobacco juice to a point just beyond my bare foot. I pulled my toes in under my robe.

"Captain Daniel knows what he's about," said Pierrot. "He'll keep those guns trained on the English."

Small and dark, Pierrot saw and understood more than the others. I leaned forward to catch his next words.

"He'll never let them sail into this gulf. Between the two of them, him and his brother, they will claim this land for God and the King of France. Not necessarily in that order," he chuckled. At this, the other men looked uneasy and quickly touched their hands to their forehead, chest and shoulders, in the magic sign they used against evil spirits.

"Claim this land," they had said. Later, when I asked the meaning of the word "claim," Antoine said that it meant to take for your own. I thought about that all night, as I lay beside my mother in our wikuom. How could anyone take the land for their own? Like the sky, it was too vast to be held or contained. And like the sea, it had its own laws, which we must live by or die. Exhausted from grappling with a concept too strange to comprehend, I fell asleep. I would remember my thoughts of that night.

𝓴

𝓽he days went on, stretching into Wikewiku's, the time of fat animals that the fishermen called Octobre. Shining down from the sky, Niskam's warm fingers played over the earth, turning the long grasses into gold and setting the leaves afire.

I studied the waves as they rippled over the surface of the blue waters, trying to capture the design and hold it in my mind. The waves were the exact blue of the tiny, precious shells that our women weave into belts of wampum. Carefully sewn into bags of soft skin, these shells arrived over trading routes set down by our people in the Long Ago. As a child, my mother would give me some sinew and a few imperfect beads, encouraging me to create my own designs.

"Look at the world," she would say, "and read the message that the Creator has etched into rock and tree and sky. Then write the message in wampum, so that others may share your vision."

In my mind, I tried to see the waves as they would appear in wampum: blue waters white-knuckled as they lift themselves skyward in a vain effort to reach the one who made them. From above, Niskam will smile at them, shimmering in his joy. It is not success, but the attempt, that pleases him.

The fishermen, too, were watching the waves. An urgency was upon them to leave, before the winter gales made it impossible. The hard, dry fish, burned white by the sun, was stacked in piles, ready to load onto the ships. Kettles of fermented spruce were bubbling on the fire. Before our people taught them to make this drink, many fishermen did not survive their stay in our land. The hard biscuits they lived on made their teeth fall out and their skin turn black. Now, they were careful to load wooden kegs of the spruce drink onto the ships, in case of shipwreck or delay.

Charles was also preparing to leave. Taking one of the tables on which they cleaned the fish, he had it scrubbed clean and covered with a white cloth. Another cloth flapped above his head, protecting him from Niskam's reach.

Hunters arrived from all over the island, bringing him the furs they had caught and cured in their villages. As each fur was laid out before him, he thrust his fingers into its depths, then scratched signs into the large white book that rested on the table. As Charles savoured the feel of the fur, the hunters' eyes strayed to the piles of thick white blankets beside him. Iron knives and gleaming copper kettles were laid out in orderly rows on the beach. Even now, I was sure, each hunter could hear the parting words of his wife, as she told him to be sure and bring home one of these kettles.

Nearby, some fishermen were doing some trading of their own. While their goods were not as fine as Charles's, they offered what they could. Our people were just as eager to supply them with their old furs, softened to a fine sheen by time and wear. As Antoine and I sat watching each group covet the possessions of the other, my eye was caught by a flash in the trees. It was Amassit who had sold even his robe, and was running naked. Looking quickly away, I saw old Johann for the first time without the red kerchief he always wore on his forehead. Another fisherman had traded his golden tooth. Much later, I saw it hanging around the neck of one of our hunters.

I was glad our people would soon return to hunting for food, while the French returned to their own land. Antoine would not be among them, for he planned to stay the winter with us. Just as she did for the young hunters, my mother helped him prepare his winter clothing. She made his breeches and long cloak, while I worked on his moccasins. Each moccasin was made from a single skin, removed in one piece from the leg of a young moose.

I had been careful not to let Antoine see me working on them. Instead, I sat with my mother, or among the other young maidens who were curing skins for their betrothed. It was the first time that I ventured to take my place in this circle. The maidens knew I had no betrothed: none of the young hunters wished to take a chance on mixing my blood with theirs. But the young women still made room for me as I advanced shyly, Antoine's skins in hand.

"Taqtaloq says my beading is the finest he's ever seen," said Mimikej, flipping her long black hair behind her shoulders, in a gesture of pride.

"Then he is blind with love," giggled her cousin Maskwi. "Wait until you're married and his vision suddenly clears. If I were you, I would take extra lessons from Mouse, to prepare for that sad day."

I ducked my head, as everyone turned to look at the beadwork on Antoine's skins. I was working on a half-moon, in white and deep violet beads.

Mimikej was not happy to see the attention diverted from herself.

"Well there's more to marriage than beadwork," she said, crossing her arms and sitting back to watch the reaction. Instantly, she had the complete attention of all the girls.

"Have you ever seen the stags in rutting season?" she went on. "Thin, gaunt, barely able to keep their eyes open? Taqtaloq wouldn't notice if I decorated his clothing with the last of the summer's berries!"

The rest of the girls hooted, casting bold glances at the group of young men, as they took turns shooting the muskets, chests bare even at this time of year. I could see by the stiffness of their necks that they were aware of the girls' laughter.

Our women had the reputation of being insatiable. Whenever they retired to the women's wikuom for five days each moon, their husbands made loud remarks about how they could finally get some rest. Among all the peoples on this coast, our women were the most sought after as brides.

I wondered what the European women were like. Most of the fishermen, I knew, had left wives behind. Each day, as they watched the waves, I felt their strong desire to be back in their own land. But Antoine had no wife. One day, after I had gathered up enough courage to ask, he shook his head and pointed to the cross around his neck. I understood what this meant. Among his own people, Antoine was a shaman.

I often saw him sitting apart with the fishermen, performing magic rites to cure them of their illnesses. I knew, from our own customs, that young men who wished to be shamans practised chastity during the time of their apprenticeship. Antoine, no doubt, had not yet completed his period of trial and testing.

I was content for it to be so. After their apprenticeship, shamans tended to marry quickly, with few of the usual courtship rituals. Among themselves, the women whispered that it was a good time for an ungainly woman, or one of low status, to find a husband.

All this I pondered in my heart, as I sat sewing Antoine's moccasins.

k

*M*eanwhile, our friendship grew. Antoine seemed not to mind helping me with my woman's work. Nor did our hunters chastise him for it: few among us would dare to reproach a shaman. One day we were helping to repair the fish fences at the mouth of the stream. Our women were trying to work quickly, before the tide turned. Antoine was hopeless in this, as in most tasks. While he had the strength to pound in the stakes, he did not possess the art of weaving the strips of wood close enough so the fish could not pass through. In the end, I had him simply pass me the strips as I wove them.

"How does it work Mouse?" he asked haltingly.

"The fish float over the fence as the waters rush in. Later, as the waters recede, they are trapped in the shallows, and easy prey for our hunters."

The river was swirling around our knees when we finished. Later, as night fell, our men would gather on the bank, one holding a torch as the other took aim with his spear. One of my favourite memories from childhood was watching the long row of lights along the riverbank at night.

These days, Bright Eyes was too busy with the hunters to spend long hours before the fire. Now, instead of listening to tales of Kluskap, I heard stories of Antoine's god. Like Kluskap, he was the son of the Creator, sent to conquer evil. But while Kluskap had banished the evil giants to the very edge of the world, Antoine's god had defeated them by his death. How, I asked myself, could one defeat evil by dying? This I could not understand, nor could Antoine explain it to me then.

Both gods had vowed to return one day. I once had a dream that the two were playing a game of waltes long into the night. The silence was heavy and thick, broken only by the occasional click of the bone dice into the wooden bowl. All the people, both hunters and fishermen, were standing behind them, silent, waiting to see the outcome. The fishermen stood behind their god, at a respectful distance, while the hunters gathered around Kluskap. Stretching far out beyond each group, as far as the eye could see, were the dead.

I myself stood silently between the two groups. I knew I would have to make my choice soon, before the game ended and the winner declared. I wished to join Antoine, yet each time I decided to make a move, I felt the silent plea of my ancestors, willing me to cross to their side. I stretched my neck to see which opponent had the greater number of counting sticks, but the small piles were blocked from my view.

Few of these battles, fought out in the dream world, disturbed my waking mind. The days flowed placidly around us, as we filled baskets with smoked fish and dried berries. The fishermen would soon be gone, and we would withdraw to the deep forests. There, under the canopy of trees, we would be protected from the cold winds and freezing droplets that blew in from the sea.

One day, after Bright Eyes returned, he and I set off for the high meadows, to gather the hard red berries known to us as su'nl. On our way, we saw the fisherman known as Raphael standing on the edge of a deep pool, fishing with hook and line.

A newcomer, Raphael burned with a strange fire, one that burned most brightly in the presence of Antoine. I often saw him leap to help as Antoine struggled to lift a heavy burden, or tie up a boat. When not watching Antoine, Raphael spent much of his time fingering the heavy beads he carried at his waist. But now, it seemed, he had found a new pastime.

"He has been here for many days," Bright Eyes whispered as we passed by the pool. "Let us not disturb him. Every man, even a stranger, needs a quiet place in which to think."

Silent and deep, the pool was a favourite among our people. Fine, leafy trees and a large overhanging rock gave shade to the fish who returned every year to deliver up their young.

More and more, Raphael sought out this peaceful place. While the other fishermen sat in circles, mending nets and singing songs, he escaped into the forest, carrying a log taken from the beach or a few scraps of metal. Before long, he had fashioned himself a wooden dwelling. Some nights, he even slept there.

While the other men were ignorant of Raphael's doings, nothing escaped Pierrot's black eyes. One day, he too was gone from the circle. Bright Eyes and I happened upon him on our way to the berry fields. Fishing in the pool with a mischievous smile on his face, Pierrot waved gaily as we passed.

It was not long before we heard the shouting.

"Thought you'd steal my salmon, did you? Followed me here, like the sneak you are."

Bright Eyes's hand on my shoulder, we retraced our steps to the pool. By the time we arrived, Raphael was sitting on Pierrot's chest, knees gripping his neck. Pierrot, red-faced, was trying to heave himself up.

"Those fish are mine! I was the first to stake this claim. That shack is proof of it!"

Pierrot struggled to get his breath.

"It was a joke. I was trying to rile you."

"Have you never heard the eighth commandment, "Thou shall not steal. Thou shall not steal?" Raphael's neck looked like it was about to burst.

We, an old man and a girl, were helpless to intervene. I was turning to run for help when I felt Bright Eyes's hand on my arm. Raphael had rolled off Pierrot, who had scrambled a safe distance away before calling out:

"One day, Raphael, that temper will be your destruction." Pierrot stepped aside just as a stone whistled by his head.

Bright Eyes and I quickly made our way back to the berry fields, where we sat for long moments, shaken. I was the first to speak, translating the men's words to Bright Eyes

"I do not understand, Bright Eyes? What was stolen?"

"I do not know. They can have no claim on the fish, who offer themselves to one man or another as they choose."

And though we bent our minds to the task, we could not explain the strange behaviour.

*

"**W**ell, what do think of old Raphael, making such a fuss over a bit of fish?"

Pierrot had come upon me as I was cleaning ferns for the pot, their delicate green heads curled shyly onto the stems. I moved quickly to scoop them out of Pierrot's way as he flung himself down beside me.

"He must have been very hungry."

It was the only explanation Bright Eyes and I could offer.

Pierrot shook his head. "No, not hungry, angry – that I dared dip a line in his pool. Course, I knew he'd taken a liking to it. But there must be thousands of such pools in this huge, empty land."

Had I heard the word properly? In my understanding, "empty" meant without contents, as when as a kettle holds nothing of what it was meant to contain. But our land was filled with every good thing it was created to hold: fish and game, trees of every kind. Bright Eyes, who loved trees, said it would take his lifetime and mine to see even one of every kind.

To be sure, I repeated the word to Pierrot.

"Yes empty, not used, as it was meant to be. Look, Mouse, at all the land your people are not using. One day, we will show you how to clear it, so you can plant vast plantations of corn and tobacco. You can build fences to protect it."

As soon as he left, I fled to Bright Eyes.

"Pierrot says our land is not being used."

The old eyes that looked up at me were amused, serene.

"Of course it is not being used. It is being held."

I sagged to the ground in relief. Of course, of course, he would have the answer.

"Held for whom?"

"For whomever wanders onto it. For whomever has the wisdom and skill to take what he needs while leaving it safe for the next wanderer. So it was with our ancestors, and so it will be for the generations yet unborn."

I thought, as I snuggled down beside him, how Bright Eyes could always keep the shadows away. But later, alone on my boughs, I could not forget the look of excitement on Pierrot's face as he described the vast fields of corn and tobacco.

◆

*t*he day finally came when the fleet of boats was ready to set off. The small fishing boats huddled close to Charles's large ship like a bevy of small ducklings. Antoine explained to me that out there on the waves other ships, like birds of prey, were waiting to swoop down upon them.

The morning before the boats sailed, Charles and Antoine spent a long time walking up and down the beach together. Charles seemed caught between the desire to sail and his concern at leaving his brother. As Charles stepped into the longboat, four of the young warriors he had taught to shoot stepped up behind Antoine, forming a protective guard. Antoine seemed not to notice their presence, as he watched his brother sail away. Turning, he strode up the beach and ducked into his wikuom. I did not see him for the rest of that day.

Few people except his new guards and me noticed Antoine's withdrawal. Our people were too busy preparing for the move into the forest, planned for the next day. Overwrought with excitement, children and dogs raced through the village, tipping over kettles and scattering bundles. In vain, mothers called to gather them together for the trip.

With the morning sun and with one last call over their shoulders, the mothers set off, knowing their children would either catch up or travel with another family. Among our people, children are welcome at all firesides. There, they know they will find a woman like their own mother, fussing to wipe their noses and make sure they have enough to eat. I have seen some children stay away for as long as a moon, travelling from wikuom to wikuom, tasting another's cooking and listening to favourite stories told in new ways.

Eventually, however, they begin to long for the unique smell and soft breast of the woman who bore them. Returning home, they savour the bowl of warm stew thrust upon them, and the feel of their mother's hands in their hair.

My mother and I took down our wikuom together, carefully rolling the sheets of birchbark then piling them on our small sled. I pulled, while my mother helped push over the rough areas.

When we arrived at our new campsite, my mother's first act was to take out the giant clamshell she carried with her and un-wind the sinew that bound it together. There, nestled between layers of clay lay the coals from our last fire. The wind blew cold as my mother bowed over the hot coals, shielding them with her slight body. Nestling the coals in some dry moss, she blew on them until she was rewarded with the small but stalwart flame – the same flame she had first struck as a bride and carried over the years, from shore to forest, forest to shore. Trapped in the coal, it had made this journey more times than I.

"I remember him sitting there, watching as I lit my first fire," she said, speaking of the young husband who had died so many years before. "My hands were shaking as I struck the stones to-gether. I watched for that first spark as if our happiness, our life together depended on it. There we sat, admiring it as we would our child. It is the only living thing we ever made together."

Hands on knees, my mother leaned back, watching the fire. As quietly as I could, I slipped away.

I did not see Antoine that day or the next, but he finally ap-peared at the large, communal fire, lit to celebrate our arrival at the new camp. It was the first time he had joined the village in one of our feasts. I was anxious to see what would happen and I did not have long to wait.

Bright Eyes was telling a long tale about Nukumi, Kluskap's woodchuck grandmother. It was she who had taught him the difference between good and evil.

Antoine had been sitting quietly, scratching marks onto his birchbark. At the end of Bright Eyes's tale, he looked up.

"Jesus had a grandmother. Her name was Ann."

He went on calmly scratching onto his birchbark.

The people around the fire sat back in surprise. They knew, from hearing him at prayer, that Jesus was the name of Antoine's god. But until now, I had been the only one to hear Antoine's tales. Cloaking their surprise, the Elders nodded in careful respect, giving this grandmother the esteem due an Elder.

"Did she come from the sky, as a bolt of lightening?" asked the chief. With his stomach full and his people safely settled, the manner of her coming mattered little to the chief. This was a ruse, designed to draw the story out of the teller. We watched to see how Antoine would react.

He took a moment to consider the question.

"No, she was born in the usual way. As was her daughter, Mary. But Ann had raised Mary to be such a virtuous maiden that the Creator chose her to bear his son."

Here Antoine stopped, struggling to find the right words in our language. "He sent a heavenly creature with bright silver wings to obtain Mary's consent."

"Ma'li, Ma'li," we whispered, struggling with the maiden's name. Then, one thought swept the group and we turned in a body to Antoine. It was Bright Eyes who formed the question.

"But the Creator has no human form. How was the act accomplished?"

"As a thought in the Creator's mind," Antoine answered. "The child was formed in the moment the maiden said yes."

The chief's wife broke in. "And the child was given to Grandmother to raise, just as Nukumi raised Kluskap," she said triumphantly. All the grandmothers in the circle nodded their heads. It was only right that such a special child be raised by wisdom and age.

"No," said Antoine. "The chief, an evil man, sent orders to kill the child. The child's mother and the husband chosen for her had to flee in the night, far away from their village."

Here was a startling thought: an evil chief. Our own chiefs were chosen only after many years of careful observation, only when the Elders were convinced of his worth. The chief who sat beside us now wore the thinnest of robes. Each time his wife made him a new thick robe, he gave it to a widow or an orphan in our village. His wife complained loudly to all who would listen, but we knew her secret pride in her husband.

Having examined this thought, our minds turned to the desperate flight of the young couple. How could the Creator allow an infant and his young parents to be driven away, perhaps to the edges of the world where giants roamed?

We made our way to our beds, each of us rapt in thoughts of such a journey and its dangers. We were content to have the story end as it did. The best storytellers let the threads hang, for us to pick up and weave into our dreams. Adolescent boys would fight beside the valiant young husband, as he slew the cannibals at the edge of the world. Maidens would dream of the exalted young mother, who carried such a special child in her arms. Grandmothers would sit with Ma'li's mother, Ann, left behind to wait and worry.

I dreamt of Antoine. Tonight, he had won himself a place around the fire. Eager to compare the reality with their dreams, the people would ask him to continue the story for many nights to come. I saw myself at his side, watching the shadows on his face and dreaming of the time when his apprenticeship should end.

The next morning I arose eager for the day to pass and the night to come. So occupied was I with my thoughts that I did not at first notice the barking of the dogs. Gradually, however, I saw the dogs were racing from all directions, to a clearing on the edge of the camp.

The two hunters who stood on the edge of the clearing had deliberately walked upwind, knowing our dogs would signal an early alarm. Well-trained, the dogs stood in a semi-circle around the strangers, barking. They would go no closer, unless the visitors showed aggression. Knowing this, the newcomers showed no fear, but waited quietly for our chief to appear.

At any other time, I would have been excited by the arrival of neighbouring hunters, with its promise of feasting and new stories. Today I was angry, knowing that Antoine's stories would have to wait. The chief would be eager to learn any news brought by the hunters. In resignation, I carefully erased all traces of frustration from my mind. Even in all the excitement, someone might sense it and remark upon it afterwards.

The newcomers spoke a language similar to, yet different from ours. "Broken speakers" we called them, for they seemed to swallow whole parts of words. Bright Eyes says that in the Long Ago, our two peoples spoke the same language and that the others changed their speech after a quarrel, so that we could not understand them. If so, the ruse failed, for by listening closely we could understand their language, just as they could understand ours.

Any quarrels between our people and theirs must have been resolved long ago. For as long as anyone can remember, our emissaries have sat at their council fires, discussing problems common to our people. Should we ever forget the ties that bind us, we have only to look to the wampum, where the promises of friendship are encoded for all time in the pattern of the shells.

The two young hunters carried messages for our chief and council, who retired to the sacred circle just beyond the village. In this way, if the news was shocking, they would have time to ponder it, before presenting it to the people. Today, however, no one worried that the news was bad. The youth of the messengers, and their arrival in early winter, suggested they wished to spend the season among us. Should anyone have the boldness to ask, they would no doubt reply that they wished to improve their knowledge of our language. Yet we knew that they really came in search of brides. Sometimes, it happened that a village did not have enough maidens of a suitable age, and young hunters were forced to seek wives elsewhere. Of all women, ours were most famous for their ability to satisfy their husbands.

There were various reactions to their arrival. The young virgins bent their heads over their beadwork to hide their excitement. Both men were strong and handsome. More importantly, each wore fine skins, lovingly decorated by a mother or sister. From this, we knew they were not alone in the world.

"Aie! They look like younger brothers," said Maskwi, who had crept up and was standing at my elbow. Everyone knew that younger brothers were petted in the family, and that their betrothed could expect to be showered with fine gifts. I shook my head at this sign of wishful thinking. Already, the girls were weaving dreams around these two young men.

Even the maidens with suitors were excited by their presence. Any pretended interest in the newcomers would make their own betrothed more attentive, and more eager to marry quickly. Our own young men were not so pleased with the visitors' arrival, as they saw themselves competing for a prize they thought won. It would not do, of course, to display open aggression. But they could look forward to wrestling matches, in which to display their strength and agility. Muscles were flexed in anticipation.

Everyone in the village looked forward to a winter of flirtations, and a host of weddings when we returned to the shore. But it was not to be. Just two days after their arrival, one of the young men fell sick. His companion joined him the next day. We were horrified. What if these young men died, and we had to carry their bodies back to their village? How great our shame, when we confessed our inability to protect these beloved sons and brothers.

In desperation, the entire village gathered at their bedside, hoping that the shaman might draw on our strength to cure them. In vain, we laid cool hands on them, to arrest the hot red tide that washed over their skin. But we could not stop them in their determination to reach the Land of the Ancestors. The first spirit departed at dawn, the next at nightfall.

A wail arose. We tore our garments and rubbed red ochre on our faces and our arms. We were not able to save them, but we could honour them and their families with our grief. We painted the bodies and gave them our finest weapons as grave gifts, to use in the kill. The families would at least have the comfort of knowing that the young men would not go hungry in the next world.

After five days of mourning, the chief chose twenty of our finest young men to bring the bodies back to the families. But on the very day they were to leave, two of these men fell sick. Afterwards, the sickness struck everyone. Some recovered, some did not. The very old and the very young did not survive. In vain, mothers tried to hide young children. Even the shaman, with all his magic, did not escape. He did not die well. Cowering against the wall of his wikuom, he screamed that the spirits were feeding on his blood.

Of all the people, only Antoine and I escaped the sickness completely. No one was surprised that I prevailed – I of animal blood. The dogs, they said, also remained healthy. But what was the source of Antoine's strength? We had seen, with our own eyes, how weak his people were. They could not endure the cold, as we could. They wore many layers of cloth and still shivered, while our hunters proudly displayed bare skin under their cloaks. Our men strode barefoot into icy streams, to hunt salmon, while the fishermen huddled around fires on the bank.

During the time of portage, they stopped once each hour to rest, drinking kettlefuls of the strong black tea they carried with them, made from a leaf unknown in Cibou.

As engaging as bear cubs, they could be both comic and harmless, as they struggled with the simplest aspects of daily life. Yet, like bear cubs, they too were trailed by a lumbering shadow of death and danger. We watched with dismay as they fought among themselves. It was not uncommon to see a fisherman draw a knife against one of his own. Always, our people hung back, afraid of being afflicted with the same madness that sat so plainly and so heavily upon the fishermen.

Even with Antoine, people had kept their distance. But now the sick opened their hearts to him. To the children whose mothers were dead, he gave a warm, maternal love. To the warriors, he was the humble and discreet servant, who bore away their soiled garments, burying them at night in the forest. To the grandmothers, he was the devoted elder son, who lovingly returned the attention received as a child.

As mothers mourned their children, rocking their bodies and keening in their grief, Antoine would sit nearby, his head slung so low it seemed weighted. Later, when they were ready to hear it, his voice reached out, to charm and to comfort. To the heavy-hearted, it seemed the one bright spot in a dark world.

We spent long vigils together, I holding the vessel of water as he wiped the faces of the sick and stroked their burning temples. Even in the midst of such misery, I welcomed this time with him. I was a silent witness as he comforted the sick with stories of his god, who walked among the people and cured them. Several times, said Antoine, he even brought the dead to life.

k

i presented the moccasins to Antoine just before the snows came. It did not happen in the way I had imagined it, all those hours when I worked on those moccasins in the circle of maidens. His thanks were kind and warming, but his eyes were preoccupied. His mind, I knew, still lay with the sick as they struggled on their deathbeds. Having seen him as all things to all people, I knew that he could never devote himself to one woman, as a husband. My dream began to die.

*A*nd yet our comradeship continued as before. A special time for us was the hour after our evening meal, when the burden of the day was lifted. At such times, we chatted quietly or sat side by side, wrapped in a cloud of thought. I bent my mind to the task of understanding this sickness that had come upon us. If ever there was a time for Kluskap to come and save his people, it is now, I thought. But the gods don't listen to the opinions of young girls or little mice.

Antoine did not spend his evenings as I did, brow furrowed. Sadness lay heavy upon him like a cloak, but so did acceptance. The sickness had come upon us like rain and Antoine always lifted his face to the rain in the same way he lifted it to the sun. When I could stand it no more, I asked him his thoughts about this thing that had killed my people. Even our enemies to the south, with their murderous forays, had never wrought such destruction on our land.

"Well, it is a burden common to man. In France, there are whole buildings, hospitals we call them, devoted to the care of the sick. As novices, we are called upon to serve in these hospitals when choosing our vocation. I did not have the gift that some of us have – Jesuit doctors are the finest in the world – so I chose to teach in one of our colleges instead. During these past weeks, I have been thankful for the training I received."

He had seen this sickness before. Yet I had never heard of such a thing. Nor, I was sure, had Bright Eyes, keeper of our tales. Such stories, had they existed, would surely have appeared at our firesides. Not even Ku'ku'kwes herself, wisest of our healers, had ever spoken of such a calamity as this.

"It is the intention of my order, that is to say my brothers who are to come, to build hospitals in this land, as we have in all the others. Already, there are those who eagerly await their chance to sail to this country. May they come quickly, for I cannot fight this sickness on my own. Even the water was a problem...." He interrupted his musings to smile at me. "Though heaven knows, Mouse, you wore yourself thin in the service of your people, trudging back and forth to the river under the weight of those buckets."

Astonishment piled upon astonishment. Not only had Antoine seen this before, he expected to see it again, here in our land, where such a thing had likely never happened before.

Antoine was still speaking. "We, the Jesuits, wage a continual war against all the ancient enemies: leprosy, scrofula, bloody flux...."

The words themselves took shape in my mind, ranging themselves across my line of vision like a row of evil giants. Even "hospital" was an ugly word, though Antoine spoke of it as a place of healing. I glanced at him now, sitting there so meek and serene. Antoine would never wish his ancient enemies upon us. But there was a danger in landing on our shores, he and his kind, laden with answers to problems that did not yet exist.

I was afraid to voice the thought, and yet I could not keep silent. "How does it come among us, Antoine, this sickness? Does it fall from the sky? And why did it descend first upon the broken speakers?"

Antoine was surprised by my question. "Surely your people become ill, Mouse?"

Well, yes. The very oldest among us suffered from pain in their feet, to the point almost where they could not walk. And it sometimes happened, very rarely, that one of us will harbour a growth in the stomach, an evil thing that begins in the gut and grows until it bursts, killing its host. But such things begin in the body, among a very few. They do not descend from the skies, as this one seemed to, upon all of us at once. I told Antoine so.

"Then what is different here?" he asked, as though to himself. "You are always on the move. Perhaps it is difficult for disease to find a harbour among you." He seemed to plunge ever deeper into thought. "And yet it has come to you now."

It had. The first of the giants had descended upon us – and if Antoine's words were true, more would follow. Our people were only now beginning to recover from this scourge. Could I tell them of what was to come? I could not: they were too weak. Even Bright Eyes had not yet arisen from his boughs. And so I remained quiet. But it was a weighty secret for a young girl to carry. I did not know then it was just the first of many.

*i*t was Siwkwewiku's – spawning moon. In normal times, this month of freezing nights and warm days is a time of celebration, when we capture the sweet juice of the snaweyey tree. The sweet crystals glitter on children's lips and fingers, and even the smallest babies are given hard lumps to suck. Their mothers say it comforts them in their slumber, and indeed it must be so, for I have seen their tiny lips moving even as they sleep, as though still savouring the sweet taste.

Normally, it is our women who pierce the trees, while the hunters go in pursuit of the animals. But the sickness had taken so many of our women that the chief had decreed that everyone who could walk, including the warriors, proceed to the tree stand with reeds and wooden buckets. We trudged slowly over the snow on our wooden frames bound with sinew.

Antoine was with us in this, as in every activity. Swaying awkwardly on new frames – a gift from the chief – he followed as I made my rounds of the trees assigned to me. He watched closely as I notched the sun side of each tree with my knife, then pushed a sharpened reed into the hole. Over the reed, I hung a small bucket made of the tree's own wood. Any other wood would darken the flavour.

When we returned to collect the sap the next day, Antoine looked excitedly into the bucket.

"It's just water."

I laughed at the face he made, so like that of a child robbed of a treat.

"No Antoine, it is the spirit of the tree. And like all spirits, it can take many, many forms. You will see"

I tipped the liquid into a larger vessel slung at my hip, returned the bucket to the tree, and trudged over to the great communal kettles, where the older women were tending the fires. These fires would burn until the sap finally turned white and bitter, marking the end of the season. A good run could last more than a moon.

My next task was to turn the stones in the fire until they were white hot, then plunge them in the kettle. As they cooled, I scooped them out to replace them with more stones, keeping the sap at a constant boil. It was a long, hot chore.

Antoine's task – even more tiring than mine – was to keep away from the fire the small children who had survived the sickness. Gathering them round, he sang a French song about a small bird who had followed a star to the birthplace of a king. The fire was soon forgotten as the children flapped their arms and crossed their fingers over their head to make stars. In the way of children, they asked Antoine to sing it over and over, until I knew every word. Later, he told me the song was a noel.

Antoine was hoarse long before the sap thickened. He was rescued at mid-day, when the children were carried sleepily off. Antoine looked as though he too would like nothing better than to curl up beneath the trees. But he pulled himself to his feet and looked into the pot, where the syrup bubbled and grew thick. At his enquiring look, I shrugged and gestured to old Ku'ku'kwes. She alone decided when to take the sap off the fire.

Niskam was already beginning to slip behind the mountain when Ku'ku'kwes finally gave the signal. Refreshed from their nap, small children came running. Older brothers and sisters followed not far behind, too dignified to run.

Taking a ladle, Ku'ku'kwes began pouring the thick, sweet liquid onto the snow, making fanciful designs as she did so: now a deer, now a boat. The children seized on them, laughing as they sank white teeth into dark candy. We adults worked quickly to store the cooled sap in vessels of bark, sewn tightly with moose hair. By the time we had finished, the sky was black. That night around the fire, each person had a long rope of the candy known as sismoqn to suck on.

Our chief glowed to see the children happy once more, sickness and loss forgotten for this night at least.

"You, Ka'qaquj," he said, pointing to a little boy whose eyebrows ran in a thick dark line across his forehead. "Do you know how this sweet gift came to us?"

"The Creator gave it to us, as he gives all things."

"And do you remember why we have to work hard for it?"

The black line grew even thicker. Though other children were squirming with their knowledge, our chief kept his eyes firmly on Ka'qaquj, willing him to remember. His faith was rewarded.

"Because the people had grown lazy?"

"Yes," said the chief. "In the Long Ago, syrup flowed thick in the tree, rather than thin and watery as it does now. But one day, when Kluskap came to the village, he found that the cooking fires had gone out and the people nowhere to be seen. Though the fish were leaping in the river, there was no one to spear them. Even the bears were wandering around the camp, breaking into the wikoums and destroying all that the people had worked so hard to build."

"'Where are my people?'" cried Kluskap. After searching for a little while, he finally came to the sugar stand. And there, what did he find?" This time, the chief pointed to Kawi.

Flushed with the honour of being chosen, the little girl rose to her feet, arms stiffly at her side, fingers spread wide.

"He found them all lying under the trees with their mouths open," she announced in a loud voice.

Some in the crowd grinned openly, but the chief nodded gravely at the solemn little speaker.

"And so it was, Kawi. When Kluscap saw them, his rage was great. 'You lazy people,' he said, 'You neglect the good work I have given you and do nothing except lie there drinking the syrup of this tree.' And seizing a vessel, Kluscap filled it with water from the river. Then climbing the nearest tree, he poured water into the top. It was a magic vessel, for the water never stopped flowing until he had filled every tree with water. And from that time on, we get the syrup only after many days of hard labour."

The chief's stern expression held for a moment, then vanished in a laugh.

"But children, do you know a secret? It makes it all the sweeter." And closing his eyes, he gave himself over to the sweet taste of the candy. As did we all.

*

*t*hat spring we returned to the coast later than usual. The move could not be made until the dead had been buried and the sick were well enough to make the journey. We were more lightly laden than we had been that fall. Sleds bumped lightly over the ground: most of our belongings had been left behind with the dead, to ease their passage into the next world.

When we emerged upon the coast, the bright colours and activity came as a shock.

"Antoine!"

The shout rang out, joyous, through the clear morning air. Below us, Charles was waving an enormous blue-feathered hat. Impatient of the path, he began to scale the cliff toward us. As he climbed, the hat prevented either brother from getting a good look at the other. But when their eyes finally met, I saw the look of shock on Charles's face. Following his gaze, I also turned to look at Antoine. With Charles looming so large and brown before us, it suddenly came to me how frail and white Antoine had grown. Charles clutched his brother to his breast, careful not to grasp the fragile frame too tightly. I watched as he struggled to compose his face into a bright mask.

"Been fasting have you?" he asked, black eyes snapping. "You know, Antoine, that the Holy Father excuses his missionaries from the Lenten fast. He does not have so many shepherds that he can afford to lose one in the field."

The words were spoken to cover a deeper fear. But Antoine simply laughed, then grasped his brother tightly to him. Feeling the strength that still lay in the grip, Charles seemed to relax.

"Have you letters for me brother?" Antoine asked as they walked down the path together.

"From your superior, yes." Charles spoke to Antoine, but his eyes were on me. It was the first time such a look had been directed toward me and I felt my face grow warm. Antoine also saw the look, and stepped quickly in front of me. "Tell me Charles, have you any bread? I have not tasted wheat these long months."

I knew his sudden interest in food was simply a way of turning Charles's eyes from me to himself. Grateful for the reprieve, I turned and ran down the path.

For the rest of that day, I took care not to be near the brothers. Unlike Antoine, Charles delighted in the look and feel of a woman's body. The year before, he had taken one of the young widows, enjoying her for the entire summer. She had been one of the first to die when the sickness came. He would be looking for another to take her place.

Such arrangements were common in our village. Many of the women, my own mother among them, had let the fishermen climb into their furs. They were invariably widows, reluctant to accept the place of second or third wife to a hunter. So instead they accepted the attentions of the fishermen, whose gifts allowed them to live independently.

But I was a virgin. Had I a father, he would have made it clear to Charles that I was not to be touched. I had only my own wariness to protect me. My own childhood ever before my eyes, I vowed to stay away from Charles. No child of mine would be subject to a life without family and protectors. But some vows can be difficult to keep.

k

*a*t first it was not hard to avoid him. As before, his mornings were spent with the young hunters, teaching them to shoot. They trained with none of the light-hearted laughter of earlier days. Each shot was a blow struck for a friend who had perished on a bed, weak and sick. Each man, I knew, was driven by single thought: if an early death were to come, it must be a glorious one.

My time with Antoine was now limited to the mornings, when Charles was busy with the hunters. I had been telling Antoine all the tales I had learned from Bright Eyes as a child. He listened quietly, sometimes scratching on the birchbark he carried with him.

"Once," I told him triumphantly, "Kluskap served a whole village from a single birchbark dish. Fifty hunters and their families ate from this dish, and still there was food left over." Antoine seemed startled at this story. He opened his mouth to speak, but another voice forestalled him.

"Mouse is learning our language quickly, brother."

Standing behind Antoine, Charles was careful to speak respectfully. But I, who could see his eyes, saw the long glance he gave my body. There was something else; something deeper within me gazed back. I was intrigued, despite my fears.

"Mouse has taught me a great deal more than I have taught her," replied Antoine steadily. "She and her people have the same longings for the next world that you and I have. They too believe in a Creator, whom they know as 'Kisu'lk.' They do not yet know his son, but they would understand his teachings. Never have I seen such Christian love and brotherhood as they displayed this winter." Antoine smiled. "It brings to mind the words of Monsieur Lescarbot."

"Who?" said Charles, who had attended little to this speech.

"The poet who wintered here with your friend, Champlain. 'If we commonly call them Savages,' he said, 'the word is abusive and unmerited, for they are anything but that'."

"Was it not also Lescarbot who wrote, 'I admire their shape and well-formed faces'?" asked Charles, fixing his eyes on mine.

"Why have you come Charles?" snapped Antoine. We both looked at him in surprise.

"Yes well, right now I'm more concerned about the true savages – the English," said Charles. "They're on the prowl, anxious for a piece of this coast."

"How do you know?" Antoine asked. "We've seen no sail."

"The fishermen on the far shore have sent me a message," said Charles. "Something about a Lord Ochiltree – damned difficult name to pronounce. Do you know him?"

Antoine thought a moment. "From Scotland, I believe. And what's more, a Stewart."

"So the King is behind it. I wasn't sure."

Antoine was thoughtful. "This is not good news for the Church."

Charles snorted. "At this moment I'm more concerned about our fishermen. It seems this Stewart is charging them a full tenth of their catch for safe passage. These men have been sailing those waters for nearly a hundred years, and a sprout of the Scottish nobility tries to charge them for passage. He knows there's a fortune to be made in the cod fishery and will try to steal it from France – but not on my watch. Did I tell you I was thinking of taking a little cruise up the coast?"

"No, Charles! Champlain himself is waiting for you in Quebec. His investors will not condone a postponement of your voyage."

"The cargo will keep," said Charles. Then, as I watched, another idea was born and grew.

"Antoine. Give me Mouse."

"What?"

Antoine's surprise was great, but no greater than my own. I had been trying so closely to follow the difficult words that my own name came as a shock.

"I must speak with the chief, to let him know the danger," said Charles. "The English cannot be allowed to settle here. Mouse can help me persuade him."

"I can go as your interpreter. Leave Mouse out of it. She's a child."

"And have it said later that a Catholic priest helped me persuade the chief to attack an English fort? No, it would endanger your mission if things went wrong. Let me have her Antoine: you know better than anyone what the English will do if they land here. One sight of your black robes and they'll have you on the next boat to England, or worse. And once they put rum into the hands of the hunters, that will be the end of the Christian love and brotherhood you admire so much. I've seen it happen Antoine: rum for furs."

"I understand Charles. But I cannot speak for Mouse. It is her decision. And yet," he said, turning to me, "I would strongly advise her not to go. This is not your quarrel, Mouse."

I had already stood up. I had heard enough to know the English would take Antoine away – and that I could prevent it.

Charles took off his hat and bowed low, as I had often seen him do. Always before, he had been laughing, and the children would roll on the ground in glee to see the blue feathers sweeping the sand. This time he did not laugh. Our eyes met.

"Come Mouse," said Charles, hat sweeping out again to point the way. Our women usually walked behind the hunters, but Charles pushed me in front of him on the path. The people along the way paused to watch our progress: it was strange for the Mouse to be accorded such an honour.

As always at this time of day, the chief was sitting in front of his wikuom, carving the bright, white stone into arrowheads. He had no need of arrowheads, for all the hunters in the village vied for the honour of presenting him with their best. He sat there merely as an invitation to approach. At this time, even the smallest child could venture close.

I did not bow, as I had seen the fisherman do to Charles. Bright Eyes had his own ideas about why they did so.

"The fishermen surrendered their power long ago, Mouse, to brutal men who would not give it back. Among us, it is different. Our chief is like the mirror that hangs from Charles's belt. A good chief takes our power and reflects it back to us. That is why we are so careful to choose one who is worthy of the task. For he carries our hopes and fears, never forgetting that they belong to us."

I had no standing, none at all among our people. But I was not afraid as I stepped forward and addressed the chief. "This man, wishes to speak to you about a grave matter. He has asked me to put his words into our language."

"Then tell him to sit. It pains my neck to look up at him," said the chief. The chief's face remained completely impassive. I caught the humour in his voice, though Charles did not.

I motioned to Charles to sit, and took my place beside him. Charles began at once.

"Your people are in great danger."

At this, the Chief looked around. It was the hour when the sun was highest in the sky, and the women just beginning to serve the bowls of stew. The dogs sat near them, too well trained to approach the food, but seizing on any piece of meat that fell to the ground. Apart from Charles's own ship, there was not a sail on the water, for all the French were at the fishing grounds. Hunters on the edge of camp were alert for the least footfall of an enemy. But at this moment, they were flirting with the young girls who brought them their stew.

The chief raised an eyebrow, then turned back to Charles, waiting for him to continue.

"An evil chief from across the sea has settled not far from here, with many warriors." This was the first I had heard of the warriors, and I checked with Charles to make sure I had understood correctly. He nodded impatiently and motioned to me to translate.

The chief's eyes had caught my confusion. "Is this evil chief from among your own people?" he asked warily.

"No, he comes from a land long at war with ours." Charles had fallen into the trap. I was not surprised. He was young and our chief was wise.

"We have made no promises to fight beside you in your quarrels," said the chief. "You have made no promises to fight beside us in ours. Through all the generations that your fishermen have been coming to these shores, there have been no wars."

"But these men want to govern the oceans!"

I saw a tiny movement, a flicker, in the corner of the chief's mouth. "Then they are foolish and will be beaten against the rocks of their own greed. The waters are ungovernable. Any man who attempts to subdue them will be swallowed up."

Charles took a breath and tried again. "With the help of your hunters, my men and I can overtake the strangers and send them back to their own land. But the strangers will build a fort here and turn its guns on your people if you do not help us."

"I did not say I would not help you."

I repeated the words with amazement. Until now, I had followed each turn of the chief's mind. But this last twist baffled me. I knew our chief had no fear of our village being overtaken. For many generations, we had seen strangers arrive on our shores – weak from their journey, out of food and water. Ignorant of how to survive in this land, they needed our help in even the smallest matters. No, our chief did not fear them.

So intent was I on my thoughts, I almost missed the chief's next words.

"Our young men have lost their confidence this winter, battling an enemy over which they could not triumph. Together, you and I will give them an adversary they can defeat."

He leaned in closer toward Charles, as one conspirator to another. "When I was a youth, we played a game in which we crept up to our adversaries undetected. The winner was the one who could take the feathers off his enemy's head without being discovered. We excelled in this art before we ever touched a bow."

The chief shook his head in sadness. "Too many of my young men have been lost to disease. I cannot risk bloodshed. And so, it is my request that the enemy be outwitted, not taken by force. That is my first condition."

I caught the flicker of delight in Charles's eyes and remembered that first day, when he had pulled the coin out of the chief's ear. They were alike, these two. For both, the victory would be sweeter if won through strategy.

"Done," said Charles. "And the other?"

"You will take Mouse with you."

Charles and I looked at each other, a moment only, before I lowered my eyes.

"A battle is no place for a child," said Charles.

"Then she can stay on the ship," said the chief. "If this ruse is to work, you must have the power of speech with our hunters. Mouse will give you that power."

When I left, Charles and the chief were smoking the sweet tobacco, all need for words at an end. I made my way to my mother's wikuom and immersed myself in the preparation of the evening's meal. What did the chief mean by sending me with Charles? It was true that I was the river along which the words would flow. But was there another reason for putting me in Charles's path? All winter long, I had felt the chief's eyes on me, seeing that I did not sicken and die as the others had. Was he afraid, as my mother was, that I stood too close to the animal world? Did he fear that I would join my blood to that of his people?

My thoughts were interrupted by the sight of Antoine striding along the path towards me.

"It is madness for you to think of joining this attack, Mouse."

He was upset, I could see. But though I looked for it, there was no sign of jealousy. He was simply afraid for my safety.

Turning, he looked intently into my eyes. "I am going to the chief, to insist you be left behind." He did not say what else was surely on his mind: could his brother be trusted alone with me?

I saw Antoine later, speaking to our chief, with clumsy words and hands flying in the air. He did not sit quietly on his heels, as Charles and I had done, but strode back and forth, up and down, black robe flapping in the wind. The chief smoked contentedly, watching this rare entertainment. But lively as it was, it would do no good. I knew that I would sail with Charles and that Antoine would not stop me. If he were to try, all wikuoms would be closed to him, at the chief's order. And for reasons unknown to me then, it was important to Antoine that he sit at the people's firesides.

К

*C*harles and I spent long hours with the warriors. The young men resented my presence, especially Taqtaloq, who had bullied me as a child. Although they knew Charles needed my help, they continued to snub me, looking only at him as they spoke. I was careful in their presence, cautiously backing away from the circle each time I rose to leave. Among our people, it is said that a woman who steps over a man's legs will rob him of his strength, so strong is the magic we hold between our thighs. As maidens, we learn this lesson early. Taqtaloq and his friends had been quick to push us roughly onto the ground whenever we ventured too close to their legs. Now, sitting so close to him, I was careful to stay well to the rear.

And yet I sat fascinated, watching as they wove together the strings of the plan, much as our women weave the wampum. At first, I could detect no pattern, but gradually it grew into a simple and bold design, the joint creation of Charles and our warriors. No woman, surely, had ever sat in on such a council, unless it was Kluskap's grandmother Nukumi.

I also sat with the fishermen as they patched their sails. Knowing I could now grasp their language, the fishermen chewed their words in the same way that our women chewed the stew they fed to their babies. They spit out only the words they thought could cause no harm, but I gobbled them anyway.

Today, their words were spit out with vehemence. "A Stewart! And not even a Catholic Stewart, like the beloved martyr Mary, dowager of France. But a Protestant like her son, the heretic James." Raphael's voice rose excitedly. "It's a heresy that is creeping across Europe, and now it has reached out to this land. But the holy fathers will never see this coast be snatched from their hands. I swear it by Saint Mériadek."

As he spoke, he grasped the small wooden case he wore at his neck, twisting it open then kissing its contents. I knew what lay within: a sliver of a human bone. We in Cibou did not carry human bones on our person, though there were people to the south who did. Among us it was whispered that our southern foes used their teeth to strip the flesh off enemy bones. Had Raphael done the same? If so, how powerful was the magic he carried? A wild thought came that I should rise and step over his legs to poke at the fire. But as usual, I sat quietly.

While Raphael spoke, the other men sent secret messages to each other from the corners of their eyes. It was Pierrot who finally spoke up.

"It's not the English beliefs we have to worry about. It's their greed. And now here's this greedy little duke, or whoever he is, demanding our fish. Every day he sets out from his fort and circles like a gull over the banks, hoping to steal a bite of fish he did not catch."

Pierrot drove the awl savagely through the canvas.

"Rosemar! Leave it to the aristocracy to give a fishing station in the North Atlantic a maidenly name like that. I'm telling you, I'll be there to cheer when Captain Daniel strings him up."

"This is our land," cried Johann, his voice like the great bell I sometimes heard on Charles's ship, calling the men together.

"And it has been our land for a hundred years, since Cartier claimed it for France. My own great-grandfather sailed in his wake. My father used to say...."

I was no longer listening. "Claimed ... our land." The words were burning a path through my mind.

"Look Mouse," said Pierrot, seizing upon my confusion to prevent another long speech from Johann. Quickly, he drew a line in the sand with his finger. On one side of the line, he sketched a square dwelling, of the type the fishermen build. "This is the English fort." On the other side, he drew a second building with a banner above it, like that which flew over Charles's ship.

"Here, we are, the French, in Cibou. But soon...." He swept his forearm across the drawings, erasing them. And in their place, he drew a large circle, with Charles's banner inside. "One day soon, all this land will be French again."

I stood, shaken. What of our people? Were we also to be contained within that circle, we to whom Kluskap had given the whole world? I knew we could never be held within such a sphere, not when our animals and ancestors roamed freely. Then a more frightening question rose to my mind. Were we to be shut outside, kept from the sacred land where Kluskap slept?

I wanted to erase the lines that lay there so ominously in the sand. Bright Eyes once told me that thoughts formed here in the Land of the Living can assume form, be made real in the spirit world. Perhaps they were taking shape there even now.

Johann looked up and saw my face. "Mouse. I think I hear your mother calling." It was a joke I had often heard the men use among themselves. My own mother would never call out for me in front of a group of men. Still I was grateful for the chance to escape. I looked back only once and in doing so, saw Johann's long hand snake out and swipe Pierrot across the back of the head.

i spent the remaining time close to my mother and the other women. On some days, I felt Antoine's eyes upon me; other days, I felt those of Bright Eyes. I avoided them both. Each, in his own way, saw too much.

Charles took no notice of me at all. He was too excited by the challenge, animated by the danger. When the day finally came for us to leave, his laughter boomed across the water, his red cape lifting on the wind.

Watching him, I thought of our men who, bright with paint and feathers, would offer themselves as targets. Only when the bait was taken and the enemy in pursuit, would they turn with sudden, deadly intent. Charles, too, would excel at this game. At the last moment, the laughing black eyes would turn opaque and flat, with no depths to which a foe could appeal. The thought made me shudder, in fear and in fascination.

The young warriors ignored the crowd that had gathered to wave them off. Resplendent with paint, their hair braided into fierce designs, they leapt aboard and tried to look busy arranging their weapons. I crept in behind them, a light bag in my hand, tucking myself into a small corner behind the ship's rail.

From my position, I saw Antoine walking down to the beach, black robe gathered up into his belt, feet bare. The bag over his shoulder held his most precious possessions: his black book, a metal cup, and a white cloth alive with flowers. This cloth covered the table on the days when Antoine's god came to share a meal with him. I had not yet seen this happen and was not sure whether I wished to be present for such an event. Should his temper prove as capricious as that of Kluskap, it would be best not to approach too closely. Off our own shores, the stone maidens stood as constant reminders of his wrath.

Antoine was walking toward the ship when Pierrot ran up to him, and spoke urgently in his ear. I saw Antoine struggling with a decision, his eyes turning toward the vessel. After a long moment, he turned back to follow Pierrot, who had already begun running for the village.

"Well, that's taken care of," said Charles to the French officer at his side. "While I applaud my brother's honourable impulses toward unprotected maidens, I cannot risk his presence. The English would string him up from the mast if ever they board this ship ... which they will not."

"What did Pierrot tell him?" asked the officer.

"That the chief's wife had a boil to be lanced before we sailed. I'll ask his forgiveness for the lie in the confessional, it won't be the first time ... nor the last, I imagine."

As he was speaking, the sailors were pulling anchor and preparing the sails. Slowly, the great ship began to pull away, as the current pulled it past Kluskap's canoe, past the stone maidens and into the sea beyond.

I had no fear of sickness. I had been on the water before, in the great sea canoes of our people. But I had never been on such a ship, one that rode so high above the waves.

Nor had I been to the other side of our island. In Cibou, the mountains loom over the village, their great escarpments falling straight down to the water. On their surface, glitter the bright rocks from which our men make their arrowheads. But not long after we embarked, the land began to change. The great hills flattened and the trees became ever smaller, more stunted. Unlike Cibou, wooded down to the sea, here were large areas of wetlands, studded with small mossy clumps. And unlike our long, golden beaches, these shores were strewn with boulders large and small. I felt it would hurt my feet to walk on them.

As we neared the place where the day is born, the waves crashed onto the rocks with greater force than I had ever seen. Cold sprays shot out from the rocks straight up into the air. This was a grey, inhospitable place, so unlike our own protected shore. Yet its very wildness called to something in me. Watching

Charles from my corner of the ship, his chest heaving as he drew in great gulps of air, I guessed he felt the same. "This must be how he is on the open ocean," I thought. I felt a stab of envy – and something deeper.

From time to time we passed a fishing chaloupe, just big enough to hold three men. Each of the three sat holding a line, jigging it up and down in the water with a quick, jerky motion. At night around our fires, our hunters had taken turns mimicking this womanly, patient way of fishing. Now aboard Charles's ship, they dared not mock the fishermen in front of him. But each time we passed a chaloupe, they turned to each other with a snort and a secret hand gesture, one I had seen them use for other things.

It was to be a short journey of two days and one night. I slept alone in a small space between decks. All night long, I heard the footsteps of the watch as they trod the boards over my head, calling out at regular intervals as the night progressed. Noises were comforting: they told me I was not alone on the vast sea.

The next morning, I was awakened – not by an event, but by the absence of one: the ship was no longer moving. That could only mean we had reached Johann's secret cove. He had given Charles careful directions before we left:

"Be careful Captain, to land on the far side of the bluff. It's Stewart's single blind spot, one even he is probably not aware of. Probably thinks he has got a view of the whole area. That's why he chose to settle there – that and the fishing of course. Prime fishing right off the Scotia shelf, cod as fat as...."

Charles had given him no chance to finish this speech about the quality of the cod. Johann's eagerness to hop down any trail on which his mind led him was one reason he had not been invited on this voyage. Charles needed to ensure that the thoughts of all his men were concentrated on the battle ahead.

"Mouse!" I could hear Charles descending the ladder to where I slept. I rubbed my eyes to remove traces of the night and smoothed down the hair flying around my face.

"I must speak to the men. Wait until I call, then come down the ladder to the hold." This, I knew, was a thought for my maidenhood: Charles did not want me descending to a roomful of newly awakened men. On this day, which could mean death for some, I felt safe in the hands of a man who could hold so many ideas in his mind at once.

When the call came, I quickly descended the ladder to where the men lay. Charles was sneaking them into enemy territory in the belly of a whale; the time had now come to spew them out onto the beaches. From there, a handful of the warriors would proceed to the fort. They would take no French weapons, wear no French clothing – nothing to indicate that they were anything but simple hunters with furs to trade. Charles had handpicked these furs himself, fine thick pelts, so alive to the touch that they still seemed to contain the spirit of the animal that had sacrificed itself for this purpose.

I accompanied the rest of the warriors onto the beach, scrambling above the watermark to avoid the spray that dashed upon the stones. Charles remained on board, preparing to meet Lord Stewart on the ocean. "Every blessed day," Pierrot had said, "Lord Stewart's ship sets out from the fort and circles like a gull...." For the first time, I was afraid for him: for Charles, and not Antoine. Perhaps a rogue wind whispered in his ear, for he turned his head and his eyes sought mine across the waves. Then he closed one eye, in the private signal I had often seen among the fishermen. And that small, intimate gesture made me even more afraid, for myself this time.

i sat beside the French officer, Philippe d'Aumont, translating his final words to the warriors. I did not notice the second sail on the horizon, until a whoop from the others brought it to my attention.

At its appearance, the handful of traders set off immediately for the fort, announcing their presence with loud noises and spirited conversation. The fort's dogs would signal their arrival long before they came in sight. The rest of us remained in the cove, eyes fixed upon the ocean.

Bright Eyes had told our people many tales of war: they filled our history. I had often imagined the noise and speed of battle. What I had not foreseen was the sight of these two ships, each a beautiful white bird moving silently toward the other, as slowly as Niskam arching across the sky. Watching, I felt suspended in the Long Ago, in a land where cannibal giants walk, gods rise from a bed of snowy mountains and great white birds float towards a distant yet implacable goal.

D'Aumont – as accustomed to the sluggish tempo of great naval battles as I was not – had turned away to supervise the midday meal. The heat of the sun made me drowsy, and I may have napped a little, for when I looked again, the white-winged birds were almost upon each other. They would soon be caught in a death grip. It was time to move.

Unlike the traders, the rest of us approached the fort secretly, in the way of our people, so lightly that not even the fort's dogs could be sure we were human. From our hiding place among the trees, we watched them run in circles, whining in confusion. We knew that they inside the fort were not attuned to their dogs, as we were to ours. They would simply tell them to be quiet and return to the business of trading.

There on the edge of the forest, an agitation, an excitement, flickered through the trees. All winter long, our young men had faced an enemy they could not see. Now, one of flesh and blood lay just within reach. Whatever the strength of that enemy, I knew it could not prevail against the desire that burned in the hearts of my people.

For now, they would have to contain themselves. Normally before a battle, they would dance, calling up the forces that burned inside. Bright Eyes had explained it to me once:

"This is a power that begins in the heart," the old man had whispered to me, as we watched the warriors rise and fall in unison, matching their feet to the beat of the drum. "Kept there, it burns uselessly. But released by the dance, it moves from its prison, to strengthen the arm and lend quickness to the feet."

Often on the eve of a battle, Bright Eyes himself would play the drum, encouraging this power to run along the paths he had set out for it.

There was no drummer here and these warriors could not dance. But as I watched, they began to tap a hand along a thigh, an arrow lightly against a bow. Their voices rose and fell in a whispering chant, indistinguishable from the wind among the trees, but frightening in its power. It seemed as if the whole forest were pulsating with this strange force. As I watched, the men grew bigger and more deadly. Before my eyes, each seemed transformed into the likeness of his animal ancestor: bear, cougar, wolf. Forearms swelled, skin shone, hair bristled. Eyes grew dark, as the power that had animated their mind only moments before left to strengthen the body instead.

Bright Eyes said it was best for a woman not to be in the path of this power when it was called forth. On the eve of a battle, maidens were kept away, for their own safety. Even married women were kept from their men, for in a woman's arms this force would be expended and dissipate. Later, the women would play their own role in helping soothe their men back into a more human form.

There in the woods, I could feel the dark heart beating all around me. Let the summons come quickly, I thought, for this power could not be contained long. Could they feel it in the fort, this brooding presence hidden in the trees? I thought not. The men of Charles's land had always seemed unaware of the forces that swirled around them.

From our hiding places, we could see men outside the fort. As instructed, each warrior was marking a victim, a bird to truss. These strangers were hardly distinguishable from the French fishermen who lived among us. There was none who looked like a leader among them. As Charles had predicted, their leaders were either on the ship or within the fort, grasping at the fine furs. The labourers working outside had just downed tools to eat their own midday meal: some slept, others sat in small groups, smoking and talking. Their view blocked by the bluff over which we had just scrambled, they remained unaware of the sea battle taking place just beyond their line of vision. So when the great boom came across the water, they leapt to their feet in surprise, shouting words I could not understand.

The tension in the trees rose to unbearable levels, yet no warrior broke the line. All eyes were fixed on the banner riding high above the fort. With its fall, we would know that the traders had overcome the leaders inside. My eyes were burning as they fastened on the bright piece of cloth. And yet I almost missed it when it fell, so quickly did it happen.

I ducked my head as ochre-streaked legs raced past me, and voices rose in war whoops. Unlike the slow dance of the naval battle, this did not take long. When I raised my head again, I could see that most of the strangers were on the ground; some were bleeding. Above each victim stood a warrior, fighting his own desire to deal the death blow. But even as I watched, each conquered his passion for blood, even Taqtaloq, the bully. Not one of the strangers was killed. It had all happened as Charles had said it would, a victory worthy of Kluskap himself.

"Mouse!"

It was d'Aumont.

"Here," I answered from my hiding place.

From within the fort, the traders had emerged with a small group of prisoners. Under d'Aumont's direction, all the strangers were rounded up, bound, and led to the small enclosure with the pigs. Then all of us sat to await the return of the two ships, now headed toward shore. The strangers, no doubt, were hoping to see English guns come to their rescue. But we knew Charles Daniel.

They arrived just before sunset. A cheer went up from the warriors, as we saw a red cape appear on the deck of the strange ship. Through d'Aumont's glass, I could see Charles directing the lowering of the longboat. Another figure also stepped forward, his coat the same colour as the porpoises that swam beside our canoes. Brilliant white cloth peeped out at his neck and wrists, and on his head he wore a great hat with white feathers. As he stood there, glittering in the sun, I wondered how he had kept himself so clean. I had been on our ship for two days and already my legs and arms were smeared with tar. If there had been a battle aboard ship, this man at least had not been involved.

Standing in the longboat, he removed the plumed hat to keep it from blowing off in the wind, passing it to a man at his side. As he stood there, bareheaded, I saw before me the embodiment of all my mother's fears. Even I could see he was not entirely human: his eyes were terrifying white balls, with no colour at all. It was only when I dared peep again I saw they were of the very palest blue, ringed with red. His hair as white as that of our most aged Elders, yet the strength of his body told me this was a young man, of an age with Charles and Antoine.

The man's face betrayed neither grief nor anger at the sight of his men among the swine. In our chief, such impassivity served as a cloak, a protective veil over his true passion: the care and concern for each member of the group. This stranger surveyed his men as though they were worth no more than the pigs among which they stood.

He was not bound, as the others were. As he stepped out of the boat, Charles jumped out behind him and stretched out an arm toward d'Aumont. From the way d'Aumont bowed low before the stranger, I knew there would be no pig pen for this particular captive. Introductions concluded, he withdrew to lounge on a rock.

Charles moved to the five warriors who had overcome those inside the fort, clasping their shoulders with both hands and laughing. Proud to be singled out, the men clasped him back.

He moved on to the larger group of warriors, who greeted him with whoops and whistles. Charles's own attempts to imitate them were met with even louder howls. Glancing over at the men in the pig pen, I saw their faces grow white with fear.

As Charles looked around, he caught sight of me standing a little apart. Too late, I remembered Bright Eyes's warning about how a battle will heat a man's blood to boiling. I wanted to run, but remained caught in his gaze. Would he try to claim me there, before all these men?

I felt the grip of terror, as he pulled his sword from its hiding place and moved quickly up the beach toward me. And still I could not move. As I stood there before him, his sword flashed out, its bright gleam almost blinding to my eyes. Above my head, a brilliant red flower traced an arc in the air, then fell lightly into his hand. Bowing, he presented it to me.

In that moment, I forgot I had once loved Antoine.

*

*W*arriors and sailors lolled in the sun, casually waving their weapons at the strangers who were taking the fort apart, board by board. The wounded sat in a small group, removing nails and wooden spikes and dropping them into buckets, ready for shipment. Rope was coiled according to size. The bundle of materials on shore grew higher and higher, ready to stow in the ships.

Lord Stewart took no part in the work. Like Antoine, he too could sit for hours with a small book in his hand, entranced with the turning of the pages. And yet he was nothing like Antoine, who could never turn away while others were suffering.

At other times, he tucked a small wooden box under his chin, stroking it with a stick to produce long, mournful sounds. Even as the remnant of his fort was consumed in a huge fire, he seemed transfixed by the sounds of his own making. I can see him still, sitting on the shore, eyes closed as if in a dream, while beyond him the flames sputtered and crackled to the sky.

Through these days, all I saw of Charles was a cape, darting in and out of my line of vision. I was glad of it: this thing between us could not be resolved under the eyes of so many men. But it was coming, I knew.

When it was time to leave, Charles captained one ship, d'Aumont the other. We on Charles's ship stayed by the rail, watching the smouldering ruins of "Rosemar" grow smaller and smaller. The warriors were jubilant to be spending all their time on deck, instead of in the airless hold.

It was the strangers who now filled the hold, row upon row of tightly bound figures.

"Like rolled herring," said Claude, one of the sailors sent to guard them, now on deck for a breath of air. "They who thought to steal the catch from French fishermen will be shipped to our king as a nice hors d'oeuvre."

Lord Stewart was given the captain's cabin, while Charles joined the other men on deck. It was there, on the open ocean, that he came to me.

"Look Mouse," he said, leaning against the rail and pointing. "Straight out there, beyond the waves, is La Rochelle. We could go there now. We'd stroll through the fair, sample the honey and foie gras. Of course you'd have to try our Pont l'Evêque – best cheese in the world."

"We'd stop first at the booth of P'tit Mathieu. 'Come lovely lady,' he'd say, 'a small glass of cider, with bubbles to tickle your nose'."

Charles reached out and stroked his finger across the tip of my nose. "What would they think of you there, I wonder?"

I was not ready, not yet, for him to touch me. And so I searched instead for something to say.

"Johann tells me your land is very far away, a journey of many, many days."

Charles smiled. "And yet, if you look straight ahead, you can just see the spires of the cathedral." Turning toward the rail and drawing me close, he stretched out his arm, making a line for me to sight along. I could see nothing, as he well knew, but I could feel his breath on my face and I drew back.

He smiled again and moved a little away. "Did you ever wonder how we find this place, Mouse, in the vastness of the sea? While you cannot see it, there is a path across the ocean, from France to Cibou. Those who stray from that path, or are blown off by storms, are never seen again."

I looked out at the ocean and its vast sameness. Charles sensed my confusion.

"It is indeed a riddle. But I will give you the key: the path is not in the water, but in the sky."

I looked up then, not at the sky, but at him.

"Look at the sun, Mouse. Right now, it is at its height. But this evening, it will be just there, on the horizon."

"And your sailors follow its path!" I interrupted, triumphantly.

Exactly right," he said, eyes saluting my quickness. "The sun – Niskam – is our guide across the ocean. Every day at noon, we meet with him in council, so that we may follow in his footsteps."

I, who knew Niskam as the great being who strode across the sky, understood how only he could point the right way to sailors. Once, I had climbed up on the bluff overlooking our village and seen one of our sea canoes far below. From there, I could see where they had been, and where they were going, as even the men in the canoe could not. But I was too far above them to shout down my knowledge. How could Niskam, who rode so much higher, communicate his thoughts to those below?

"But how does Niskam signal the right path to take? For surely there are many paths on the ocean."

"Ah, another riddle," said Charles. And one that challenged him as well, for he took a moment to put his thoughts into words. Finally he pointed to the deck.

"Do you see, Mouse, how you are standing on the very edge of my shadow?"

He grasped my fingers lightly in his own. "Walk with me a little."

Hand in hand, we moved several paces along the rail.

"You see?" he said, measuring the distance between us. "As long as you stay on the very edge of my shadow, we will always remain the same distance apart. So it is with our ships. It's as if we sail within the shadow of the sun. To stay on the path, we must move no closer and no farther away from the being you call Niskam."

"But what of the night, when Niskam has completed his day's journey? Your ships sail on through the night."

"Yes they do, but always within the shadow of the fixed star, which we know as the Polar Star."

"So that is why, each day at noon, and every night, I see your pilot with a bright metal disk, communing with the skies."

"Exactly, Mouse. You are quick. It is called an astrolabe, and with it he takes the measure between us and the sun."

"Too quick by far," he repeated, as though to himself.

"Pardon me Captain," said d'Aumont, "but Lord Stewart is asking for you." I jerked my hand away from Charles's. As he left, I reflected upon the powerful magic I had just heard.

"We underestimate them, the French," I thought. They come to us weak from lack of food and fresh water, flung upon our shores as if by accident, children in need of our instruction. But Charles was no child – nor was Antoine, in spite of the fact that he could not make a bed.

i saw little of Charles during the rest of the voyage, and nothing of Lord Stewart. I did, from time to time, hear the whine of his instrument – a distressing sound, like the moaning of the wind in a great storm when it seems as if all the world must be swept away. I held my hands over my ears to block it out. The warriors did nothing so womanly, but from their grimaces, I knew the sound was vibrating in their teeth, as it was in mine, and it robbed the voyage of much of its joy.

Antoine was waiting on the shore when we arrived. Charles jumped out of the longboat and waded toward him, arms outstretched. Antoine went rigid in his brother's grip, but Charles seemed to take no notice. He then turned toward the chief and embraced him as well. Our chief looked surprised, but he returned the embrace, as Antoine had not.

I felt Antoine's eyes upon me as I slipped up the beach. I understood his fears for me, and was relieved I had nothing to show him. When I raised my eyes to his, he nodded and turned back to his brother, to hear his account of the battle. I was grateful to escape: the presence of the two brothers at once was becoming too much to bear.

My mother was in the crowd. I tried to persuade her to return with me to our wikuom, but she would not be drawn away. Our people had formed two lines, raising their voices and clicking their tongues in salute to the warriors who passed by. Parents proudly watched victorious sons; maidens eyed potential husbands. For some of the younger warriors, it was the first time they had received this tribute. Joy burned behind their passive faces, I knew. But they walked in proper dignity, unlike the sailors who waved to the people on each side. One Frenchman even grabbed the widow who shared his wikuom and pressed his lips to her neck. Embarrassed for her, I turned away.

A gasp from my mother drew my attention back to the crowd. I did not have to look to know it was Lord Stewart.

"White eyes, he has white eyes," my mother whispered urgently.

I had expected her to turn away in horror, as I had. But her voice grew soft and thoughtful. "Like Netaoansom, Kluskap's sister's son, he who was born of the ocean foam."

"It is not Netaoansom, it is not he," I whispered back, the words hissing through my teeth. I tugged at her sleeve, "Look, they are bringing the rest of the prisoners."

The strangers were being escorted from the hold, eyes squinting against the sun. After lying on their backs for more than two days, some had to be helped to walk. These men – who looked like all the fishermen we had seen over the years – held no fascination for my mother. Her eyes kept returning to Stewart.

What dreams, I wondered, had filled my mother's mind as she sat by the fire, listening to Bright Eyes spin tales of Kluskap's dazzling nephew? She was not yet too old yet to take a man. I shuddered to think of this cold thing entering our house.

Lord Stewart's men were led to the caves along the shore, where our captives are held. Lord Stewart would remain in the captain's cabin of his own ship, along with his body servant and a few officers. I had seen enough to know that this one prisoner – who must be a great chief in his own land – would be treated with respect. At such times, I wondered if the land across the seas were an upside-down reflection of Cibou. Our chief – in his ceaseless care for his people – lived in a humble wikuom and ate the simplest food. This Stewart, who cared nothing for his men, was given the very best food and lodging. It was perplexing.

My mother and I returned to our wikuom, to dress for the great feast. Cooking fires were already beginning to smoke. Round white stones lay sizzling, ready for the dugout kettles, where they would make the water boil. Pits lay smouldering, to receive the great piles of clams and quahogs stacked on the beach. Cooking was the work of the married women: the maidens were too busy braiding coloured beads into each other's hair and rubbing fragrant oil into their skin. Later, they would sit beside the warriors and fend off advances, hoping to inspire a more serious offer.

I normally remained at my mother's side, among the married women. Knowing I would end the night covered in soot and kettle juice, I prepared to put on my oldest robe.

"Not that robe, Mouse."

Turning to her sewing basket, my mother pulled out a new suit of white moose skin, so bright it shone in the wikuom's dark interior. The beading along its edges must have taken days of sewing. Such a thing had never been seen in our poor home.

"It's for you," my mother said shyly. "The chief gave me the skins himself, and excused me from all other duties, so that it would be ready in time. It is a reward for your work over these last days."

"I'll braid your hair for you," she added.

It had been a long time since I had felt my mother's hands in my hair.

"**C**ome Mouse," my mother said later. "The village will be gathering."

I peeped out the flap. "It is too early. People are still sitting beside their own firesides." In truth, old Siklati was the only one still at his own fire, snuggling beside it for warmth. But it was still daylight and I was embarrassed to be seen in these fine new clothes. The old Mouse was disappearing and a new being taking her place. It could not be stopped, but it could be slowed. And perhaps, if I were careful, it would not be played out before the whole world.

But my mother would not be deterred. She had also dressed carefully, feathers in her hair and dark eyes deepened to mystery with soot from the fire. I did not ask why a woman who planned to spend the night behind the cooking pots would be dressed in this way, and I did not want to know.

As we walked toward the beach, my mother tapped me on the back, in the old signal to lift my spine and lower my shoulders. And so it was that I, who had hoped to slip into the shallows under cover of darkness, was forced to enter under full sail. And, just as the crowd always gathered to see the tall ships enter the harbour, they also stood to watch as Mouse took her place by the fire.

Antoine also watched as I stepped into the circle. Of all people, he was the last I wanted to see. "It is still I," I wanted to cry. But even as my mind formed the words, I knew they were not true. Forcing myself to act naturally, I stepped up to his side.

Just beyond him, the chief was advancing, dressed in his cape of wild turkey feathers. Behind him walked the war chief and Elders, followed by the warriors. Together, they advanced toward the fire, which they slowly encircled twice, sunwise.

I explained the rite to Antoine.

"They are paying homage to Niskam ... saluting the great force that animates us all."

There was a long silence. "You must know, Mouse, that the sun exists only to give us heat and light. It is a servant, not a master."

This confused me ... for I knew how the sailors of his land looked to Niskam to guide them across the water. Caught between so many conflicting ideas, unable to hold them all in my mind, I did what I had never done before. I turned from Antoine, pushing my way into the crowd. But the crowd would not have me, and pushed me back into the inner circle.

Our chief had already begun his speech.

"Look up," he said, one hand thrown to the sky. "There, above your heads, lies the Road of the Ancestors. It is along that great pathway of stars that spirit runners travel from our world to the next. Watch as their flaming arrows go before them, a sign to our ancestors who wait by their firesides for news. This night they will celebrate the great victory won for them by their sons' sons, these warriors here before you."

But even as we watched for spirit arrows high above our heads, something else caught our attention: a shower of stars from Charles's ship, rose high in the air then fell toward the dark waves. One world a reflection of the other, I thought. It was the false stars that drew the people's attention. In a body, they ran down toward the water for a closer look, leaving chief and Elders no choice but to trail behind.

It was in the light from these false stars that a longboat advanced toward the shore. And as we watched, a figure suddenly rose and separated itself from the dark mass: Charles.

Skillfully, bowing almost to his feet, Charles managed to make it look as though the chief and Elders had advanced to accept this tribute. Together, they proceeded back toward the fire, Charles careful to remain a step behind. Everyone took their places as before, waiting for the ceremony to continue.

From a velvet bag beneath his cape, Charles extracted a mass of bright gold, and beckoned the war chief to step forward. Separating a large, crescent-shaped object, he hung it around the war chief's neck. Everyone gasped as it gleamed in the light of the fire.

"This is to honour the bravery of a fine captain," said Charles.

"What did he say?" I heard those around me ask.

"He has bestowed on this chief the war name of 'Keptin'," replied Bright Eyes, who had caught the word.

"Keptin, Keptin," the people whispered, enshrining the word forever in our language.

One by one, each of the warriors was called forward to receive his own, smaller tribute. Knowing the food would soon be served, I was turning to look for my mother when I heard Charles call my name. For the second time that night, hands reached out to push me toward the inner circle. Charles's black eyes glowed in the flames as he hung the last of the bright gold objects around my neck. "For courage in the face of battle," he whispered, his hands freeing my hair from the chain that encircled it.

Not knowing where to look, I ducked my head and escaped back into the crowd. Charles followed, red cape signalling his intentions to all.

"Wait for me, white lady," he said, catching and fingering the tasseled edge of my sleeve.

"Do you know, Mouse, that in our tradition the white lady – a spirit to you – will steal a child away and put a fairy child in its place. Only in this case, it seems that the white lady herself has taken the place of the child."

Black eyes blazed down into mine.

"And when she's not busy stealing children, she lurks under bridges, waiting for simple, unsuspecting men to return from the fields. They say she forces them to dance, spinning ever faster and faster until finally she flings them to their death."

He moved closer still. "I, for one, am prepared to risk such a fate."

I did not know how to play this game. But Charles, I knew, was ready to teach me this and more.

"Come," he said taking me by the hand, "I'm eager to taste the great red beast cooking in yonder pot." Together we watched as one of the older women pulled at a claw, hauling the giant red creature from the kettle.

"The spider of the sea," he mused, watching as I cracked the shell with a wooden mallet. "Larger even than the spiders of Dieppe."

"Hmmm." I was struggling to extract the white flesh from the shell without breaking it, so as to hand it to him whole and complete. Together, we ate of the jakej flesh, then started on the oysters that had lain baking in the deep, smouldering pits.

"You know, Mouse," Charles began, chewing determinedly on an octopus tentacle. But his words hung in the air as he wrestled with the slippery flesh. His eyes betrayed his frustration as he struggled to conquer the dense mass. Again, he tried to speak, with no more success than the first time. I laughed, perhaps the first time I had done so in his presence.

"The next time we women chew the deer hides to soften them, I'll invite you to join us," I told him. "Such fine teeth should not go to waste."

"Oh really," he sputtered when at last he was able to speak. I could see from his eyes that he had thought up a too-clever response, but stopped it before it reached his lips. I admired the grace that let me emerge the victor in this, our first battle of words.

At the exact moment we could eat no more, a dancer appeared – then, on the far side of the camp, another. Arms and heads covered in white feathers, they moved toward each other

– weaving, swooping, feinting, now attacking, now retreating –
at a pace so slow they seemed suspended. The women and old
men who had not sailed with Charles were unable to solve the
riddle. But we who had been there knew that some battles move
slowly, on a plane beyond our understanding, and that not all
wars are won by the swift.

"I should capture them to sell to a theatre troupe in Paris,"
Charles said, turning to me. "I'd be a rich man, providing
that...." But his words were lost in the roar that greeted the next
dancer.

It was the first time a Frenchman had joined our dancers.
Dressed all in white, he ran with tiny steps toward a group of
sailors. In his hand he carried a large handkerchief, that he
pressed to his nose whenever one of the sailors got too close.
Then flapping it over a rock, as though to wave off any particles
found there, he seated himself, pulled out a comb from his pocket and began to blow, eyes skyward.

Seeing Lord Stewart thus portrayed reminded me of my
mother, whom I had not seen since we left our wikuom. Perhaps,
I hoped, she had eaten too greedily of the oysters and left early. I
could not free my hand to go and seek her out. Nor, by then, did
I want to.

&

"*C*apelin!"

Everyone at the feast turned as one toward the waves, in
search of the tiny fish that came to us but once a year. Rarely did
they catch us by surprise. With the advent of the summer fogs,
our people would gather on the beaches night after night, waiting for the magic moment of their arrival. Perhaps the Creator
had sent them early this year, in return for the great victory won
by the warriors.

Driven by one mind, the crowd seized bags and baskets and were running towards the water, responding to the age-old call of the capelin. I leapt to my feet, pulling Charles with me.

"What's happening, Mouse?"

"Come Charles, come! You may never have another chance!"

A moment only to remove our outer clothes, Charles's fine hat flung onto the sand. Then we were running into the surf, each grasping one end of an enormous basket. The tiny fish butted their heads against our legs, as we filled the basket again and again. All around us, people were dipping their containers and running to the shore to empty them, laughing with wild excitement. Caught in the spell, we lost all awareness of time, as again and again we lifted the heavy basket brimming with fish. There was no fatigue, no thirst, just a mad delight with the gift that had come to us so suddenly.

Then, just as suddenly, it was over. The fish were gone. How long had it lasted? A faint lightening of the horizon told us that the night was almost gone. I looked at the man beside me in the surf and saw that the wild tune hammering through my blood had found its echo in his. Wet, fully aroused, he looked tensile and dangerous. But I knew no fear as I stepped into his arms.

k

*h*e was playing with my toes. "So soft," he said, nuzzling. "The toes of a newborn. No, a mermaid, captured during the night and transformed into a woman before my eyes. Tell me lady, will you stay here with me, or escape back into the sea?"

I knew that I would not be the one to escape back to the sea.

The night we had just spent together had caught me as securely as the creatures trapped in the fishermen's nets. Entwining arms and legs around Charles, I gripped him tightly. And we began again.

*L*ater, I slipped out of the abandoned fishing shack where we had spent what remained of the night. Charles wished to speak to my mother about what had just happened between us. But I needed time to think about what lay ahead, before he and my mother took the decision out of my hands.

Too shy to be seen in my clothes of the night before, I skirted the village and ducked into the wikuom from the forest. My mother was still dressed in her own fine clothing. So she had not spent the night there either. Each of us undressed with her back to the other. I did not want my mother to see the marks of the night before. I suspected that she felt the same.

"When is he coming to speak to me?" she asked. "He should be here now."

"He thought so too. But I wanted to speak to you alone."

"Perhaps you were right to do so. It gives me time to go to the chief for counsel. This is the first time a stranger has taken a young, unmarried girl."

I could not let her go to the chief.

"Mother," I said, gripping her by the shoulders and turning her to face me. "We both know that no warrior will ever marry me. Nor will Charles Daniel bind himself to Cibou by taking a wife." I took a deep breath. "Since no husband will take responsibility for my life, I must be free to choose for myself. Otherwise, I will be forever blown like a feather in the wind of a thousand counsels. Do you understand?"

She nodded, distressed at the enormity of my decision, knowing there was no other choice.

"I understand. I will tell the chief."

"There's no need. He knew long ago – before I myself did."

"So," I said, changing the subject to distract her, "You have found your Netaoansom. I hope you were not disappointed in him."

Her look of shock told me I had guessed correctly. "How did you know?"

"You yourself have just told me. But how was the thing accomplished? Charles himself told me that Lord Stewart was locked in his cabin, under guard."

"Even men who are kept under guard must eat. I was one of those who was rowed out to the ship with food for the guards and prisoner."

"And will you be going again?" I asked, fearing the answer.

"Yes, tonight," she whispered.

I had just received the gift of freedom from my mother's hands and could not deny her the same privilege. But I worried for her – she who had known such pain. Lord Stewart, I was sure, would only bring her more.

There was one thing more to do before I returned to Charles's arms. That same morning, I sought out Bright Eyes, to ask him about the special leaf I had heard spoken of only in whispers in the women's wikuom. He looked at me long and sadly. "Such a thing does exist, Mouse, but it is given only to older women, already mothers, whose husbands are dead and who choose not to bear the child of another. I will not risk giving it to someone so young, who has yet to bear her first child."

"And whose child will I bear Bright Eyes? Captain Daniel's? You, one of the few with courage enough to sit at the fire of an outcast, would not wish such a thing on a child."

In the end, he gave me the potion. With the first taste, I felt the eyes of all the children I would never bear, staring at me from the Land of the Ancestors. I tilted the cup and drank it down to the dregs.

*W*e had the whole summer before us, Charles and I. Stewart's ship remained in Cibou, while d'Aumont sailed Charles's to a place called Canada. Champlain would be displeased, he said, not to receive delivery of his supplies from Charles's own hands. But he could not leave Cibou unprotected. Lord Stewart had allies up the coast who might decide to rescue him – if they knew where to look.

Charles and I slept in a small hut built for us near the site where Charles planned to build his fort. I did not know at first what he expected of me. He kept me close, wrapping himself in my hair as we slept, a light hand drawing me close as he sat giving instructions to his men. I did few of the things that a wife would do. Once, when I slipped away to repair a tear in his clothing, a laughing voice called me back:

"Bring them here Mouse. Old Jean Marc cares for all my possessions and would grieve to think that I had replaced him with youth."

When meals were brought to us from the ship, he took my plate from me and fed me with his own hands. I was confused by this behaviour, as was the whole village. Young wives watched him, then looked to their own husbands who sat waiting to be served, barely noticing as their wives struggled by with heavy burdens.

But as they envied me, so I envied them. I was strong enough to carry such burdens, had prepared my whole life to do so. Just as we wasted no part of the animal that sacrificed its life for us, no ability among our people was allowed to lie unused. Survival in our land demanded nothing less than the full strength of both man and woman. As much as I wanted Charles's hands on me, I longed for the chance to put my strength to the test, but he gave me no opportunity.

Instead, I tried to learn as much as I could about his ways. I listened and watched as he and the ship's carpenter bent over large white sheets. "It must be exactly the same as Rosemar, built by his own men with his own materials," Charles was saying. "I want the tower of my fort to be the last thing he sees as he sails away to prison in France. That will teach him to erect an English fort on French land.... What is it Mouse, are you ill?" he asked.

He was getting too close, I thought, and will end by knowing my thoughts. And when he did, he would know that I had no wish to live on French land. I was suddenly glad I would never bear a French son. For then where would my loyalties lie?

During those early days with Charles, Antoine and I took care to be on different sides of the village. But as Charles would be separated neither from me nor his brother, we eventually came to share our evenings at Antoine's fireside. The two often spoke of Lord Stewart:

"Stewart's expedition was funded by Sir William Alexander, intimate friend of the old king ... and we both know what that means. You've heard of him Antoine?"

"Alexander? Of course. He has some small talent as a poet."

"And even more as a politician. King James made him Secretary of State for Scotland. The king also granted him a vast fief in this country, which Alexander promptly burdened with the name 'Nova Scotia.' I would have expected more from a poet."

"A tragedian, to be precise."

"Yes, well, he'll be reduced to light comedy when I finish with him. Lord Stewart was to establish Alexander's authority in the region, but now we're using their men and their materials – of the best quality I might add – to build ourselves a fine little fortress, right here in Cibou. They'll be the laughing stock of Europe."

"The Lord deplores such arrogance, Charles."

"Then I beg his forgiveness – and yours. Come Antoine, it is late, and Mouse is so sleepy she will fall into the fire if we do not retire soon."

Sometimes I did fall asleep, my head on Charles's knee as I listened to the low murmur of their conversation. I awoke to fragments:

"...marry ... putting yourself and her in a state of mortal sin. You may marry a woman of this country, Charles, and suffer no penalty for it. The church will bless your union."

"Ah, but you've forgotten our father's ambitions for us Antoine: you a cardinal's ring ... me a lord's estate. But sea captains rarely become great landowners, unless they marry well."

The wine bubbled into Charles's cup. "You know, brother, I predict my value on the marriage market will rise the moment I deliver Lord Stewart into our king's hands. My deeds will win for me what my dash has been unable to do before now. Our father would be proud."

"Our father's ambitions seem small and petty out here Charles."

"Not to me."

ᴋ

*I*n the morning, it was easy to believe that such words belonged to the realm of dreams. The days flowed placidly around us. Mornings were spent at the fortress, just beginning to take shape under the prisoners' hands. These men were eager to trade their caves for an extra measure of food and days working in the bright sunshine.

"You can't keep men who are used to hard, physical labour trapped in a hole in the ground," said Charles. "They will become desperate, and seek to escape, no matter the cost to themselves.

These men are craftsmen, and less of a threat to us with tools in their hands than with their hands bound."

I could see the truth in his words: the prisoners gripped their tools the way our warriors gripped their spears. I could not understand the words they spoke among themselves, but I could see their minds were set upon the challenge of wedding wood to metal.

I often sat and watched as Charles and the ship's carpenter struggled to understand the words and gestures of the English giant, as he jabbed a large finger over the sheets spread on a table before them. On the day they raised the roof, French and English formed a long glistening body, that heaved and strained as if animated by a single mind. Afterwards, when the task was done, they clapped each other on the back, and raised cups together.

The sailors from Lord Stewart's ship were another matter. Not once did Charles turn his back on them. The caves in which they were kept were guarded by our fiercest warriors, faces fearsomely painted, hair stiffened with bear grease and bristling with the spines of the porcupine. Once a day, they were let out for an airing. Their guards were led by Taqtaloq, who seemed to delight in poking the prisoners with his spear, or knocking them over with his foot. Charles, who would never have permitted such treatment of his own men, simply stood and watched.

"The dregs of Bristol's streets," he said to Antoine as we sat over our evening meal, "dragged from the holes in which they were hiding, to serve Lord Stewart. Violence is all they know and violence is what they will have. When I took Stewart's ship, five were lashed in the hold, their backs covered in stripes. I too must govern by terror, though I lack his taste for it."

Such discussions of Lord Stewart's tastes made me uneasy. After the first night, he was allowed more freedom and was frequently rowed from the ship to the beach. On such days, my mother waded into the water to greet him, reaching into the boat for his instrument, or his books. He paid her no attention, aside from a harsh warning to guard his possessions from the water. Carrying his burdens, she trudged behind him up the beach, where she had a fire prepared and a hot drink waiting. He spent his days stretched out on the sand, absorbed in his book, while she sat quietly beside him, shading his eyes from the sun. It pained me to see it.

I heard his voice for the first time on a day when Charles presented him with a bottle of wine. I knew he was speaking Charles's language, but could not catch the words at first. As I focused on his lips, I felt the white gaze upon me. Seeing his interest, Charles moved quickly, turning so I was lost in the swirl of his cape. But he was not quick enough and I felt the man's mind reaching out for me as we made our way back up the beach.

It was an interest that should never have been aroused. But Charles seemed unable to resist his company: the two men often shared a meal on the ship, and a pipe afterwards. At such times, Lord Stewart watched me as I sometimes felt my own mother watching, to see if I were animal or human.

On such evenings, each man assumed a relaxed air, to throw his opponent off guard. As my ear grew accustomed to Lord Stewart's tones, I was able to follow most of the conversation:

"That was quite an accomplishment for you English, snatching our governor, Monsieur de la Tour, from Acadia," said Charles.

Stewart stretched out a hand to the bowl of nuts on the desk. "Information obtained, no doubt, from your spies at the English court."

"Of course. They tell us that Governor de la Tour has quite captivated your king."

"And married one of our queen's ladies."

Charles was surprised at the news. "You know what the Bible says about marrying foreign wives: they induce one to run after strange gods."

Stewart looked at me. "Indeed."

Charles laughed and reached out to stroke my ear before turning back to Lord Stewart.

"What did you think of him, de la Tour?"

"A braggart. All winter long, we heard of nothing but Acadia, with its virgin soils and thick pelts. But on that bloody great rock from which you plucked me, there was no soil at all and hardly enough vegetation to feed a hare. I could almost thank you for rescuing me." And Stewart bowed to Charles, who bowed back.

"Ah, but Baleine – our name for the land on which you found yourself – is not Acadia. That land is located farther south, on the peninsula. It was named for Virgil's Arcadia, and does remind one of that poet's paradise." Charles rose to his feet, glass extended, in a pose I had not seen before. Nor could I understand the language in which he spoke. Seeing my confusion, Charles translated the phrases for me:

Narcissus flower

And fragrant fennel,

does one posy twine with cassia then,

and other scented herbs,

Blends them,

and sets the tender hyacinth off

With yellow marigold.

Lord Stewart cracked a nut between his teeth. "Excellent performance Daniel. By a linguist at that, though I prefer Sir Philip Sidney's description of that fair land."

Assuming the same pose as Charles, he too began to speak, though I could not understand the words. I did not expect him to translate them for me. Nor was I disappointed in that expectation.

Watching them, I remembered the time a rival storyteller had arrived in our village. All night long he and Bright Eyes had battled – and in the morning, each had a new respect for the other. So it was with Charles and Lord Stewart. Around and around they circled, neither losing territory, neither gaining ground.

· "I have not yet had the honour of meeting your brother, the priest," said Lord Stewart. "Does he think I'll devour him?" Watching him crack the nuts between white teeth, I felt he would welcome the chance.

Charles laughed. "You must excuse Antoine. I'm afraid our squabbles are not sufficiently interesting to divert him from his goal."

"Which is?"

"Saving souls, converting the people of this land."

Stewart raised an eyebrow. "It is an admirable objective, providing they have souls to save. Have we established that they're human?"

Charles looked at me. "I can assure you."

All my life, I had sat at the feet of others, gathering words, testing their weight in my mind. But this burden was almost too heavy to bear and I felt a sudden longing to dash it at their feet. Long practise kept my face smooth.

Lord Stewart rose, to flip through one of the books from Charles's shelf. "That is why your country will never be able to hold this land: too much time spent toadying to the Church."

"The two are not incompatible. Once converted, these people will become full subjects of the King of France."

Lord Stewart lifted astonished eyes from his book. "What purpose could that possibly serve?"

"You are new to this country, Stewart. It is impossible to rule by force in a land so vast. French policy is therefore one of alliance, not conquest. One day we will be a single people."

"A French people, of course."

Charles bowed.

Lord Stewart went on. "It is so like the French to believe that all differences can be solved in bed."

"And so like the English to think that all must be resolved at the point of a sword."

k

*t*he next morning, I sought out Bright Eyes.

"Come share this stew with me," he said, pressing a large bowl into my hands. In his eyes, I would always be the little girl who never had enough to eat.

"What happens, Bright Eyes, when two peoples collide? Must one always give way to the other?"

The old man poked the fire with his stick. "You have never been to the big island – that most ancient of lands which the fisherman call 'new'."

As was his way, Bright Eyes turned from my question to trace a large circle of thought, a path for me to follow as I could.

"On that island lived a people named for the great auk. The Beothuk were tall, much taller than we. And they painted their skin with the red dust of the earth."

"Have you seen them Bright Eyes?"

"Not since my youth. When the strangers came, they turned their faces from the sea and disappeared into the forests, never to return. They may be there still, but I think not. Their forests are stumped and barren, not lush with life as ours are."

"Why would they choose to do such a thing?" I whispered, horrified at the thought of an entire people turning their back on the sea, on life.

"Because they could not face the changes that would come. And so they chose instead to seek out a place where change could not find them."

"It took courage to go," I said.

"Yes Mouse, but it also took courage – great courage – to stay, as our people did."

Bright Eyes leaned forward, staring into the flames. I waited, knowing there was more.

"Of course unlike the Beothuk, we of Cibou had been warned of the Frenchmen's arrival."

"By whom?"

"By a young girl, newly grown to womanhood, as you are now."

"How did she know such a thing?"

"It came to her in a dream. One night, as she wandered in that other world, she saw a small island floating toward her. On it were tall trees and living beings."

Bright Eyes looked out toward the water, where the masts of the fishing boats swayed in the wind.

"As the island approached, she was able to make out a man with fair skin and hair on his face." Bright Eyes laughed, rubbing his own chin ruefully. "As you know, Mouse, we the people of Cibou are not hairy, as the French are."

It was true. The faces and chests of our men are as smooth as stripped saplings.

"The next night, the young girl brought her dream to the fireside, to entertain the others. Think of the people's surprise when, the very next morning, such an island did appear. To those on shore, it looked as if the trees' branches were covered with bears. Seizing weapons, they rushed down to the shore, intending to shoot the animals. But as the island approached, they saw not bears, but hairy men, just as the young girl had predicted. Our people were so surprised by the appearance of these men that their first words were 'Who is that?'"

I smiled. Our word "wenuj" meaning "Who is that?" is the word we use for "stranger."

Bright Eyes chuckled. "The holy men were angry that the dream had been given to the young girl. But Mouse, it is not always to the aged and wise that great understanding is given. Sometimes it takes a pair of new, fresh eyes to see what lies just before us."

It was then I told him my secret. "They are planning to change us, Bright Eyes, into something we are not."

The old man was serene. "Yes, they will change us. It is the fate we accepted in the same moment we turned our faces toward them. And we will change them, though it may take many generations. You and I will watch from the Land of the Ancestors."

It was not the answer I had been hoping for. As I sat there, brooding, Bright Eyes poked an elbow into my side.

"I have heard it said, Mouse, that all their stories end happily. It is not so with us. Our stories go on and on, over many generations. People face one trial after another, and through it all, are strengthened. So that nothing that comes can destroy us."

It was true. We were strengthened by our troubles, and by our stories as well. Perhaps that was the role of the storyteller: to fire all hearts with courage. I began to feel better. Then a thought came to me.

"What of Father Antoine? His stories do not all end happily."

"No, they do not, for he is a true teller of tales. It may be that his will endure, long after he himself has gone."

ℳ

i returned to find Charles in the newly built fortress with Lord Stewart. The Englishman did not seem at all distressed to find himself in this French stronghold, built with the very wood and nails of his own Rosemar. Lifting the pot of mulled wine from the hearth, he poured as if he, and not Charles, were the host. Seeing me, he raised an eyebrow toward Charles, who shook his head. Although I had tasted the drink once before, I had never yet accepted a cup of wine from Charles's hand. I had seen what it did to the fishermen.

Sipping from their glasses, the two waged their quiet battle: who was more fit to rule our land?

"You cannot simply transplant the European system, Stewart. You English sweep in, pushing before you all that stands in your way. Whereas we creep gently along the river, to the very heart of the continent."

"And do you ever think, as you advance, that the forest is closing in behind you? One day, Daniel, you will turn around to find yourselves in the middle of a vast continent, cut off from all that is familiar."

Lord Stewart watched as the wine crept up the sides of his glass. "Our way is superior, if slower. We will secure the coast before attempting to move inland. Then step by step we will advance, clearing and planting as we go. You will see," he said, pointing his glass at Charles, "Our farmers will win more gains than your – what do you call them – coureurs de bois?"

"But not this winter," said Charles with a smile.

I stole a secret glance at his opponent. Was it wise to taunt a vanquished foe in this way? But Lord Stewart only laughed.

As I listened, I remembered Pierrot's circles in the sand. The edges of Lord Stewart's circle would push against the people of Cibou, crowding us out. I drew closer to Charles.

But Charles was drawing away. That night, as we lay upon our spruce cushions, he sought his peace as usual in my body. But for the first time, it was not to be found there. Afterwards, he lay awake, thoughts churning.

"Does it ever come early, Mouse?"

"Of what are you speaking, Charles?"

Susan Young de Biagi

"The ice."

And then I knew: he was anxious to be off. I forced myself to focus on the ice so that he could not read my thoughts, as he sometimes could, even in the dark.

"It is not yet time for the ice, Charles. Niskam has not yet called it forth from the Land of Ice and Snow. He himself still rides high in the sky. Niskam will not fail you, Charles. He will be there waiting as always to guide you on your path across the ocean."

"But beyond the mountains, in Canada, surely it comes earlier. If the great river freezes, d'Aumont will be unable to return with my ship." Then to himself, as if I were not lying there beside him, "I cannot sail Stewart's ship back across the ocean with such men."

So even he, I thought, is plagued by the spirits who whisper in the night. And this, beyond the sewing and the carrying and the body, is the duty of a wife: to stand beside him and fight the giants. But he would not let me. And so instead, I told him all I knew about the ice, and tried to guess at his fears. As the night wore on, I beguiled him with story after story of the Land of Ice and Snow, where the ancestors' hair was white and hung with icicles. I told him of battles fought with icy spears and great blocks of snow flung onto unwitting enemies.

"But all," I said, "are subject to Niskam, who can defeat them in a moment. Sleep, Charles, Niskam himself rides above d'Aumont's shoulder."

And although he slept, caught securely in the net of my hair, I grieved to know that I would never truly penetrate the circle of his thoughts. I remained, as always, the outcast, doomed to forever ride on the very edge of his shadow.

$t$he chief came to our fireside as we were eating breakfast. Turning to Charles, he spoke slowly and formally.

"I have come, Keptin Daniel, to invite you to the moose hunt."

Charles sat up. It was his first sign of interest in something other than his ship in many days.

The chief turned to me, "You will come as well."

In the women's wikuom, it is said that men use the hunt to escape the concerns of wife and children. The woman's involvement begins only with the animal's death, when we cut up the carcass and prepare the skins.

"Will the hunters not be offended by the presence of a woman?" I asked.

The chief spoke quickly, too quick for Charles's ear.

"Not as offended as they would be if Keptin Daniel managed to scare off the moose, or affront its spirit. You will explain the rites to him, then remain close by his side to avoid dangerous blunders."

I nodded. Moose are noble creatures, freely offering themselves up to the hunters. They are also proud and touchy, with spirits that linger long after the kill, to ensure their bodies are handled with proper reverence. Some hunters will first cut off the ears, to guard against the spirit overhearing a careless word. The fact that our chief was willing to take such a risk showed the respect in which Charles was held.

Charles spent the rest of that day practising with bow and spear. I smiled to see how much he looked like a boy before his first hunt. I used the time to seek out some footwear that would protect his feet from the cold, icy bogs where the moose roamed.

I was excited: with Charles participating in the hunt, we would bring home far more than the usual joint of meat allotted to my mother and me. I carefully planned what I would do with every part of the moose, for among our people no part of the gift is wasted. We women use its long, stiff hair to ornament deerskin robes and birchbark baskets. The sinew lining its spine is beaten into fine, silky threads, while the hide is rolled into cords for our snowshoes. Out on the ocean, the wind fills the moose-skin sails of the hunters' canoes. And generations after its death, the moose's bones still rattle in the waltes bowl.

We set off the next morning before dawn, climbing straight up the mountain. Although Charles kept an effortless pace with the hunters, he seemed not to know what to do with his spear. I caught the sneer on Taqtaloq's face and easily guessed his thoughts. Charles was not keptin in this, Taqtaloq's domain.

Charles hardly noticed the warrior at his side. In the long wait for d'Aumont, forces had gathered within him that he could barely contain. He was eager, too eager, for the kill. I hoped I could keep my promise to the chief.

Niskam was directly over our heads when we arrived at the bog. A fire was lit so the hunters could enjoy a hot drink; the chief had pulled out a twist of tobacco and was savouring the smoke. All around us, men were quietly sorting through their arrowheads, or sharing tales of past hunts. Only Charles remained standing, circling like a cat.

"When will it begin, Mouse?"

Beside us, Taqtaloq was combing his long hair and watching with an ironic smile.

I snapped my head back to Charles. "It has already begun. This is the track where the moose will pass. We have only to wait for the animal to offer himself."

"Wait? If all we will do is wait for an animal to blunder by, I could have more profitably spent the time preparing for d'Aumont!"

He squatted, then stood, then squatted again.

"Let us go after him, you and I!"

Over Charles's shoulder, I caught the chief's look of alarm. Though he could not understand the words, he had heard the impatience in Charles's voice. Drawing Charles aside, I whispered into his ear.

"Do you remember, Charles, my words of last night? It is the prey who chooses the moment of the kill, not we. Should he choose to elude you, you could search this whole bog without once seeing him. It would be like chasing the mist."

Charles hooted. "I'd like to see the animal that could outwit me. As a child in Dieppe, I spent my days tracking the wild deer, which are far more fleet-footed than this great, clumsy beast."

I winced at his arrogance. "Please choose your words more carefully, Charles. You will offend the prey."

Charles leaned closer, a dangerous smile on his face. "Tell me, Mouse: do you really think this moose understands French?"

A shadow fell over us, and I looked up to see Taqtaloq at my side. Squatting, he offered Charles a twist of tobacco then jerked his head at me, appointing me as translator. I grit my teeth, but prepared to obey. Young girls do not ignore the commands of a warrior.

"Ask him if he would like to take part in a little competition."

"What kind of competition?" asked Charles, in reply to my question.

Standing, Taqtaloq pointed in the distance, to a huge boulder precariously balanced on the very edge of the cliff. The rock was split with a deep cleft.

"The winner will be the one who drives his missile into the very heart of the rock."

"And the weapon?" asked Charles. I saw his fingers tighten around the spear.

But Taqtaloq, a master of the spear, was too proud to engage in such an unfair contest.

"I will use your pistol and you my bow."

It was a clever challenge. Each man had some small skill with the other's weapon, but not so much that the outcome could be easily predicted, even by the combatants themselves. As Charles measured the distance with his eye, I could see he was tempted.

"What is the wager?"

Taqtaloq pointed to the pistol at Charles's belt, its hilt heavily crusted with fine stones.

Charles hesitated. At night in our wikuom, he often twirled it in his fingers, testing its balance and watching the play of lamplight on its stones. When he slept, it lay hidden under his blanket. Never had I seen him parted from it.

Charles's eyes narrowed as he studied Taqtaloq. I also studied the warrior, trying to see him through Charles's eyes. What could he have of value that could possibly interest the Frenchman?

"Very well, I accept," said Charles, after a moment. "And if I win, you will return to Europe with me in the autumn. Our king has expressed an interest in meeting a man of this country face to face."

I saw Taqtaloq start and draw back. When the fishermen first came to our shores, said Bright Eyes, some of our young men had sailed away with them, thinking it a fine adventure. None had ever returned. I had also heard it said that Taqtaloq was to be married. Brave hunter that he was, not even he would wish to face Mimikej's wrath when she discovered his betrayal. For my part, I suspected that death in France might be a better bargain than a life spent with Mimikej. Still, I was surprised when Taqtaloq accepted the challenge.

Charles leapt to his feet, grateful to escape the tedium of the hunt. "Then let us begin."

"No," said Taqtaloq. "This is the moose's hour. We will meet afterward." And putting his bow into Charles's hands, Taqtaloq took his leave.

His mind busy with thoughts of the contest, Charles was content to leave the time of the kill up to the moose. The huge male appeared shortly afterward, lumbering heavily toward its destiny. Instantly alert, the younger men grasped their spears while the older hunters stood bow to shoulder. By custom, the chief shot first, a fine thrust that wounded the animal in the neck. Another arrow brought him to one knee. This was the sign for the younger men to move in, spears extended. I watched anxiously, as Charles pressed forward, to the very edge of the circle. Wounded moose have been known to turn suddenly on their attackers in one last, deadly charge: a life for a life. It is a gamble our men willingly accept.

I need not have worried, for it was over in a moment. The hunters were just turning to salute each other when a great "monnnnkkkk" sounded close by. I looked up to see a huge cow, standing with head lowered and four legs extended rigidly, as if bracing herself to face her mate's death. Mercifully, the hunters turned upon her and dispatched her with a few quick thrusts.

"Well that was worth the wait."

I looked up to see a laughing, excited Charles. Quickly, I put my finger to my lips, in a gesture I had seen the brothers use. Already, the chief was speaking the words to release the animals' spirits. Reverently, he took a handful of tobacco from his pouch and put it into the mouth of the bull. Nearby, Taqtaloq had lit a plait of sweetgrass and was waving the smoke toward the beasts, helping their souls waft skyward in a cloud of fragrant smoke. Watching those long, strong hands, I thought how they would soon be clasped around the butt of a pistol – his future decided.

The rumour had run through the crowd that there would be a contest later that day and, with the two moose bundled onto the sled, the hunters began casting secret glances at Charles and Taqtaloq. At last, Taqtaloq stood and beckoned toward Charles. Together, they moved toward the cliff where the boulder stood.

As the challenged one, Charles was the first to shoot. His stance was awkward as he balanced the heavy bow and his fingers gripped the arrow far too tightly. But with its release, the arrow fled into the cleft of the rock. All eyes turned toward Taqtaloq.

The warrior's face was wooden as he moved toward the target. He who had thought to shoot for a jewelled pistol was now playing for his very life. Pistol arm stretched out rigidly from his body, Taqtaloq showed none of the Charles's easy grace with that weapon. The sound of the shot echoed in the valley, but no eye was quick enough to follow its path. The crowd set off as one toward the rock. Grabbing my hand, Charles pulled me after them. Only Taqtaloq remained behind. A quick glance over my shoulder revealed the warrior standing alone against the black wall of carcasses.

As we approached, we could see Charles's arrow, standing erect between the two halves of the stone, its fletching rippling in the light breeze. The hunters were crowing, ready to name him as the victor, when the chief held up a hand for silence. Pushing his fingers deep into the cleft of the rock, the chief felt around for a long moment, and then beckoned to Charles. I had to look no farther than Charles's face to guess the outcome. The prize had eluded him: there would be no trophy to present to his king.

That night, with no jewelled pistol to play with in the lamplight, Charles lay rigid at my side.

"Little good it'll do him," he said, speaking of Taqtaloq. "I've given him no ammunition."

He turned to me then, black eyes fierce.

"That man will come to regret ever having taken something of mine."

Several days later, all work on the fortress was stopped in honour of the wedding of Taqtaloq and Mimikej. I was not among the circle of maidens who attended his bride as she dressed. Nor was I invited to join the married women who would counsel Mimikej in the secret ways of pleasing her husband. Our customs had no place for one who was neither maiden nor wife.

I was glad to remain outside: praises for the fine, strong husband and his virtuous bride would surely have caught in my throat, choking me. For I knew that happiness could not dwell long in their wikuom. Mimikej saw only her own beauty, soon to be enrobed in the finest of wedding clothes. Taqtaloq would be conscious only of the honour he was conferring on her.

I spent the morning working on a pair of skin leggings for Charles, who would need them when the weather grew colder. After a restless night, he had hurriedly drunk the spruce beer I brought him then set off for the beach. Calling to me over his shoulder, he said that he would return in time for the festivities. It was the first time he had left me behind.

When we first came together, Charles had given me a pair of scissors. Head down, trying to accustom myself to the new tool, I was surprised to see Antoine's black robe before me. I looked up, shielding my eyes against Niskam's rays. "Your brother has gone to his ship," I told him. "He will return when the shadows lengthen."

"Yes, that is his way," said Antoine, with a hard smile I did not understand.

He dropped to his heels beside me. "I have come to talk to you, Mouse, not to my brother."

Susan Young de Biagi

He paused, looking into my eyes. "Are you happy?"

It was a foolish question. The French, I knew, spoke of happiness as a thing to grasp and hold forever. Fishermen spoke of the days when they would return to their land, sit beside their own firesides, and never again know want, or fear. But to us, fear often came as a friend, sweeping from wikuom to wikuom – I know not how – whispering to us to be on guard against the enemy that lurked outside.

Anger, too, had its uses. Once, when I was very small, a group of fledgling warriors, too young for wisdom but old enough to be dangerous, had formed a circle around me, taunting me about my animal ancestors. My mother, who never raised her voice to a man, entered the circle – small, dark, spitting, and not to be trifled with. Oh yes, anger has its uses, permitting one to stare, undaunted, into the very face of life.

Was I happy? Not knowing how to answer, I simply bent my head to my work.

Antoine tried again. "The other women are helping to prepare Mimikej for her wedding. Why are you not among them?"

I bent my head even farther, concentrating on a sinew that refused to pass through the hole I had made for it. "Mimikej has too many women fussing over her costume already. Too many hands will spoil a beautiful creation."

"Exactly right," he said, reaching over to help me tug at the stubborn sinew. "And yet, the Creator did not intend for us to be alone. Sometimes, an extra pair of hands can mean the difference between survival and ruin."

Suddenly impatient, I wrenched the cord through the hole, and was dismayed to find it dangling, useless, in my fingers. I threw the skins in their basket, and turned to the man at my side. "I understand what you are saying, Antoine. You are warning me that, with your brother, I will always be alone. But you forget that I was born to be an outcast."

"Thankfully, we do not always become what we were born to be."

Antoine absently twisted the third finger of his right hand, as if pulling on something that was not there.

Anger rose in my throat. "And what of Taqtaloq, who was born to be a bully?"

"The burdens that Taqtaloq assumes today will change him. How? It remains to be seen. If he is wise, he will turn to heaven for help."

I rose to my feet. "You would, perhaps, prefer to see me in the hands of such a man?"

"Married, and protected by a man of your own people? Yes, Mouse, I would."

"It is good to see you together again, as it used to be."

The two of us turned, startled. It was Charles, who had not gone to the ship after all. Had he heard our conversation? I thought not: his face was open, eyes clear. Whatever had plagued him in the night was gone. He drew me to his side and tugged my braid, as he sometimes did when feeling playful. "We three have a wedding to attend."

"Not I," said Antoine. "I have an appointment with my breviary."

"Then we will leave you to it. Come Mouse. And I will explain to you how your weddings differ from ours in France."

I followed; I could not do otherwise.

k

*O*n the morning after the wedding, Charles once again left for the ship without me. Seizing a basket, I set off for the shore, where I spent the morning gathering shellfish. My mother and I would spend the winter alone, and in need of food stores. Tomorrow, I would smoke the oysters, a winter treat my mother loved.

The beach was empty when I arrived. People were recovering from the wedding, just as they had been on the day the brothers arrived. And although much had happened since then, I was still alone.

The oysters lay thick and plentiful on the shingle. I worked quickly, ever mindful of the tide. But even after a whole morning's labour, I was still restless. Storing my basket under a cool tree, I made my way to the fishermen's camp. The camp was empty at this hour, but I could see the chaloupes just offshore, bobbing on the water. The men would be in before long, and grateful for a cup of tea. Eager for another task, I busied myself around the fire.

Pierrot was the first to land, eyes dancing as he saw me. Settling himself comfortably at my feet, he began to indulge in his favourite game: tormenting old Johann.

"The fish will be fine where they are," he said in reply to the old man's indignant pointing to the boats. "Here's Mouse with tea. It would be an insult to refuse."

He reached out a hand for the steaming gourd. "Ah, but it was cold on the banks this morning, Mouse. Of course, I had my friend with me," he said, patting the small flask in his pocket. "But there's nothing can match the gift of tea from a lady's hand. My mother would always wait for my father and me on the shore, her bonnet the beacon we'd steer by."

Pierrot's memories had to keep for another day, as I was soon busy handing out cups to all the men. Raphael scorned the cup I offered him, going off by himself a little distance down the beach, where he began kindling his own small fire.

"Ignore him, Mouse. He's not one for company."

Cup in hand, Pierrot began wandering among the boats, merrily chiding their occupants for the size of their catch. As I tended the fire, I watched Raphael pulling his large string of beads through his fingers, lips moving in a constant and regular rhythm. At that moment, he stiffened. Following his gaze, I saw a longboat pulling toward shore with two passengers: my mother and Lord Stewart.

My mother, as was usual, leapt out of the boat first, a large bag on her head.

"Jezebel, Jezebel." It was Lord Stewart, calling her back on a high, whinnying laugh.

Jezebel: the strange sound of it fell harshly on my ears, but my mother leaned back into it as though it were birdsong.

As she waded back to the boat, Lord Stewart slung another bag around her shoulders. From the bow of her neck, I could see it contained a weight of books.

Raphael continued to watch them. Kissing his beads, he hung them around his neck and began walking toward the beach. I shaded my eyes to watch.

"Good morning."

Antoine was standing before me, cheerful as the day.

"I've been looking for you, Mouse. I have something for you."

"A husband perhaps?" I had not entirely forgiven him for his words of the day before.

Antoine laughed. Never had I seen him in such a good humour.

"Nothing so valuable. It is only...."

Antoine raised his head at the shouting on the beach, then began to run, skirts flying. I followed quickly behind.

Lord Stewart was standing on the beach, blood dripping from his hand. My mother had already torn off part of her robe, and was binding the wound. Two of the sailors were holding back Raphael, who was straining toward Antoine.

"Father, Father! I had the heretic in my hands, but this... this bitch," he said, gesturing toward my mother. "She came between him and the knife. Had it not been for her, this devil would even now be in hell where he belongs."

Antoine's face was whiter than I had ever seen it. The slight grimace of distaste he always tried to hide around Raphael was replaced by open horror. But the fisherman was too agitated to see it.

"I did it for you, Father. Together, we can rid the land of these heretics." Raphael spit on the ground at Lord Stewart's feet.

Antoine raised a hand, as though to ward the man off.

"It is an evil thing you have done. You must ask the Lord to forgive you. I cannot."

He then turned to the sailors holding the crazed man.

"Ask the fishermen for rope to bind him good and tight, then take him to my brother on the ship. I will tend to Lord Stewart myself."

Turning his back on Raphael, he put one arm under Lord Stewart's elbow and beckoned to me with the other. Raphael's anguished pleas of "Father, Father," followed us up the beach. Though each one hit Antoine like a blow, not once did he turn around.

Lord Stewart's smile was charming as he stopped and turned to Antoine. "We have not yet been introduced, sir. I am James Stewart of Killeith. I would extend my hand but as you can see...."

Antoine bowed briefly from the neck, then made as if to continue up the beach. But Lord Stewart refused to move.

"You know. I find I can't regret this ridiculous act. From one moment to the next, I seem to have become ... 'sufficiently interesting'."

I drew in my breath at his words. Lord Stewart looked me up and down, and in his eyes I saw a tribute to my quickness. I fixed my own eyes on Antoine, and kept them there.

Antoine was confused, then angered, by the remark. "Your amusement comes at a terrible cost, Lord Stewart. That man will give his life for that one moment of madness. You will admit it is a high price to pay."

"A fisherman's life? The man should thank your brother for relieving him of the tedium."

In Lord Stewart's land, perhaps, such light treatment of death was a thing to boast of. But I had watched Antoine gently holding the faces of the dying between his hands.

Lord Stewart tried to infuse his voice with some measure of regret.

"Come, Father. I apologize. I have long awaited our meeting, and now see what a wreck I have made of it. How can I atone? I know. I will beg your brother to spare the man's life."

No matter what the surface, Lord Stewart saw none but his own reflection. I fell back in disgust.

"We must find a way to save him," came the fierce whisper at my side. "They will not stop until they have taken his life."

The words, I knew, were not for Raphael. Looking down at my mother, I saw her face was streaked with blood where she had swept back her hair. Glittering black stars had consumed the soft brown of her eyes. Talons gripped my forearms and would not let go.

Breaking free, I ran, past the fisherman's camp, past the sorrowful face of Pierrot, to the silent hut I shared with Charles. Much later, I remembered the basket of oysters hidden in the cool of the trees. I left them where they lay. No oysters would console my mother for the approaching loss of her Netaoansom.

❧

"Well, little girl. You certainly manage to find yourself in the thick of it. All the while I thought you safely at home, you were watching that fool put his own head in the noose. Well, there you see what a head filled with religion can do. At least he managed not to involve my brother in his crime."

"Is he...?"

"What, dead? Not yet. My brother will want his hour with him, to make sure he gets a swipe at heaven. He'll swing in the morning."

Charles waved aside the soup I ladled out for him. "I ate on the ship. But sit here beside me and tell me how it happened. It's lucky for me your mother was there to save Lord Stewart's precious neck. A dead body, even a pickled one, wouldn't make quite the same impression in Paris as a live lord, wearing his chains like a bracelet, bless his dear foppish soul."

Charles reached over to the rub the back of my neck. "Do try, Mouse, not to place yourself in quite so much danger next time. You're too engaging to lose."

Charles hand strayed down under the neck of my robe, to the small, hard pebbles beneath. I knew he did not love me, but I could not help my body's response. I was young, and he was skilled.

The loud crashing through the trees could not be ignored. Antoine did not have our talent for walking noiselessly through the bush, but even he did not usually make so much noise. I jumped back and Charles laughed.

"And I thought Jesuits were supposed to be subtle. Angel Gabriel with his horn could not have made such a flourish."

"Not so much levity, please Charles. There's a soul in agony this night."

Charles made a small, impatient sound in his throat. "Your capacity for forgiveness astonishes me. I admit," he said, raising a hand to silence his brother, "forgiveness is your trade. But even you must see how this fisherman has compromised you. By the time this story reaches London, everyone will be raving about Lord Stewart's miraculous escape from an assassin priest. From now on, every lookout on every English ship will be scanning these shores for the sight of a black robe."

Antoine waved a careless hand. "You exaggerate Charles. Besides, Lord Stewart knows I had no part in this crime."

"You do not know Lord Stewart as I do, brother. Think of it: would he rather it be known that he was attacked by a common fisherman, or a zealous Jesuit, educated in the finest college in France?"

"You could be right. But we have weightier matters to discuss. I have come to ask you a favour."

"You know, Antoine, that I cannot spare his life. The decision has been made, according to the articles of war. As admiral, I cannot contravene what is decided in court martial."

"I do know. I want you to accompany me to the ship."

Charles cast a long dark glance at my body. I felt the heat rise to my face.

"I've just returned from the ship, Antoine. Ask one of my men to take you."

"No, Charles. Raphael has requested your presence. There is something he wishes us both to hear."

Charles reached down to re-buckle his sword. "As you wish. Come Mouse, we can sleep on the ship."

Antoine put a hand on his brother's chest. "Leave the child here, Charles. You know what it's like the night before...." Antoine could not even say the words.

But Charles would not relent. Young as I was, I knew what role my body would play that night. In spite of his levity, the taking of a man's life was a sober thing. Charles would bury himself in me, seeking the unconsciousness that comes at such moments.

There could be no such relief for Antoine. On the morrow, I guessed, Antoine's face would still bear its full weight of grief, while that of Charles would be as smooth as a child's.

Antoine stamped out the fire while I prepared a bag. Anxious to get the thing over with, Charles was already far ahead of us and standing impatiently by the longboat. Across the water, every light on the ship was ablaze.

On board, the few sailors who had stayed behind to man Stewart's ship were huddled in small groups around huge barrels, grimly pouring rum down their throats. A few were doggedly trying to sing. Now and then, one toppled over and the others pushed him into the shadows.

Antoine was studying them with a look of disgust.

"Will you not intervene, Charles?"

"Who do you think ordered the barrels to be opened? By dawn, they'll be so hung over they'll just want the deed to be done, so they can crawl back into their hammocks. And by tomorrow eve, the whole thing will seem like a dream."

"I hope the executioner will be sober at least."

"Yes, but I've a whole barrel put aside for him, for afterwards. He'll be snoring along with the rest of them by noon."

Charles made for the hold, pulling me along behind him. Antoine barred the way.

"No, Charles, really not. I consented to Mouse coming with us to the ship, but she cannot now go where we go."

"And what do you suggest, that I leave her above with a ship full of drunken men? Maybe I can stash her with the executioner, to listen to his maudlin stories."

Antoine's frustration was clear, but he said nothing as he turned and helped me down the ladder. Here, in the belly of the ship, the noise from the decks above was muffled. Charles opened a door and the three of us entered a small closet, lit only by the moonlight streaming in through the tiny porthole. There, in the semi-darkness sat Raphael, beads in hand.

Antoine went up to the condemned man, taking his hands in his. "I have come to hear your confession, Raphael, and remain with you this night. My brother has also come, as you requested."

"There is only one deed that remains unconfessed, Father: the one I shall hang for. And for that I will not ask forgiveness. It is why I have asked your brother to be present."

He turned to Charles, "I wished to tell you, Captain, that I do not blame you for doing your duty. Murder was, and is, in my heart, and I am willing to pay with my life. My one regret is that I did not succeed."

Charles nodded, commending the man with his eyes. But Antoine's eyes held only sorrow.

"You know, Raphael, that had you succeeded in killing Lord Stewart, you would have condemned him to hell?"

The man's lip jutted out. "A fitting place for heretics."

"And yet our Lord died for this man, so that even he might escape condemnation. It was a gift our Lord gave him, one that you tried to rob him of."

"Anyone can see that Lord Stewart does not belong to Him!"

"Not yet. But while he lives, he may."

"While he lives, he will try to stop your work here, Father. How can this one soul be weighed against the multitudes who will be saved by your work?"

"Our Lord did not die for the multitudes, Raphael, he died for us one by one. Would you add to his pain by stealing even a single soul?"

Back and forth they went. After a moment, Charles tugged at my arm, and together we backed out, leaving Antoine alone with the condemned man. Once on deck, I leaned against the rail, breathing in the fresh, clear air.

"I do not understand, Charles."

"Nor do I, Mouse, nor do I."

*C*harles was pulling on his breeches when I awoke. "Stay here, Mouse. There is no need for you to be on deck."

But I was already reaching for my robe. I would not lie cringing beneath the blankets while a soul took its first steps into the unknown. We, the people of Cibou, have always stood arm in arm against the approach of death.

Outside, I could feel the cold deck through my moccasins. A young drummer was already beginning a low rumble. The men lined up along the rail were making a hasty attempt to straighten their clothing. Striped caps were pulled down low over their eyes. I looked for Lord Stewart, but he was nowhere to be seen. His absence was likely Charles's decision. Lord Stewart, I felt sure, would have savoured his moment of revenge.

Charles had left me with one of the few sailors who was still sober, giving strict orders that I was not to pass beyond the poop deck. From afar, I saw Antoine emerge out of the hatchway onto the deck, followed closely behind by Raphael. Hands bound tightly behind his back, he stumbled on the first step. Antoine caught him just before he fell. Charles raised a hand, signalling a halt to the drum. "Prisoner, do you have anything to say in your defence?"

Raphael's voice was clear.

"No sir. But I will say to all men here present that I die a confessed Christian."

Then kissing the cross Antoine held out to him, he stood quietly waiting, noose swinging from the yardarm above his head and heavy weights tied to his feet.

Charles took a step back. "Seaman, do your duty."

The huge man spoke a few words to the prisoner, who nodded. But instead of reaching up to the rope, the executioner suddenly heaved his vast bulk against the condemned man, tipping him over the rail and into the sea. My eyes flew to Charles, who watched with serene calm. Murmurs of approval arose from the sailors around me. It was, perhaps, the death each man would have chosen for himself.

Back at my side, Charles explained away my confusion.

"The sentence was death by hanging, a damned slow way to die. I've seen them dangle there, choking, for more than a quarter of an hour. The law had to be obeyed, of course. But can we help it if the man slipped at the last moment?"

"Slipped? He was pushed."

"Well, as a Christian he would never have jumped, though some will. Still, he welcomed the favour. The executioner, as you saw, was careful to ask."

Antoine was slowly making his way to our side. The men patted him awkwardly on the back and shoulder as he passed.

Charles took him by the arm and pushed him into his cabin.

Antoine turned, white-faced, to his brother. "You saw the last moments ... how long...?

"Seconds. You can comfort yourself on that point. I see that he confessed."

"Yes, he confessed."

"And received absolution?"

Antoine nodded. "I told him this day he would see his Lord."

Then falling into Charles's arms, he cried until he could cry no more.

ƙ

*i*t was several days before I saw Antoine again. I was searching for plants along the riverbank when I saw him approaching from the other direction, a sack full of leaves dangling from his hip.

He called out as soon as he knew the words would carry.

"You'll remember, Mouse, that I have a gift for you."

Coming closer, he reached into his robe and pulled out a tiny, polished stone that glinted green in the sun.

"I found it in a riverbed in France, when I was a small boy. It's been in my pocket ever since. Do you see that hole? It was carved, I believe, with an ancient tool, by a craftsman a thousand years dead. At least, that's what I always told myself. It deserves to hang upon the neck of a pretty lady, but of course I had none to give it to. My mother and sister both died young. And I've always known I was meant for the Church."

Stretching out his hand, Antoine dropped the stone into my palm. I looked down at the green object glowing in my hand.

"It sometimes happens that a man will happen upon a treasure and try to hold it for a time. Eventually he will relinquish it, knowing it was never his to keep. As for the stone, its value is neither scarred nor diminished by its time in his hands. For no matter its history, it is still a jewel of great worth."

And turning, Antoine left me to find my way back to the village alone.

k

*t*here was a pattern to the days that followed: each day, Charles would leave me for a little while longer. He spent long days on the ship, poring over sea charts, and a growing number of nights on board. Warriors were posted at the high places, to watch for d'Aumont's arrival.

It was hard to know how to fill my days. At first, I tried to rejoin my old friends, the fishermen. But they did not speak as freely as before. I had lost the advantage of invisibility. Over the past moons, I had helped negotiate the agreement between commander and chief, translated orders to the warriors, been in the front line of battle and slept in the captain's arms. I was no longer the little mouse who sat at their feet and nibbled at the words that fell like crumbs. But who was I? They no longer knew. Nor did I.

From afar, I feel my mother's eyes, watching. She was angry to see me abandoned so soon, while Charles was yet in Cibou. I knew her resentment would not soon be forgotten.

The air was so burdened with waiting that we felt its pressure on our skin. I passed the time sorting through the beads in my collection, separating them through my fingers and letting them fall to the ground in languid waterfalls of colour. I watched events play out slowly before me: Charles advancing up the beach, laboriously, as if wading ankle deep through the sand; Lord Stewart sitting frozen, book in hand, a finger eternally poised above the page. Even Niskam stood fixed in his place, waiting for d'Aumont's return.

At night, I lay sleepless on the pallet I had once shared with Charles.

"Daughter!" The whisper was weak, but insistent. Searching in the darkness for a robe, I slipped out of the hut.

"Come," said my mother, catching me by the elbow, digging her fingers into my skin. Beyond, in the trees, I could see someone moving. I tried to pull back, but she only gripped harder. Two men stepped out of the shadows.

The stone had fallen. In her desire to free Lord Stewart and avenge herself on Charles, my mother had made a tragic mistake. I wanted to run, but could not.

One of the men stepped forward. I searched my mind for a name: Lambert, Lord Stewart's body servant, who had received his master's hat that first day in the longboat. Why not Stewart himself? Then I remembered the brilliant white of the man's collar and sleeves, on the day his ship was taken. I remembered too,

Lord Stewart calling out to my mother in order to heap more bags upon her head.

"Mouse. That is your name, is it not?" The words were spoken in French, no doubt the reason why this man had been chosen. In the next moment, he revealed other qualities that made him valuable to Lord Stewart.

"Well Mouse, we need your help," he said, smiling as though for the first time in his life. "Jezebel here has put herself in great danger by helping us flee the ship. She will be safe only when Lord Stewart reclaims his property."

I knew my mother would never be safe in the hands of such men. Seeing the disbelief in my face, the man dropped the mask and assumed another, with frightening ease. It came to me that he wore many such masks. And when all were peeled away, there would be nothing left but air.

"I could tell her what kind of man you are."

"Oh please. It would be very amusing." With this he stepped back, leaving me to choose the words that would sway my mother. But as I looked into her eyes, alive with a light that was almost madness, I fell silent.

It was a short walk to the caves where the rest of Lord Stewart's men were held. The questions chased each other in circles. The plan was undoubtedly Lord Stewart's. But how had he conveyed it to my mother, who spoke only the language of our people? The two must have been planning it for long nights: Lord Stewart struggling to convey the plan with signs and drawings, my mother struggling to understand. He had few virtues, Stewart, but patience was apparently among them.

My thoughts were interrupted by the man at my side. In a pleasant voice, as though recalling the day's activities, he gave me the words to say. "You will ask for Andrew Haddington, say it after me Mouse, Had-ing-ton, yes that's right, and William

Baxter. Tell the guard that Captain Daniel is planning to sail in search of his ship, and requires two of Lord Stewart's sailors as crew."

"And if they do not listen?"

"Everyone knows that Captain Daniel gives his orders through you. They'll listen."

I sifted through my choices: the two men could not understand the words I spoke to the guards but my mother could, and might warn her new companions of any trickery. Nor could I risk a secret message to the guard. If he reacted in alarm, it could mean my mother's life.

It all happened as they had planned. The two men hid in the trees with my mother as I announced my presence. The guard, Kloqntiej, had me stand before the gate and shout the difficult names into the cave. Though roused from sleep just moments before, the prisoners were alert and wary. Kloqntiej motioned to two of his warriors to accompany us.

I was unprepared for the suddenness of the strike. I fell back as one of the warriors crumpled against me, his head bleeding from the force of Lambert's blow. My gaze caught in that of the dying man, I did not see the rest. When I finally looked up, the second warrior was staked to the ground by his own spear.

I heard a small keening sound in the forest and turned to see my mother, wakened too late from the dream that had held her captive these many weeks. As Lambert hauled her to her feet, his companion freed the hands of Haddington and Baxter. They moved quickly to hide the bodies. Then Lambert turned to me.

"Now, clever girl, you will tell us where Captain Daniel keeps the muskets. We know they are not on the ship."

And in that moment I understood: with the muskets, even four men could overtake the warriors, armed only with spears. They would be able to free all the men held in the caves. The few French sailors on Charles's ship could not hold it against such a force. The ship would be gone long before d'Aumont arrived with Charles's own men.

Lambert pushed me and my mother in front of him as we began walking. With the approach of dawn, the forest filled with birdsong. One note stood out among the rest. Unaccustomed to the birds of our land, the men noticed nothing unusual, but I knew the sound. Bright Eyes had a special whistle for me as a little girl, known only to the two of us. From somewhere, he was watching. A moment more, then the sound was gone.

Beside me, my mother was sniffling. I kept a hand on her elbow to propel her forward, but was busy with my own thoughts. Charles was asleep in the fortress, a single guard at his door. The muskets were locked in the small room beside him. They would have to kill him to get the muskets, and kill him they would, unless Bright Eyes warned him in time. The most important choice of my life lay before me: would I lead them to Charles, or risk my own mother's life?

Bright Eyes's whistle came to me again: it could only mean that he had alerted Charles. This time, though, Bright Eyes did not go unnoticed. Lambert looked up to see the old man standing on a ridge just above our heads. With a flash of Lambert's knife, my friend was gone forever. My mother's mouth was wide open, but Haddington's fist silenced her before any sound could emerge. Gripping her mouth, in which a tooth was hanging, she stood quietly beside me, in shock.

Bright Eyes lay suspended on the ridge above us, his spirit already flown to the Land of the Ancestors. Our people would change them, he had said, as he and I watched from the spirit world. His long vigil had already begun.

Lambert pulled on my hair, urging me to move forward. Though shaken at being discovered, the men were still determined to carry out their plan. In the violence of the last moments, not a sound had been made: we walked through the same, peaceful pre-dawn forest, alive with birds.

Perhaps the men had persuaded themselves that Bright Eyes was simply an old man unlucky enough to stumble upon us. This time, however, they were more wary of discovery than they had been and kept glancing at my face. Knowing the danger, I was careful to clear my mind of any thoughts of Charles and what must be happening at the fort. Nor could I bear to think of Bright Eyes. I focused instead on the red neck scarf of the man in front of me. Later, when it was all over, I would be haunted by dreams of that vicious blaze of red. In moments of distress, it still rises before me, a banner of every disappointment and every failed dream.

The men knew their route. We had circled behind the village, coming to the edge of the forest just behind the fort. There was no activity, not even a wisp of smoke. The men grinned at each other. Baxter put a rough hand on my neck, pulling me along with him. My mother kept a shaking hand on the edge of my robe.

Lambert signalled for me to call Charles from the other side of the door. But as I leaned on the heavy oaken door, it fell open. Stewart's men, hoping to catch Charles by surprise, were themselves surprised by a circle of Frenchmen with muskets trained. Charles himself was seated, fully dressed, on the edge of the table, one leg swinging, a pistol aimed at Lambert's head. He glanced casually at me, eyes blank, before moving his gaze to my mother. I could not tell what he was thinking – or what he would do.

"Take this scum and lock them in the caves," he said to his men. "Throw Lord Stewart in with them, and make sure he has neither book nor fiddle. Leave the women here."

As the men were leaving, Charles came to stand before me, pistol in hand. Black eyes remained blank as he brought the barrel to rest just under my jaw, pressing it into my skin.

"Charles!"

Antoine burst through the door. Charles dropped the pistol, disgust on his face.

"Heavens Antoine, don't surprise me like that. I could've shot the girl."

"Surely you know that Mouse had nothing to do with this plan!"

"Of course, but I had hoped to ascertain the details from her mother, before your dramatic entrance ruined everything. You know Mouse would have sacrificed herself before revealing her mother's involvement. She must have diverted the guards somehow." He put the pistol back in its sheath and sat down again on the table.

Ignoring Charles's words, Antoine guided me to a chair and poured me a cup of water. He was angry, I could see, but his grief went deeper than his anger. He turned back to Charles.

"Bright Eyes is dead...," he said dully, "Mouse's mother now an enemy of her people – perhaps Mouse as well, unless we can persuade them otherwise." He struck a hand onto the table. "The fault is ours, Charles, yours and mine. This is what comes of giving in to our passions."

Charles passed a hand before his eyes. "My passions, Antoine, not yours."

"Not entirely. The first sin was my mine, for it was I who singled her out the day on the beach, a little girl with eyes like the sister we lost."

Antoine's voice dropped, speaking – not to Charles – but to his god. "Had I known it would come to this, I would never have taught her our language. Forgive me, Lord."

I had had enough. Large drops of blood were falling from my mother's mouth onto the floor, as they sat scissoring me out of all responsibility for my own life. Inside me, a nameless, dark thing lifted its head. I rose to my feet and, gripping my mother by the arm, left the fort.

*M*y mother and I remained in her wikuom throughout the turbulence that followed. Every day, I expected warriors to come for us. No one came. My mother lay with her face to the wall, weeping for Bright Eyes and the part she played in his death.

I knew they would bury him on the third day, according to our custom. In search of a fitting tribute, my eye fell on the copper cooking pot Charles had given me. I had often wondered what he had intended by the gift, as it was clear he had no wish to taste my cooking. Seizing a mallet, I began flattening the pot, delighting in every blow struck. I was wiping the sweat from my eyes when Pierrot dropped down beside me.

It was a clever choice. Charles and Antoine knew I could not rebuff my light-hearted friend.

"They have sent me for you, Mouse. It is time."

He looked down at the shiny, battered object at my feet. "Was that a cooking pot?"

"It was."

"And now you are turning it into … what? An ornament?"

"It was never intended to be more than an ornament," I said, giving it a final, savage blow with the mallet.

Leaving the vessel for Pierrot to carry, I went to fetch my mother. I could not risk leaving her behind. Failure to attend the burial would be taken as proof of guilt on her part. I had earlier given her a draught made with Bright Eyes's own herbs, and sat beside her to make sure she drank it. By the time we were ready to leave, she walked as one dead. At least she would be unaware of the whispers around her.

Pierrot ran to grasp my mother's other arm, and together we steered her toward the burial ground. I kept my eyes down as we approached. Just as I had feared, a black robe and a red cape fluttered on the very edge of my vision. I turned quickly away, searching for Bright Eyes.

Susan Young de Biagi

He was sitting upright, chin on his knees. The old robe had been replaced with a fine, new deerskin I had seen the chief's wife curing for her husband. As the closest thing Bright Eyes had to a daughter, I bent to fasten my gift around his chest. A gasp went up from the crowd as the copper glowed red in the fire. No warrior had ever been sent to the Land of the Ancestors in finer armour.

The drumming had already begun, the men's voices spiralling up to the sky. Our chief wrapped Bright Eyes from head to foot in a second skin, then bound the whole with cords. The men placed him carefully upright in the round pit dug for him.

Our chief stepped forward, into the circle.

"Here he sits, honoured Elder, victim of infamy." Had our chief been a lesser man, this would have been the place to stop and look at my mother. But such petty gestures were beneath him. Turning instead to the people crowded around the pit, he called out in a ringing voice.

"Warriors, have you nothing to ease his passage to the Land of the Ancestors?"

One by one, the warriors stepped forward with their newly fashioned weapons, flinging them into the hole. A waste, I thought, for Bright Eyes was no hunter. Even there, in the Land of the Ancestors, he would have to earn his keep as he had always done, with his tongue. For surely, surely, there is as much need of storytellers there as here.

*

*t*he next day, I heard a scratching on the outside of the wikuom. Opening the flap, I was surprised to see the chief. My mother had fallen into a stuporous sleep, and I left her inside as I joined the chief by the fire. As is our custom, I waited for him to speak.

The chief pulled a brand from the fire, to light his pipe. I sat and watched as he pulled the great clouds of smoke into his lungs. This, I thought, may be my last moment of freedom. It had been so short: the time in which I gathered into my own hands the threads of my life.

Too late, I realized that the short span of time – from the night Charles first took me, to the moment my mother arrived with Lambert – had been a space in which to act. Niskam himself had tarried, giving me the gift of time. But lulled by the very slowness of events, I had chosen instead to watch and wait. And as I dallied, others had seized the opportunity: my mother, Lord Stewart, Charles. And suddenly, events had swirled, speeding out of my hands. All this I pondered as our chief sat savouring the smoke.

"You are young," he said, surprising me, as usual, by his ability to read my thoughts. "Thankfully," he chuckled, "life does not grant us a single mistake. When you are as old as I, you will have the great honour of looking back over a lifetime of them."

"I have forfeited the chance to make my own mistakes," I responded, dully.

"And that, too, is a failing of youth," he smiled, "to watch your opportunities float away on the tide, thinking they will never return. And as they embark on their journey over the waters of the earth, it seems they never will." He drew deeply on the pipe, watching the embers turn red.

"But then one day, you look down to find them once again at your feet. And that, Mouse, is wisdom: the ability to recognize them when they return to you once more."

It was a gift. As I looked up in sudden thankfulness, the chief patted me on my knee. Then he stood.

"Come, Mouse, let us walk together a little."

I knew what was coming before he formed the words.

"Your mother...."

"Was not herself," I said, quickly breaking in, then shamed to silence by my own bad manners. Not offended, he gestured to me to continue. And as we walked, I told him her dreams of Netaoansom – and how those dreams were shattered in the moment the first warrior fell to the ground.

"And yet those warriors had families, who demand justice," said the chief. "Keptin Daniel will administer justice to his own people, but it is our duty to deal with your mother. The Elders will meet in council tonight to decide the matter. We will expect you and your mother at the council fire."

He put a kind hand on my shoulder. "The Elders are wise, Mouse, and will sift every grain of sand twice before making their decision. You can trust your mother to them." As I watched him turn down the path that led to his wikuom – robe in tatters and moccasins worn through – I felt humbled by his care in seeking me out.

I was beginning to feel hopeful as I made my way home. The forest was now in deep shadow. Had we walked so far, the chief and I? Where was the light of our fire? As I moved between the trees trying to find my way, my foot hit a stone. All strength drained from my body as I recognized that stone, one of the big ones round our fire, laid there by my own hands. It was then I knew: the flame that my mother had guarded so tenderly since her earliest days with her young husband – that flame had gone out. And my mother, drugged with sleep in the wikuom, neither knew nor cared. I sat down and wept the bitterest tears of my life.

*L*ater that night I escorted my mother to the council fire. Our people are too civilized to stare directly into the face of one so overcome by shame as my mother was. But I felt their thoughts: some were curious, others kind. Many were hostile.

I could not read the thoughts of the Elders as they moved slowly to their places: old women leaned on the arms of strong young grandsons; white-haired men shuffled proudly on alone, refusing – on this most important of occasions – the aid of a stick. As the Elders took their seats, I searched their faces and found them as blank as those of small children, with no judgment written thereon. Later, I would wonder about those faces: how innocence can somehow be fanned to new life from the very embers of pain and disappointment. But in that moment, I was simply relieved it was so. Easing my mother to the ground, I took my place beside her. Charles was nowhere to be seen. But on the other side of the fire I saw Antoine, concern for me clearly written on his face. I quickly turned away, so that from every direction, I saw only the faces of my own people.

Ku'ku'kwes, the very oldest among them, rose slowly to her feet. Bright Eyes – how it hurt to think of him – Bright Eyes once told me that she had been born before even the first of the fishermen came to our shores. The crowd hushed to hear her voice – so light, a feather on the wind.

"Who among you will stand to speak for the fallen warriors?" she whispered.

Lentuk stood and strode to the middle of the circle. He was not a warrior, Lentuk, nor did he hunt. With no wife or children to cook for him, he lived on the food that our women prepared and left outside the door of his wikuom. Sometimes, on very rare nights, we saw him walking along the beach by the light of the moon, his cloak wrapped tightly around his body.

Lentuk's gift lay in his command of words. My heart fell when I saw that he would be speaking on behalf of the slain warriors.

"It is not just I, Lentuk, who stands before you," he began, waving an arm in a wide circle, directing our gaze to the shadows. "Behind me stand the brave warriors who fell so recently.

They cannot begin their journey to the Land of the Ancestors until they see that justice is done."

At the mention of the fallen warriors, my mother let out a low moan. I wrapped my cloak around her, feeling her head burrowing into my side.

Lentuk waited for silence, then began again. "Beyond them are the shadows of the children who will never be born to them. They, too, cry out for justice. Can you see them?"

And such was his power that, for a moment, we saw in the flames the dark, sad eyes; the upturned palms; and the tiny bare feet of these shadow children. I shifted uneasily, remembering that I had consigned my own children to oblivion before they were even born. As Lentuk's eyes caught my movement, he permitted himself a small, secret smile of victory. That smile stiffened my back and I stared back hard at him. There were no children, I told myself, only shadows caused by the flicking flames. I gripped my mother around the waist, nudging her to sit up a little straighter.

I glanced at the faces around the circle. The Elders' faces were serene, unreadable. But behind them, the crowd sat entranced. Always before, I too had sat enthralled as Lentuk wove his visions. Now I wondered: did he sit in his wikuom planning his performance? In my mind, I saw him there, saying to himself, "Here is the place to pause, and lower my head in grief. And there, for a moment, I will be overwhelmed, unable to find the strength to go on." I was suddenly glad that Lentuk had been chosen to speak for the other side.

But who would speak for my mother? I felt a stab of pain as I realized who would have stood as her natural protector: Bright Eyes himself. Was he watching from the Land of the Ancestors? Surely he was a more real presence than Lentuk's phantom children.

As Lentuk stepped back into the shadows, another figure stepped forward in a flourish of red cape.

"No!" I screamed.

Or perhaps I did not scream, for when I came to my senses my mother was still burrowed into my side and my neighbours sat calmly, enjoying the show. This was the Charles I had seen in his debates with Lord Stewart: casual, irreverent, and determined to win. And I was as angry as I had ever been in my life.

He began by bowing low, in apparent grief, to the warriors' families who sat in a small group on one side of the circle. The words were spoken in the language of our people, formal and well-rehearsed.

"I remember the bright days of summer, when these young men clustered about me, laughing, glorying in their strength."

There it was, I thought perversely: his first mistake. How could it help to remind the families of his part in hastening the death of their sons? But as I looked at the families, I saw they were entranced by this vision of young men at the height of their strength. I felt my anger burn at his victory.

Beside me, I felt my mother straighten, suddenly alert. And on her face: joy – not at the possibility of escape that had so abruptly opened before her, but for the forgiveness that Charles's presence signified. I could no longer look at either of them. Rising to my feet, I stumbled into the darkness.

*

*i*t was our chief who came to find me. My fury had abated, and shame at leaving my mother had crept in to take its place. As he stepped before me, a light hand on my shoulder, I lowered my head to avoid his gaze.

"The Elders have reached a decision," he said gently.

I nodded, tears dropping onto my robe, where he could not see them.

"It is their decision that she be banished from Cibou. When Keptin Daniel leaves, she will be on his ship, which will leave her on the coast of the big island." He looked at me kindly. "It is our hope that she will find her way back to her own people."

"I will go with her."

"No Mouse. You will not."

"But she cannot make it back alone, she is too weak. I can care for her. Please ask the Elders to reconsider."

"It was your mother's own decision. Life is harsh on the big island, and winter is coming. Your mother's people, if she finds them, will take her in and care for her, but it will be a burden on them. She wishes to spare you the indignity of coming to them as a beggar."

I rose to my feet. "I can persuade her otherwise."

"You can try. I advise you not to. Letting you share her exile will only add to the burden of remorse she carries. Let her go Mouse. And one summer, you may accompany our hunters to the big island, where you will see her again."

What could I do but obey my mother's wish? Returning to our wikuom, I found she had already been taken away to the ship. I fell onto her blanket, where the smell of her body lingered.

I did not want to fall asleep: who knew what the morning would bring? But when I did, I dreamt that huge white birds were settling on my head, pricking me with their feet and flapping their wings in my eyes. All night long we battled. When finally they left me, I was surprised to find Niskam already high in the sky. And in the distance, someone was shouting: "A sail! A sail!"

It was d'Aumont – arrived too late to save my mother, too late to save Bright Eyes. Feet rushed past my wikuom, but I simply turned over and lay with my head to the wall: two days, I thought, maybe three, for d'Aumont to take on food and water. And then they would set out, under full sail, running before the autumn gales. I had enough food: I would simply wait, for Charles, his ships, and his prisoners to be gone from my life.

I spent the days dozing. When not actually asleep, I planned designs for the wampum I would make in the winter: wampum I could exchange for food from the hunters, wampum to twine around the neck of a peevish wife. The great white birds continued to haunt me from the spirit world: I would capture them finally, I vowed, encase them forever in hard shell, pinion their wings on a background of cold blue. I would trade them to Taqtaloq, to present to his wife Mimikej. And there, I thought triumphantly, they would remain shackled forever. I almost laughed.

When Charles entered, on the third day, I did not even turn to look. I felt cool fingers on my forehead, but only squeezed my eyes more tightly shut. A sigh, then he sat back on his heels.

"My country, France, is a soft land, much softer than Cibou," he began. "There are fields, meadows, alive with flowers; whole orchards of apple blossom; silent brooks with reeds gently blowing on their banks."

Suddenly intent, he gripped me by the shoulders and turned me towards him, forcing me to look into his eyes.

"But Mouse, the flowers of Cibou cannot be transplanted, not even into the softest of French soils. I have seen it tried with women of this country. They blossom, for awhile, then fade before the summer's end."

I tried to turn away, but he held my face fast in his grip. "Always, Mouse, since our first night together, I have known that I cannot take you with me. Nor can I remain in this place. I am not my brother: my destiny does not lie here. It is out there, following Niskam's lead. And Mouse, he shines on many, many lands other than this one."

Pain flickered on the surface of Charles's eyes as he looked upon my face. But in the depths, where his soul should be, there was nothing but a vast, black ocean. Freeing myself from his hands, I lay back upon my boughs and turned my face toward the wall. I did not hear him leave, but I knew the very moment he was gone. Reaching up to my neck, I gripped the chain that held Charles's gold crescent around my neck, the one he had placed there with his own hands on our first night of love. Ripping it off, I flung it into the fire.

i ended my exile the day Charles sailed. For a man who so loved to laugh, he had left the village a strange talisman to remember him by. Among the trees that swayed in the light winds off the beach, four bodies dangled. Not for them the easy slide into the ocean. Bereft of tools and weapons, they would never be able to make their way in the next world: they were doomed to forever wander, hollow-eyed and spectral, on the very edge of the Land of the Ancestors. My joy was fierce: Bright Eyes would never run the risk of meeting them, murderous and savage, in the depths of some celestial forest. To him, they would ever be but shadows flickering in the trees.

Lord Stewart's body was not among the four that waved in the breeze. I was not surprised. He was too big a prize to leave dangling in the trees of a small village.

"A captain looks exceedingly small without his ship," Charles had once said. He had laughed in delight at the thought of the English captive sent home to face his king, with not even a ship to bolster his claims to greatness. I knew Charles would never surrender such a trophy. But what trick did he use to snatch him away from chief and council?

"I will ask Antoine," I thought. And then I remembered: Antoine was a draught I would not drink again. I spat my resolve out onto the ground, in the same gesture I had seen the fishermen use.

As I walked through the village, I saw that people had already resumed their regular lives. There was the eternal circle of maidens, preparing the winter skins and teasing any young man courageous enough to walk within range. Last year's maidens, now young wives, were already beginning to show signs of the living burdens they carried. Their days were now spent throwing heavy pots onto the fire, or struggling with skins that had ripped loose from the wikuom and were at risk of being lost in the wind.

The wind. No longer content to merely lick the surface of the water, the morning's light breezes were beginning to drink deep. Out there, on the ocean, Charles was racing before them, in a desperate attempt to outrun the monsters already snapping at his heels. The people of Cibou were preparing to seek their own refuge in the deep quiet of the forest. I was eager to be off, eager to widen even further the chasm that lay between me and Charles.

This time, I walked alone – with no mother to help push the sled and no Bright Eyes to shorten the distance with his stories. Each day, I fastened the long strap against my forehead, pulling with a strength that was not my own. My face froze into a tight grimace that would not unclench itself even at night. I could not risk falling behind, for Antoine was in the rear, lingering to help the old women and widows with small children.

Beside me, Taqtaloq urged a pregnant Mimikej to hurry. She seemed determined to frustrate his obvious desire to claim the finest campsite for their wikuom, for with each urging she found a fresh excuse to go even more slowly. She complained of her ankles, though they remained as slender as larch branches. She complained of nausea, all the while gnawing on a well-hidden chunk of dried salmon. Mimikej's mother, who travelled with them, maintained a constant whining appeal. "Taqtaloq, stop and fetch some of those berries to tempt my daughter's appetite. Do you see them? No, not those, the ones on the higher branch, that have not yet been picked over."

The fact that her pleas went largely ignored rarely deterred her, for her mind had no more constancy than a butterfly.

Susan Young de Biagi

Taqtaloq, perhaps in desperation, began to focus on other things.

"Look at that one," he said on the second day, gesturing.

"Which one?" asked Mimikej, listlessly.

"That one over there.

"Oh, that's just Mouse," she said, dismissively.

"Mouse or not, she bears a heavy burden – and bears it lightly," he said, with a meaningful look at Mimikej.

"Animals are born to bear burdens," she said. "Look at her eyes. What kind of son would anyone get from that one? Even the great Keptin Daniel himself could not get a son off her. It would be like mating with a dog: you might enjoy it for a moment, but in the end it would come to nothing."

In my astonishment, I almost stopped walking. Even in the privacy of the women's wikuom, her words had never been so coarse. Taqtaloq was silent. I longed to look at his face, to see his reaction to his gently reared bride. At the same time, I refused to cede Mimikej the victory of knowing I had overheard. Adjusting the strap a little higher on my forehead, I trudged on.

As one of the first to reach the clearing, I had my choice of good sites, near the central fire. Yet I chose to remain on the far edge of the settlement. For the first time in my life, I feared the long winter nights ahead. All the tasks were complete: the huge piles of shellfish had been smoked and stored in baskets, stores of dried and smoked salmon filled every sled, birds were carefully dipped in their own fat, then sewn into skins. Women no longer went to the berry and tea fields, and hunters enjoyed a respite from long journeys spent tracking the animals. Everyone looked forward to the time when gathering food was merely a matter of stretching out one's hand while listening to the singers and storytellers. I did not share their excitement: for me, nights around the fire meant enduring the accents of Antoine, when it was only Bright Eyes's voice I wished to hear.

I could not avoid the nights around the central fire, for my absence would be commented upon. But by building on the very edge of the camp, I could make sure the walk was a long one, and that my dreams would not be invaded by the voices of the small, determined group who lingered around the dying embers.

For the first two days, I was busy building my wikuom, along with another, smaller one for the food stores inherited from my mother. On the third day, I could tell from the timbre of the high, excited voices that there would be a gathering that night. I searched for wampum beads and threads to take along: only by focusing on the small, intricate designs could I hope to shut out the voices.

By the time I arrived, the drumming had already begun, and children ensconced in the most comfortable laps. As I had hoped, the only remaining space was on the very edge of the crowd. But while safely hidden, I had robbed myself of the light from the fire, and compelled to abandon my wampum. I felt the tides of anger rise against this small obstacle, and was surprised at their force.

"Ma'li, Ma'li," the crowd began, in a whisper that grew to a chant.

They had not forgotten the story about the young mother and her child, begun by Antoine last year, just before the waters of sickness and death swept over us. From my hiding place, I could see that Antoine was surprised. I saw him desperately casting in his mind for the last line of the story. It was soon supplied by Ku'ku'kwes, the oldest among us, though every child who had attended to the story's beginnings could have done the same.

"The chief, an evil man, sent orders to kill the child," the old woman intoned. "The child's mother and the husband chosen for her had to flee in the night, far away from their village."

Amazement flooded Antoine's face as he heard Ku'ku'kwes repeat the syllables he himself had spoken so many moons before. But the best storytellers are born, not made. And just as Bright Eyes would have, Antoine began with a question.

"And where did they flee?" he asked, giving himself time and space in which to gather up the story's lost remnants. "To the land of their enemies, where their ancestors had once laboured as slaves."

The crowd nodded, pleased. We, the people of Cibou, understood slavery. One of our oldest tales honoured the bravery of a boy who had managed to make his way back home after many harrowing ordeals in the land of the enemy. As one body, the listeners leaned forward in anticipation of the next line.

"The Creator himself had been their ancestors' guide out of that wicked country. And now, many generations later, he led the young family back there."

"Why?" each mind asked.

"Because if the Creator goes with us, we are safer in a strange land than we could ever be among our own people," replied Antoine in response to the unvoiced question. And in spite of the quickening darkness, I saw a shadow pass across his face.

"So the child grew and thrived in enemy territory. And when it was safe for them to return, a heavenly messenger was sent to penetrate the dreams of the young father."

"Was it the same creature with the bright silver wings who came when the child was to be born?"

All eyes turned to the young questioner. The chief nodded approvingly, pleased that his own child had remembered this detail.

"Exactly right," Antoine replied. "And he told the father that it was now safe to return to their own land. By that time, Muine'j, the boy was about your age. And so wise that he was invited to sit in the council of the Elders."

"Did he grow to be a great chief, leading the people into battle against his father's enemies?" The people sitting near Muine'j smiled at this glimpse into the dreams of the young boy.

"No, he did not," said Antoine. "You see, he was born to die."

The listeners confidently racing ahead of Antoine on the storyteller's path came to an abrupt stop. And one by one I saw the people wilt, as Antoine brought them face to face with the great truth: children, even the most promising, die.

He has lost them, I thought. But I could not rejoice in his failure. The people had come too joyfully, too ready to be entertained. In the long pause that followed Antoine's words, some on the edge of the crowd gathered up sleeping babies for the walk back to the wikuoms. The darkness sat upon us like a stone.

"And with his death, he vanquished his father's great foe."

Antoine's quiet voice barely skimmed the surface of the darkness. But it was enough. People sat down again so abruptly they jostled the slumbering children and long moments were spent coaxing them back to sleep.

Muine'j was impatient for the story to continue. "What was he like, this foe? Was he a giant, bristling with feathers? Did he prowl the edges of the world, looking for victims to consume?"

Antoine thought for a moment. "He is a giant, yes, but one who can make himself very small. His is a stolen kingdom, for his home is the human heart."

I would not admit it then, but I myself had encountered this giant. Every time I thought of Charles, and every single time I thought of Bright Eyes, I felt his power grow.

Muine'j's excited voice rang out. "I know of what you speak Antoine! In one of our tales, a grieving father travels to the Land of the Ancestors to seek his dead son. But when he arrives, he finds that the boy's spirit has shrunken to the size of a nut that the father carries home in a little bag. Surely it is so with the giant?"

Antoine turned to the boy, smiling. "Perhaps. And what happened then, Muine'j?"

Susan Young de Biagi

"The boy's spirit did not want to be back in the Land of Men, and escaped at the first chance. His father died soon afterward, and was reunited with his son in the Land of the Ancestors."

I was angry: angry with Antoine for telling the tale, angry with the chief's son for spoiling it. And in my anger, I felt the giant smile.

In all my life as an outcast, I had never truly been alone. Always, there had been Bright Eyes and my mother: one to comfort, the other to scold. I did not know which I missed more. For now I walked in the shadow of my people in the same way that Charles walked in the shadow of the sun: never drawing nearer, never escaping.

The advantage of being a shadow, of course, is that one can linger, unseen, in the very midst of life – a silent witness to all conversations, all thoughts.

"So what is he like, Mimikej? With such arms and legs – lithe as stripped branches – we wonder if the rest is as smooth and powerful."

Although pregnant, Mimikej still came to the women's wikuom with her friend Maskwi. At this moment, she was lounging on her boughs, small piles of fish bones scattered around her. After thinking about Maskwi's question for a moment, she shrugged. "He was very entertaining, in the beginning."

Maskwi tried again.

"He seemed very angry with you yesterday. My mother and I could see the poles of the wikuom shaking in his rage. Were you not afraid?"

"Of course not," said Mimikej, her small tongue snaking out to lick the grease from the corners of her mouth. "I have something he wants."

"All men want that. It does not mean they value the women who give it to them."

"Not that, this," and Mimikej reached down with both hands to grasp the small bulge already pushing against her robe. "You've heard the prophecy."

"That Taqtaloq's firstborn would be a great chief, sent to guide his people through fire and water? Of course. He reminds us all at every opportunity."

I almost laughed, to think that Taqtaloq and Mimikej between them could produce such a child. The prophecy had been made at the time of Taqtaloq's initiation into manhood, by the same shaman who had died snivelling against the wall. I thought it unlikely that any such event would ever come to pass. So, apparently, did Mimikej.

"That prophecy has been very useful," she said, tossing another bone onto the pile, "especially since I've been so ill. Do you know there are days when I cannot even raise myself from my boughs?" She winked at Maskwi and selected another fish from the basket.

Now I understood why Taqtaloq, the great warrior, was so often seen carrying water from the river, and hefting the stew pot for the evening meal. The other men, though not daring to laugh, permitted themselves an occasional raised eyebrow.

"That's all very well for now, but what will you do when the second child comes?" asked Maskwi.

Mimikej reached out and brushed the bones over to my side of the wikuom, before settling in even more comfortably among her boughs. "I'll think of something," she said, closing her eyes.

*

*T*he days went on, in the pattern set out for us in the Long Ago. This winter – so different from the last – was just as it should be.

Deeper and deeper we burrowed into our furs, as the snow piled high and thick around the wikuoms. We slept late, rising only after Niskam had staggered to the very top of the mountains, where he stood on uncertain feet for the rest of the day.

Those who had not been diligent the night before lumbered outside to gather sticks for the fire; others merely rolled over to throw a handful of leaves into the pot, before burrowing under their covers for one last dream. This was the best time for dreaming: great, epic adventures were lived out in the time it took for the tea to steep. Some people stored them away in their bag of memories like precious scraps of cloth, to be slyly brought out when the storytelling lagged.

Sipping my tea on cold winter mornings, I would frequently run my fingers over the shells in my collection, trying to find an exact match with the colours of the dream before the memory faded. The necklace of wampum I had planned so confidently in the days after d'Aumont's arrival was not taking shape as easily as I had hoped. The birds that swept through my dreams as separate and distinct were beginning to blur into a single, elusive image. Was it a strutting bird with blue-green feathers and black eyes that saw all? Or perhaps a dull brown creature with a brilliantly plumed head – caught, to its great dismay, in my hair. No, surely it was a great white bird, wounded in a battle to the death, its blood pooling around it like a red cape.

Until now, I had managed to avoid Antoine. But something was growing in me that would not be contained, something that wanted to lash out. And he alone understood it: for he too had met the giant, and somehow it had been slain. The story haunted me. This time, I would not let my questions be lost at a young boy's whim. I resolved to seek Antoine out.

I found him seated on the side of a small brook, his hands filled with the plants that grew along its banks. The study of healing plants was a new source of fascination for him. Over the past moon, he and old Ku'ku'kwes had formed a deep friendship. I often saw them together, he slowing his pace to match the feeble steps of the old woman, his concentration intense as he bent to examine the plants in her hand. The sight of their camaraderie – so like his and mine in the old days – threatened to call forth the giant from where he slumbered, and I had to soothe him by telling myself I did not care, that all my pain had its root in such a friendship.

I found Antoine, as I planned, alone. Like all the people of his land, he did not hear me approach until I was upon him, standing so close our toes were almost touching. As he looked up, I saw a fierce blue flame of joy rise up, before his eyelids dropped to cloak it. My own face felt carved in stone as I sank to my haunches before him.

"I've come to hear about the giant."

I saw him wince at the cold tones. "What is it you wish to know?" he asked quietly.

"Where does it come from? What does it want?"

"It wants your destruction," he said, shaking the water from the plants then wrapping them in a cloth. "Where does it come from? I do not know. Somehow, it grew in creation – as the Creator knew it would – perhaps from the very beginning. And he grieved to see it."

"So why not just remove it? Why allow its existence?"

"Some evils are not so easily removed," he said, reaching down and scooping some water into the small cup he kept hanging from his belt. Feeling in his bag, he extracted a vial, from which he tipped a single drop into the cup of water. He passed me the cup to drink. I spat the contents out immediately, appalled at their bitterness.

"In the same way," said Antoine, "evil has permeated every part of the world. It cannot be so easily extracted."

"Then there is only one answer," I said, flinging the horrid potion onto the ground. "Destroy it all and begin again. It's a simple enough remedy."

Susan Young de Biagi

I saw the pain in Antoine's face, as he absorbed the bitterness in my voice.

"It is simple enough," he replied. "But let us imagine for a moment the Creator – knowing the pain the future will bring – deciding whether to proceed with the work of creation. As he looks down, perhaps through the centuries, his eye is caught by a little mouse. And although she is not what she was meant to be, he cherishes her for her uniqueness, for in all the world there can be no other like her. And he cannot bear to see her destroyed, but yearns to see her safe, restored to a place where evil can no longer touch her.

This was not what I had come for. "It's a nice story, Antoine," I said, rising to my feet. "But I lost my taste for stories when Bright Eyes was murdered."

And yet, I could not keep away. I had spent the day planning tasks that would keep me from that night's circle around the fire: I would work on my beading, sharpen my knives. Yet somehow, as Niskam was dropping below the line of trees, I found myself on the edge of the crowd, waiting, as they all were, for Antoine to continue.

Seeing him arrive, so tall and quiet, set my teeth on edge. He and his brother both, had promised so much, took so much, gave nothing. And I, who had begun life with so little, now had even less: no Bright Eyes, no mother, no children of my own. Even the gift of weaving visions into shell had deserted me. All that was left to me, it seemed, was a fisherman's bed.

I heard my own voice speak the words that would start Antoine on the storyteller's path.

"His is a stolen kingdom, for his home is the human heart."

The words fell like stones, bitter and angry. Antoine looked across at me, relief in his eyes, and took up the battle.

"The giant takes a heart of flesh. Around it, stone by stone, he builds a prison of lies and murderous rage. With their own hands, people pile the stones higher and higher, driven on by the commands of that voice. And as they sit in a prison so thick and black it shuts out the sun, they know – deep in our hearts – that it is death the giant wants for them, death that awaits them."

Antoine's eyes were as limpid as those of an infant.

"And so the Creator watched, grieved. For there, in a prison of their own making, they could no longer come to him. And so he had to find a way to go to them."

"Just like the father who went to seek his son in the Land of the Ancestors," said Muine'j triumphantly.

Antoine smiled. "Something like that. But in this case, it was the Creator's son himself who offered to go."

"Ma'li's son," added Ku'ku'kwes.

"Yes, Ma'li's son. Under the very eye of the giant, he slips into the prison. And clothing the prisoners in his own white robes, he assumes their soiled garments. So that when the time comes for the jailer to lead them out to death, it is he who goes in their place. And it is over his broken body that they escape to freedom."

"And what of the giant?" asked Muine'j.

"He is held back with a flaming sword and cannot follow." Antoine leaned over, smiling at the young boy. "For you see, Muine'j, when the Son sets you free, you are free indeed."

They were all nodding, pleased with the night's story. Would no one ask the question? I finally forced the words out through frozen lips. "And what does it take for all this to come about?"

Antoine smiled. "You must simply open the prison door."

Something was watching us from the mountains where Kluskap slept. It confused the dogs, who whined and ran in circles. Scouts sent out from the camp returned perplexed, for no tracks had been found. Was it human or animal – or both? We did not know. Whatever was out there was hiding its thoughts from us, so that not even our Elders could read its intentions. But sometimes, we caught the scent it gave off unknowingly. A dark presence stole in and settled upon us like a blanket.

Chief and council met long into the night, Antoine among them. Warriors who had spent the long evenings carving fanciful figures for their children now fashioned stone pieces into deadly points. Together they sat, their faces worried and serious in the shower of small, silvered chips that flew around them.

I knew the men would give generously of the points that lay beside them in a steadily growing pile, but they seemed too beautiful to be used for such a deadly purpose. The stone itself came to us from the Land of Ice and Snow. Brilliant white, almost translucent, it could have been chipped from the icy giants that sometimes floated down to us on the spring seas. As a child, I would hold the arrow points in my hand, using them as a talisman to fly me to northern lands, where I would swoop down among the great, frozen chunks. Beholding them now, I realized that, like the icebergs, they too carried doom in their depths. I grabbed a handful, squeezing until the blood flowed.

With no father or brothers to protect me, I had learned to defend myself. Bright Eyes had spent an entire winter teaching me to draw a bow, sight along a line, relax my fingers in a single, liquid motion. Some had laughed at the sight of the old man and the little girl, seriously discussing the things of war. He wasn't much of a shot Bright Eyes, even in the days when he could still see the target, but he knew better than anyone the secrets of the body, the hidden parts that do not recover when pierced by an arrow.

As I grew taller and his sight grew dimmer, Bright Eyes presented with me his own bow. Drawing it out now, I remembered the old brown hands rubbing up and down its length. Bright Eyes's mind and spirit had freely gifted me with this treasure, but his hands were loathe to let to go.

"Here, that's not the way."

Bending over to retrieve my arrow from an old stump, I looked up to see Taqtaloq before me, bow in hand.

"Bright Eyes never understood that the arrow's path was as important as its mark. He taught you many of his bad habits."

I wondered why he had chosen to speak to me now. Something in me urged me to rile the beast.

"He knew enough to keep stupid little boys in their place."

"But not enough to keep himself from getting killed. Do you want to learn or not?" The voice was curt, impatient.

I longed to refuse. But whatever lurked out there might be too large to be humbled by the few warriors left in our village. If it were human, every bow – even a woman's – would be needed. I nodded.

We spent the whole of that short winter afternoon engaged in a study of the arrow's path. As Taqtaloq waited impatiently, I was the one to brush the deepening snow off the target, to seek out every stray arrow. I began to regret that I had worn such light footwear: trudging back and forth along the icy path, my feet began to freeze.

"Come, sit down over here," Taqtaloq said, pointing abruptly to a half-buried log. Removing my moccasins, he took my cold, bare feet in his hands and rubbed them until they tingled with life once more. Then leaving me to put my footwear on myself, he stood and began walking back toward the village.

"Keep your head up," he called over his shoulder.

As I watched him disappear into the growing darkness, I wondered what kind of welcome he would find at home.

k

*t*hey revealed themselves on the fifth day: human. Young Muine'j saw them first, pointing with his finger at the wisp of smoke curling up from the highest mountain. Those of us who had been carrying our bows night and day gripped them all the harder, exulting in the knowledge that we faced an enemy of flesh.

Now that they had revealed themselves, it would not be long before their emissaries arrived.

Our chief sat, as always, at the door of his wikuom. But instead of the thin, ragged robe he usually wore, he was carefully dressed in shirt and leggings of the finest hide, thickly encrusted in beads of midnight black. The emissaries would not fail to read the message. Impossible to obtain in Cibou, these beads came to us from the enemy's own lands in the south. Our chief could have obtained them in one of two ways: through peaceful trade, or from the body of a slain enemy. There had been no periods of peaceful trade in my lifetime, or in my mother's.

The whole village followed the three emissaries' progress down the mountain. As they drew closer, we distinguished a very old man accompanied by two young boys, barely past their initiation. We were not deceived, nor were we meant to be. By sending the weakest among them, they sent their own message: the forest around us teemed with warriors in their prime. Should a weapon be lifted against these ones, the others would be upon us as soon as the arrow had left its bow and before it met its mark.

The smallest children among us laughed behind their hands at their strange manner of dressing their hair. Each man sported a small knot on the very top of his head, greased to stand up high then ornamented with feathers, beads and coloured sticks.

"It's a nest," whispered Jijiwikate'j, who had just seen his third summer.

Unbidden, a vision arose before me of the mythical bird that would build such a thing. In my vision, the bird lit on the very summit of the old man's head and remained perched there until I banished it. This was an easy enough thing to do: war is a cold chaser of dreams.

With not a gesture passing between our chief and theirs, the two men sat at precisely the same time. The young boys remained standing, eyes fixed on distant points chosen at random. Such young ones, I knew, would be careful not to look too closely at us, against whom they had hardened their hearts.

Our chief waited courteously for the other to speak first. Our tongue sounded strange in the mouth of the old man. Even Antoine, I thought, had a better command of the sounds.

After the long, formal preamble required at such times, the old man threw down his opening bid.

"It is time for your people and ours to resolve our long-held animosities."

Every person among us raised an eyebrow, everyone except our chief. I marvelled at his control.

"Such animosities are buried in the tangle of time. It would take long hours to unravel them." A good thrust. Silently, we cheered our chief even as our eyes flew across the fire to his opponent.

The old man pulled out a knife, its blade carefully pointed towards his own entrails. Every one of us recognized it as French. The knives of our land were made of bone, infinitely sharper and more deadly than the metal knives, but brittle, easily broken.

"This has come to us," the enemy intoned, "hand to hand, mountain to mountain, from your land to ours. It is a marvellous thing. And our women covet it for themselves, to shorten the hours they spend with the skins."

His eyes swept up and over our warriors, who were standing at the prescribed distance from the two chiefs, their weapons nowhere in sight. What was he looking for?

"We ourselves would like to trade with you for such marvellous items. Our corn, as you know, is higher than a man's head. The juice that spurts from its kernels is sweeter than even the sap that flows from your trees."

We knew about their corn, and their blue-black beads. Some of our people had already forgotten the danger that surrounded us, so fixed were their minds on these precious items. Already, perhaps, they saw themselves in peaceful trade: French metal flowing into the southerners' hands, corn and beads into ours. The French fort on our shores would make us the elder brother in such a partnership.

All around me, the eyes of our people were growing opaque, lost in dreams of corn and beads.

"No!" my mind screamed.

"Such a decision cannot be made in a day." Sharp and clear, our chief's voice woke his people from their trance.

"Of course not," replied the other serenely. "Our camp, as you can see, is there on the farthest mountain. And there we will withdraw, to await your emissaries."

The old man then rose to his feet. "I am very content to end this long estrangement between our peoples. And I hope that the next time we meet, it will be to smoke the pipe together."

It was another brilliant stroke: their tobacco, long and sweet-leafed, was much finer than our own, short and stunted as it was by our long winters.

As they left, the two boys helping the old man up the mountain, our people broke out in excited babble. The chief was silent as the Elders withdrew.

I guessed that some slept peacefully that night, wrapped in dreams of corn and beads and tobacco. But I could still feel the presence upon us, heavy and deep. Bow at my side, I resolved to sit up until dawn. I did not have even that long to wait.

*

"*t*reacherrrrrry!"

A woman's voice screamed high and long into my ear. Crouching on arms and legs, I slipped out the small back flap into the woods. Our warriors were already there – had been there all night I now realized – encircling the sleeping village. The men on either side of me permitted themselves a single look, nodding as I took my place beside them. As I reached back to draw my first arrow from its quiver, I glimpsed Antoine just over my shoulder. One eye closed to fix his aim, all his concentration was on the enemy beyond. Following his lead, I quickly marked my own victim.

The enemy's behaviour was confusing. While a small enemy force engaged us, the majority ignored our line of warriors, concentrating on the wikuoms instead. No matter how many arrows we let fly, they would not be deterred. Even the small wikuoms containing the food stores were ransacked and overturned.

Above the screaming women and barking dogs, I heard Antoine's sudden shout in French. "They're looking for the muskets! They think we have the muskets!"

The words hammered against the red fog in which I was enveloped and I shook my head to clear it. And as I did so, understanding came in a flood.

Even a large force of bowmen, as they were, could not hope to prevail against a village they thought armed with muskets. So instead they tried to disarm us with trickery, only to steal back in the night with knives and axes. By slaughtering our warriors in their beds, the enemy hoped to claim the French weapons for themselves. But our chief's vigilance ruined their plan.

What the enemy did not know is that there were no muskets. Our wikuoms were filled with something far more valuable: women and children. And by focusing on the small enemy force that stood against us, we were leaving those loved ones defenceless. Antoine came to this understanding before I did. Already, he was pulling on the war chief's arm, trying to explain. But the newly learned words deserted him. Dropping my bow, useless now on this strange battleground, I stumbled to his side.

It took only a few words. Pulling their knives from the sheaths, our warriors fell upon the wikuoms. Suddenly weak, I dropped to my knees there on the forest's edge. The roar, already deafening, rose in intensity until it seemed that the whole world vibrated as a single, piercing scream. Even today, I cannot fully banish it from my dreams.

Most of the strangers fled in the face of the attacking force. They had come, after all, not to conquer, but to steal. Those caught inside the wikuoms were killed outright. With families in danger, the warriors would not risk taking them alive.

The largest number of the dead were our own people. In their rage at finding the wikuoms empty of muskets, the enemy had turned on the people inside. Those of us who could still walk carried the bodies to a place just beyond the camp. Among them lay the tiny, broken body of Jijiwikate'j, who had laughed so delightedly at the strangers' hair. And there, too, was Mimikej.

I saw Taqtaloq from a long distance away, running toward us, fear on his face. Stepping into the path of the frantic warrior, the chief caught him before he reached the body of his wife, holding him in strong arms and whispering into his ear. I turned away from the sight, knowing Taqtaloq would not want me to witness this first, fresh grief. His cries tore at me as I made my way to the central fire.

Antoine was already there among the survivors, binding and comforting. Ku'ku'kwes, stalwart and unhurt, followed behind him, giving each a draught from the skin she carried. I followed their lead as best I could, one of many silent shadows who wrapped the wounded in blankets and laid them before the fire.

My feet kept moving long after my mind had ceased to direct them. But in the end, I could go no farther. Feeling Antoine's hands upon me, I submitted to being wrapped in a blanket and gently eased to the ground. When I opened my eyes again, the wounded lay sleeping while those who grieved had slipped into a state of stunned shock. I had not relieved myself since the night before, and barely made it to the edge of the forest. Once there, squatting, my attention was drawn to Antoine, searching in the distance among the bodies of the enemy.

"What is he looking for?" I wondered. All at once, I saw him stoop and bend. Again and again I saw his black-robed body heave and shake until, finally, there was nothing more to give. Wiping his mouth with his hand, he rose and stumbled toward the river. I crept to the place he left and there saw the body of a young boy, one of the two who had accompanied the old man down the mountain. In his chest was Antoine's arrow.

Darkness was falling by the time I headed back to the village. Taqtaloq had not left his post beside the bodies: seeing him there on his knees, hands gripped around his spear, I knew he would spend the night guarding his wife and unborn child from the wild animals that would surely come. Filling a vessel with tea, I walked over and held it for him to drink. Raising his head, eyes dazed, not knowing even who held the cup, he drank. Then slipping away, I left him with his dead.

*i*t snowed during the night. I was too busy at first to notice this white presence that stole in so gently around us. All night long, we fought back the darkness, responding to the cries of the wounded and soothing their fears – night is an enemy to those who are suffering. It was only toward dawn – when the light crept in to comfort and console – that the wounded were finally able to sleep. Seated beside them, my head against a rock, I closed my eyes. When I opened them again, it was to gaze upon a magical landscape: one in which small icy chips shimmered from every tree branch, every stone. I shuddered, knowing the grim scene that lay beneath. My eyes fled toward the pile of bodies that Taqtaloq still guarded so devotedly. But even he could not protect them against the natural forces that were already seeking to reclaim them.

My attention was caught by a black figure on the edge of my vision. Looking round, I saw Antoine moving toward Taqtaloq, a steaming gourd in his hands. As Taqtaloq sipped the hot soup, Antoine remained stooping beside him, his hand on the warrior's shoulder. I was surprised to see that Taqtaloq did not shrug it off, but remained attentive to the words that Antoine spoke so earnestly into his ear. When Taqtaloq nodded in acquiescence, Antoine patted him one last time then rose slowly to his feet. As Antoine stood for a moment in the cold morning air, our eyes met. This time, I did not look away.

*h*is stories kept the dark away. Night after night, I would listen – a child at my side – as he beguiled the wounded with his words. Sometimes he spoke to us of his childhood in France. We thought it a very strange place, France. Families like his, he told us, each marked off a piece of land and erected a wall around it.

We shivered at the thought of animals so fierce they needed a wall to keep them out.

"How high is this wall?" asked our chief, cracking nuts for the wounded man at his side.

"Sometimes, not even as high as my waist," Antoine replied.

"Then it cannot be very effective. A wolf or a bear could easily jump over it."

"There are few wolves or bears left in France now. Our king has killed them all."

This seemed to us a very unwise thing to do, but we refrained from criticizing Antoine's king.

"He did it, you see, because wolves were attacking the ...." Antoine pressed a hand against his forehead, as he sometimes did when he was thinking very hard. He then took a stick and began tracing in the sand the outline of an animal. "It is a large beast, with a thick hide and a loud bellow. It brings up the contents of its stomach to chew."

All around the circle, heads were bobbing knowingly. "A moose."

Antoine shook his head. "No, not a moose."

"Does it have horns and hoofs?"

"Yes it does. But it is far less aggressive than the animal you know here. It will even stand patiently while we milk it."

We grimaced at this image. It was not the first time we had heard of such a thing. In the west, it was rumoured, there were people who had fallen this low. Whenever one of our own men turned out to be a slow or slothful hunter, he would be compared to these moose milkers. Among us, it was a word for laziness.

Antoine's listeners looked at each other from the sides of their eyes. We even began to feel sorry for the poor, foolish king: forced to sacrifice the bear, with its fine meat, to provide milk for an idle people.

Susan Young de Biagi

Seeing these looks, our chief spoke up quickly.

"Not all people follow our ways," he said firmly to the crowd.

Then turning graciously to Antoine: "This animal you speak of, we will call the French Moose."

Antoine looked pleased at this idea. Taking his small book from his bag, he quickly scratched the new symbols onto the page.

When Muine'j asked about Antoine's own dwelling, he pointed to the very tallest tree, saying his house was just a little higher. We craned our necks for a moment, then glanced around to see each other's reaction. Again, only our chief dared to ask the question.

"Why does a man your size need so tall a house?"

As we contemplated walls too low to keep out the animals and houses too high to fit comfortably around a man, all of us felt lucky to live in Cibou.

But later, on my boughs, I wondered. And suddenly I understood: that wall was built to keep out – not the bears and the wolves, but the hunters. Instead of freely following where the animals led, the people had retreated inside the walls until each man rested within his own protective circle, drawn by his own hand.

Pierrot's words rose to my mind. "One day we will show you how to clear it. You can build fences to protect it." The memory of Lord Stewart also came, unbidden. "Step by step we will advance, clearing and planting as we go." It was a long time before I slept.

We were baffled by the tales of Antoine's land. But we understood the stories he told of the Creator.

"Do you know," he told us sadly, "there are many in my land who have forgotten the sound of their creator's voice? They have become wild, untamed, led into the darkness. Yearning, he stands waiting for them to return, making no noise, no sudden movements to frighten them."

Antoine stopped to nuzzle the tiny hand that reached up to him. The child in his arms had not wakened since the night of the attack. Yet instinctively, she reached out for the comfort of his voice. His accents grew gentler, more hushed.

"And why, do you think, must he approach his own children so cautiously?" Antoine asked. "Sadly, they have seen too much destruction, seemingly wrought by his hand. So they hang back in the shadows, angry, afraid. And his heart breaks to see it. For though they do not know it, they share a common enemy – an ancient, dishonourable foe – his enemy long before it was theirs."

The chief spoke up. "Why not simply command their presence? The Creator has mighty weapons at his disposal."

"Bolts of lightening, showers of stars? One to frighten, the other to lure? No, he will not frighten them with displays of fireworks, nor seduce them with promises of power. They must come of their own accord, out of love. He will accept nothing less."

Antoine looked around the circle. Some could not see, for their eyes were bound. Others lay tossing, trying to throw off the blankets though the night was cold. He grasped the child even closer to his breast, and continued speaking.

"And so he stands on the edge of the forest and – one by one – he woos them. To his joy, there are some who steal in a little closer. There in full sunshine he stands, unafraid beneath their scrutiny. And they, who expect a rod upon their backs, warm to his presence. Until one day, he calls them by name and they come, because they know the master's voice. Instead of stealing from his stores, they end by eating from his hand."

The darkness had stolen in and surrounded us. Looking over my shoulder, past the circle of light cast by the fire, I saw a dark, hunched figure, swaying above his spear: Taqtaloq. Moving quickly to his side, I managed to break his fall so that he slumped to the ground unharmed. As I pushed the stiff, frozen locks back from his face, I saw that he was still conscious, though barely. Beside me, a hand pressed a cup of tea into mine, and I in turn forced it between his lips. With the help of those around me, I managed to roll him in a blanket and there – with his head on my lap – he slept.

k

*t*his was no longer a place of refuge for us. The enemy had withdrawn, for now, but they remained on the very edge of our lands. Nor could we bear to stay in a place of such death. It was not yet possible to return to the coast, where the snows still beat against the shores. So chief and Elders decided to move us to an old winter campsite, a journey of several days. The grim pile on the edge of the forest was covered with rocks, to protect the bodies from the ravages of the animals. Hunters would return when the ground thawed in the spring, to bury the people in the rites demanded by our ancestors.

Much was left behind. When we made the trek in the fall, the sleds had been filled with wikuoms and provisions, while everyone except the very old and the sick walked alongside. Now, many of those who had once pushed the sleds lay inside. Before we set out, the Elders inspected each sled, persuading mothers to leave behind a favourite cooking vessel or a pile of newly cured hides. I left behind my fine suit of white deer skin, though it weighed almost nothing. Better the wolves tear it to pieces, I thought. I had no need for it now.

This time as we moved through the forest, there was no race for the best campsites. Struggling along with a group of orphaned toddlers, I thought of Taqtaloq, who had hoped to make this journey with his own child. Now Taqtaloq remained at the very tail with Antoine, each man carrying a wounded child in his arms.

The two men spent most of their time talking. I was too distracted to attend to their conversation: it is not an easy thing to shepherd a group of wandering children, not one of whom had reached its third year. Although the snow in the forest was not deep enough to impede our progress, there were many things to distract a curious child. My days were spent persuading a determined toddler to leave behind the log she was bent on carrying – or pulling another from his hiding place in a rotting tree trunk. When we finally stopped to rest, I slept as one dead, missing the debates that went on long into the night.

One morning toward dawn, however, I awoke to a strange scene. Taqtaloq was sitting not far away, head bent beneath Antoine's hand. For a long time I lay between sleep and waking, lulled by words too low for me to grasp. But as Antoine's words ceased and Taqtaloq raised his head, I was suddenly stunned into full wakefulness. Taqtaloq's face, worn by nights of no sleep and deep grief, was transformed, illuminated, by a look of intense joy. Troubled, but too exhausted to consider the scene, I turned over on my boughs and tried to sleep.

*

Slowly, as the wounded came to life and the children were taken into families, I was able to resume my normal tasks. I was seated outside, sorting through my beads, when Taqtaloq appeared.

Susan Young de Biagi

After all I had witnessed, I was afraid to look him full in the face. But as I stole a look, I saw he suffered no such awkwardness. His hands full of tiny skin bags, he stood awaiting an invitation to sit. I moved over to make room for him on the log.

Taking his place beside me, he laid the bags carefully in my lap. "I have no use for these," he said. "But I have seen your work and would like you to have them."

I knew before I opened them what they contained. As part of the bridal gift given to Mimikej by the groom's family, they had been displayed to the whole village. She herself had been more interested with the fine skins and hair ornaments. But my own eye had been caught by the small piles of brilliant red, blue, and black beads, and I felt an envy such as I had never known. Now Taqtaloq was offering them to me.

Though tempted almost beyond my strength, I gathered up the bags to return to him.

"It is a noble gift, too fine for one such as I. One day you will give them to a new wife." I stopped in confusion. It was cruel to speak of such things to one so newly grieved. But Taqtaloq replied calmly, "I will not marry again. I once thought to ride the river of life on the flood, to a wide and tranquil sea. But it has cast me, bloody and broken, onto the rocks." He rose abruptly. "Keep the beads Mouse. You have more use for them than I."

I watched him go, amazed. Where had Taqtaloq learned to shape his grief into images, images into words? As a child, he had been too impatient to listen to the stories Bright Eyes was always ready to repeat, over and over, to the children gathered round. Some of us had learned quickly, letting our voices rise on one word and fall on another in the same way as Bright Eyes himself. The old man would laugh and say it was like shouting into a cave, to hear his own voice come bounding back to him. In this way, Bright Eyes once told me, our stories echoed back to the Long Ago and forward to the future. They were the link that bound us to our ancestors.

Only Taqtaloq had had no time for such games. Instead, he would prowl the edges of the crowd and shoot branches from his bow, aiming so they whirred over our heads; or feed the fire until the sparks flew, driving us from the circle. It was not in him to describe his life as it flowed by – or so I had thought.

Carefully, I spread a blanket out on the ground and slowly, slowly poured each shining stream of beads out of its bag. And as I watched, the form of the wampum was already taking shape in my mind, startling in its clarity: a wide river, and on its edge an eagle poised in the tallest tree, its eye plunging even to the depths; a small mouse, feeling itself safely hidden, suddenly vulnerable to the force swooping down out of the sunlight; a flurry of dark feathers and a world changed forever.

This sudden, clear vision swept all others from my mind. And there, beside a broken wikuom in an abandoned camp, on the very edge of death, I began to weave the pieces of my life back together. Thread by thread, bead by bead, I gathered up the lost parts of myself: Bright Eyes, Charles, my mother, my children. People began arriving at my wikuom to watch the necklace taking shape beneath my hands. We marvelled that this thing of beauty could come from a winter of such darkness.

"What will you do with it, Mouse?" asked Muine'j, when it was finished.

This chief's son had fought bravely on the night of the battle, then helped carry the dead through the grey hours of dawn. Though no longer the chirping, inquisitive boy who spoke up so boldly, he could still speak the thoughts of everyone in the crowd.

"I do not know. Perhaps I will give it to your father, the chief, to trade for food."

"Such a treasure cannot be traded for food. Keep it for mothers in labour to look upon, to ease their pain and bring forth strong children," said Ku'ku'kwes, for whom midwifery was the highest calling.

"It has surely been sent to you by our ancestors, as a sign of victories to come," said one of our oldest warriors. "We will carry it before us into battle.

"Let there be no more battles!" cried a woman. "Let it stand instead as a promise of peace. For the eagle symbolizes harmony among all things."

"Let me send it to my king," said Antoine, who had crept into the circle, "as a symbol of peace between our two peoples."

We turned to look at him, startled. He also looked surprised, as though he had not meant to speak the thought aloud.

Our people do not take it lightly, this giving and accepting of wampum. Carefully wrapped in old pelts, shiny from so much folding and unfolding, they are brought out at our great feasts, as reminders of promises given and received. Did Antoine know that such agreements are never broken? Did he know that the promise, once given, stood binding upon our children and theirs for all time? If we extended a promise of peace to the French king, it would be kept through all generations.

I sat uncertain, the necklace in my hands. Who was I, the Mouse, to decide the use to which it would be put?

Seeing my dilemma, the people rose to their feet and slipped away, until only Antoine and I were left. Embarrassed, he turned to me. "I do not covet your treasure Mouse. I spoke before thinking. Forgive me."

"No Antoine. It is I who ask your forgiveness. I once thrust a gift into your hands and was angry when you would not take it. I was angrier still when your brother accepted, then renounced it. I now understand that such agreements cannot be entered into so lightly. For they stand as promises between generations. And promises, once given, must be kept."

I turned to him. "Tell me Antoine, what passed between you and Taqtaloq that night on the trail?"

Antoine looked confused for a moment, before the memory came to him. "Taqtaloq accepted a gift. And in return, made a life promise."

"To you?"

He smiled. "No, not to me. To a king."

"What will happen to him now?

"Wait and see, Mouse. Wait and see."

⚓

*i*t is our custom to seize on joy when it comes, just as we bow to sadness. It was the night of Muine'j's coming of age, a night for celebration. We knew that the boy's true coming of age had taken place several months before, on the night of the attack. This, then, was not an initiation, but a confirmation. What more would life ask of one who had been tested so young, and already found so worthy?

As usual, the chief's wife tried to conceal her pride in a shower of complaints. "Not once has my husband sought his own bed in the last moon, so determined is he to bring back three times the amount of meat that people's stomachs will hold!"

She spoke no more than the truth: the pile of meat, though smaller than those of previous years, was growing daily. Other preparations were also underway: the actors had withdrawn to their own, secret corner of the village to prepare. Young girls sifted through their collection of finery, to see what would tempt this young hunter, too young to marry but not too young to cast his eye over the choices.

Muine'j himself had spent the day in the sweat lodge with his father and the Elders. Inside, the men were pouring water and herbs over heated rocks. So perfectly designed was the lodge that not a wisp of steam escaped.

All who passed by the willow lodge heard the sound of chanting, as the men invoked blessings upon the boy's head.

Inside, I knew, Muine'j was making a manly effort to withstand the heat and darkness that swirled around him. How shameful it would be to stumble out, sputtering into Niskam's gaze.

As the hours went on, people found an excuse to gather in front of the lodge, waiting for the young boy to appear. Finally, in late afternoon, the men of his family began to emerge, blinking, into the sunlight. The chief came out next, face stoic in an attempt to disguise his pride in his son. The attempt failed. We could see from the set of his neck and shoulders how proud he was that this child had withstood the test.

Muine'j was the last to come forth. The crowd rose to its feet with a series of shouts for the young boy, who emerged red-faced from the heat, water dripping over his forehead in rivulets. His mother had the honour of approaching him with a dry blanket, but was careful not to touch him. Fully cleansed, he would now withdraw to his own wikuom, to await the call to the fireside.

I too was covered in sweat. I had spent the day trudging back and forth with kettles of water from the creek and leaning over the huge cooking pots. I was wiping away the drops that threatened to fall into the soup when, through my fingers, I saw Taqtaloq standing before me, frowning.

That frown raised my ire. Well and good for him to stand there, so cool and handsome, after activities no more strenuous than fitting feathers to flint. I was shaping my lips around a cutting remark when he suddenly stooped to wedge a rock under the wobbling pot.

"That will steady it," he said, sitting back on his haunches in satisfaction.

Rising, he blew a long, cool breath across my face, rippling the hairs that lay splayed upon my forehead. I stood as frozen as one of our own stone maidens – caught unawares, as they had been, by the capricious behaviour of a young god. Taqtaloq turned to give the rock one last kick and then ran, loping, to join the crowd already gathering at the central fireside.

Defiantly, I considered wearing the same soup-splashed robe in which I had spent the day. But I feared that Muine'j – open and vulnerable from long hours spent in the very womb of darkness – might be shaken by yet another vision of a hag peering at him across the flames. So I dressed my hair carefully, and chose a clean, quiet robe. Thankfully, there was no determined mother to clothe me in white, no ardent suitor protecting a space for me beside him at the fire, no feeling that events were pushing me forward.

Charles had explained to me how ships at night take a single fix on the polar star. And though they do not look upon it again, no move is without relation to that star. So it was with Taqtaloq. Even as I applauded the dancers, laughing at their quickness, the eyes of my spirit were steadily and gravely focused upon him. Sitting there so quietly beside Antoine, could he feel the thoughts that enveloped him like a cloak?

The lesser storytellers went on first. As they droned on, I spoke sternly to my spirit: cool breath upon my face, warm hands upon my feet were not signs of love. And still my spirit kept its eyes firmly upon him, in spite of all attempts to dislodge it. Desperately, I set before it the image of the young bully boy who had taunted me as a child. It responded with a vision of a young husband resolutely carrying water, under the disdainful gaze of the other men. I reminded it of the husband who shook the walls of the wikuom in his anger. It conjured up a statue in the snow, surrounded by the bodies of the dead.

As I was struggling thus, I felt a hand on my shoulder: Antoine. "You are alone Mouse. Come share the meal with us."

I nodded, knowing there would be no need to struggle against temptation in Antoine's presence. I kept my head down as we approached Taqtaloq. When I finally stole a look, I saw that he was sitting beside Ku'ku'kwes. The old woman was not able to manage both her gourd and cup together. Even as he listened to the storytellers, Taqtaloq had the cup ready each time she looked around for it.

The food was good; the entertainment was not. In this, the first celebration after the attack, it became clear just how much we had lost: Jipjawej, the best dancer; Sespewo'kwet, who told the best jokes. Even the audience was not what it should be. Elmniket had laughed in all the right places, teaching the rest of us the art of encouragement. Apjelmit had laughed in all the wrong places, delighting when we laughed at him in our turn. Mourning, we turned to each other, in hushed little groups.

I thought, as we sat there, that Antoine had gathered unto himself a strange trio: the healer, the warrior and the outcast. Each of us had come broken in some way: Ku'ku'kwes in her body, Taqtaloq in his hope of the future ... and I? I had lost something that could not be restored to me.

To my surprise, it was Taqtaloq who spoke first.

"He will be a strong man, Muine'j. He fought well, bravely."

"He will be a good chief," said Antoine, using his fingers to scrape the inside of his bowl. I laughed inside myself. When Antoine first arrived among us, he had scraped off the excess with a small stick. Somewhere along the way he had learned that fingers are sometimes the best tools for the job.

"It is up to the people to decide whether Muine'j becomes chief or not," said Ku'ku'kwes. "He is just one of several young men we are watching." She turned to Taqtaloq, smiling, "Just as we are watching the men of your generation."

When it became clear that Taqtaloq did not know where to look, Antoine stepped in kindly. "What does it take, Ku'ku'kwes, to become a chief?"

"It takes a knowledge of when to act and when to wait. It calls for an understanding of the needs of his people, often before they themselves know what it is they require." She reached out to grasp the cup Taqtaloq was holding out for her.

"Must he be a great warrior?" asked Antoine.

"No," said Ku'ku'kwes. "That is the war chief's role. But he must know when to press forward, though it seems that all must be lost, and when to retreat, though victory beckons. At all times, he must inspire his people with the courage to follow. For as you know, Antoine, we advance or retreat as one. A chief must move with the assurance that, were he to look over his shoulder, a vast crowd of witnesses – born and unborn – would be there to urge him on. For without them, he is no chief at all."

The wind was rising in the trees, looming as dark shadows on the walls of the wikuoms. Our little group huddled closer together, as we strained to catch Ku'ku'kwes' words. My own attention was now focused on the small space between my knees and Taqtaloq's. Yet there he sat, unaware of my struggles. Was I always to be drawn to men who placed me so firmly on the edge of their lives – I who so longed to be at the centre?

"You," the giant whispered, "will always be alone."

So he was still there, when I had thought him dead. The force of the realization drove me to my feet.

Three faces looked up in surprise. Maddened now, with fury and grief, I turned and ran, stumbling over the dogs in my path. The camp fell away and I found myself running through a tunnel, caught in a cacophony of winds and barking dogs.

Antoine caught me before I reached my wikuom, spinning me around. No, not Antoine. Taqtaloq.

"Give it away, Mouse, the hatred. You cannot live with it. It will kill you."

"To whom, to whom shall I give it?" I cried, twisting against the arms that bound me.

"Give it to the one who set out on the long journey to find you, the one who cut his feet on the path."

And that is how Mouse, a poor child of the most humble status, became Marie-Ange, child of a king.

*t*he transformation became complete the next day, as Antoine scooped the water from the river and let it trickle over my forehead. Taqtaloq himself stood beside me, nodding in response to Antoine's words. As the ritual concluded, he stepped forward to wipe the droplets from my face with a rough blanket, laughing as I emerged, red-faced, from the treatment.

"So Taqtaloq is now your father?" our chief asked, confused by the rite. "Well, that is less trouble than a husband. At least there will be someone to take care of you."

I tried to correct his mistake, but he had already gone off to clap Taqtaloq on the back. I sat, writhing inside, as I waited for Taqtaloq to laugh off any idea of kinship. He did no such thing. Instead, he sat nodding as the chief laid a hand on his shoulder and spoke earnestly into his ear. Then to my horror, he raised his head and caught me watching. Trapped in his gaze, I could not look away. Seeing the exchange, the chief smiled and came toward me.

"Father, indeed," he whispered, then continued down the path, chuckling.

We were preparing, all of us, for our return to the coast. Yet a single, grim task still remained. With the spring thaw, the bodies at the old camp could now be buried. When a small burial party was organized for the trip, I asked to be part of it. Our chief was surprised that I, a young woman with no family among the dead, was willing to undertake such a gruesome duty. But there were old hatreds to put to rest. There was a woman lying there among the dead with whom I must make my peace, and an unborn child with no mother to sing the songs over his grave.

I was fastening my snowshoes when Taqtaloq approached with Antoine. Both were surprised to see me. Taqtaloq simply nodded, eyes signalling his approval at my presence. Antoine greeted me with warmth, using my new name for the first time in conversation.

Antoine and Taqtaloq had also bestowed new names upon each other. Taqtaloq now referred to Antoine as Kitpu, the eagle who bore messages from the Creator to his people. Antoine, in turn, referred to Taqtaloq as Timothé, the one who stands firm when all others fall away. Secretly, I let the name pass over my tongue. It was a good choice. Taqtaloq – our word for the small serpent that changes colour with events – no longer fit the man so determined to keep his sad pact with the past.

As we walked, I reflected on how far each of us had strayed from the paths we were born to follow. "They will change us," Bright Eyes had said, "and we will change them."

We three remained slightly to the rear. We did not speak: Taqtaloq was preoccupied with his thoughts and we had no wish to disturb him with chatter. Yet several times he reached out to grasp my arm before I blundered onto a piece of shaky ground.

I felt the chill wind of the campsite long before it came into view. Alive once with the voices of our people, this place now belonged to the dead. Wrapping a cloth around my mouth and nose to protect me against the evil odour, I separated myself from the rest of our party and headed for the central hearth. Some tea, I thought, would strengthen us for the task ahead. Reaching the hearth, I stopped to gaze at the cups scattered around: these vessels had not been made in Cibou. Instinctively, I glanced at the hillside from where death had suddenly swept down upon us in the night. Were they there still, the enemy? I knew now they had not returned to their own country, but had lain hidden in the hills, waiting for the chance to reclaim their dead.

I forced the sound through my frozen throat. "Taqtaloq!"

Susan Young de Biagi

He came at once, at a run, his hand already reaching for the arrows tucked into his hood. I held out a hand to stop him, and pointed to the fire pit.

"It has been some days since they were here," he said. "We will track them, to see which way they have gone." Rising, he laid a hand on my shoulder to reassure me, then froze with a sudden thought. I knew at once what he was thinking. He in front, I behind, we tore over the ground to the edge of the woods, where the pile of bodies had lain.

"No!" screamed my mind. "No!"

Antoine grabbed me before I could look upon the sight. But there was no way to protect Taqtaloq from the shock. Dropping to his knees, he let forth a shriek, a roar, that rose violently upward into the sky. So strong was it, that Antoine and I found ourselves leaning away from the sound, as though pushed back by a powerful wind. Behind us, people were weeping and shouting, as they took in the sight that lay before them.

"Like deer they've skinned them," cried one woman, her voice rising above the rest.

Unable to stop myself, I stole a look over the blue-red mass, then quickly looked away. I knew that whatever courage I had stored up for the task of burying the dead was not equal to the even more gruesome one that lay ahead. Fainting, I took the shoulder that Antoine offered.

Rising from his knees, Taqtaloq began running toward the hills, his head bent toward the ground. Unable to do more, I watched him until he was a small speck, a fly crawling up the mountain. He would be back with news of the enemy. And then? All around me, men were shouting their desire for revenge. Only their hatred, their desire for blood, would sustain them in this nightmare.

As always, it was Antoine who knew what to do. "Marie-Ange. Fetch me the skin from one of the broken wikuoms, and a kettle." Thankful for a task that would remove me, if only for a few moments, from the grisly scene, I turned and fled. It took some time to wrest the skin away from the poles, but I managed and then began looking for one of the small kettles left strewn at every camp. By the time I returned, I felt more prepared to face the scene that awaited me. But Antoine stepped forward to block my view. Putting a gentle hand on my shoulder, he pushed me to the ground.

As I watched, Antoine wrapped the skin around the kettle, set it before me, and handed me a stick. "Sing Marie-Ange. Sing the songs Bright Eyes taught you."

I was surprised, for I knew how Antoine feared the frenzy of the drums. His aversion was greater even than that of the fishermen, who likened our music to the howling of wolves and mocked it when they thought themselves alone. Likewise, many a night our warriors sat around their fires, imitating the flutters and squeaks that came from the throats of grown men. For us, French music was sparrow song, sweet but with no power to inspire.

Antoine knew too that I had no voice for singing. Bright Eyes himself had tried to teach me, but soon gave it up. "Stay with your wampum Mouse, that is where your talent lies," he had said, with a smile to soften his words.

Still, it was into my hands that Antoine put the drum. I began quietly, hesitantly, then slowly grew louder, more confident. And somehow, my voice began to penetrate the shouted conversations of the warriors. One by one, they came to sit beside me, joining their voices to mine. Even the women stopped weeping, and began to sing along with the drum: song after song, until the first fury of rage and grief abated, to re-emerge as a strong, quiet power that would carry us through the days ahead.

Only Antoine was unmoved by the music. As the warriors swayed to its rhythms, he alone remained standing, one hand shading his eyes, to search for his friend. Seeing his reaction, I too began to worry. Handing the drum to a woman beside me, I rose and stood next to him. Together, we walked away from the group. Rapt in song, no one noticed.

"Will he try to confront them, alone?" I asked.

"I think not. His hate will not permit him to sacrifice himself unless he can strike a mortal blow in return. No, he will return with some knowledge of their weakness and a plan to exploit it."

"And you, what will you do Antoine?"

"I will try to convince him otherwise."

"But you yourself took up arms against the enemy."

"In defence of those weaker than I, not in revenge."

The drumming behind us had begun to wane. Calmer now, people were bending their minds to the work of burying the dead. It was decided among us that no attempt would be made to identify loved ones – a nearly impossible task. All of us, men and women, seized implements and laboured day and night to dig a mighty pit. On the afternoon of the fourth day, I was standing on the burial mound, wearily throwing the last clods onto the bank, when my spade was taken from me.

He was back, the lines in his brow more pronounced than when he had left. Standing before me now was a man in full strength, with the grim knowledge of how that strength was being tested. And as I looked upon him, I fell in love – as I had never loved Antoine, as I had never loved Charles. He saw it in my eyes. And there, atop a mass grave, in the midst of soiled and weary warriors, both of us exhausted and grieving, Taqtaloq leaned his head against mine and took my mouth.

*h*e lay the gift gently in my hands: offer of a marriage into a chiefly line – to me, the outcast, offspring of an unknown fisherman and an outlaw; to me, of the animal blood.

"It would be like mating with a dog," Mimikej had once said. "You might enjoy it for a moment, but in the end it would come to nothing."

He did not care. Somehow, he had forgotten the pride of family that seemed to dictate his actions until now. But I had not. Ku'ku'kwes herself had told us that he was one of several young men being considered for chief. A wife such as I could jeopardize his position.

And so I told him no. He did not insist. Nor, to my surprise, did he ask me to become his concubine, a position to which I was better suited by birth. He simply lay his face in my hands for a long moment, then left to join the group of men hunched around the fire. Later, we would all meet beside the newly covered grave, singing the ancient songs that would hasten the spirits' journey to the next world.

I was the first to rise the next morning, hoping to make the tea before the others awoke. There was much to think about: the honour I had been paid the day before, the bleakness of a life spent alone. As I sat gloomily poking the fire, I felt someone creep up beside me – Antoine. I rarely saw Antoine before his morning ritual of shaving and prayer. Wrapped in a blanket, his short hair standing in spikes, jaw covered in stubble, he slid onto the log beside me. As I watched in surprise, a hand snaked out of the blanket and ran vigorously through his hair, making it stand up even higher. I almost laughed.

"Well, I wanted to speak to you before the others were up," he explained wryly, in French. I was surprised. Ever since Charles's departure, we had conversed in the language of my people. I had turned my back on the other language and Antoine had respected my decision. But now, he had something to say that he did not want the others to hear.

"I once said, Marie-Ange, that I would like to see you married and protected by a man of your own people. Do you remember?"

Yes, I remembered. We had been speaking of Taqtaloq, at a time when Mimikej was still alive and Taqtaloq nothing more to me than the bully I had feared as a child.

"And now he has asked you to be his wife, and you said no. Why?"

Mistaking my silence for disapproval, he became more persistent.

"He is a good man, a different man from what he once was. He will care for you, protect you."

And then I understood: he had come to plead Taqtaloq's suit. I was at once honoured and embarrassed at the thought of these two fine men, coming each in his in turn to plead for such a worthless gift.

The tears escaped so quickly they splashed into the bucket of water I held for the tea. Antoine took it from my hands and set it on the fire, before turning to me. Then grasping the edge of his blanket, he began to dab at the corners of my eyes.

"Who am I," I gulped, in loud whispers, "to marry such a man, I who was cast out of another man's bed?"

Antoine's smile was tender. "Do you remember, Marie-Ange, that I once gave you a green stone? Do you still have it?"

I nodded, searching in my pocket for the small talisman I always carried with me.

"That's not the place for it." And threading it through a piece of sinew from his bag, Antoine placed it around my neck, where Charles's gold crescent had once hung.

"I always thought it was meant to adorn the neck of a princess," he said, sitting back to survey his work. Then leaning closer, he captured my eyes with his. "Never forget, Marie-Ange, that you are a child of the King, of the royal house of David. And – above all others – you are the one Taqtaloq wants. And now he lies back there, awake and grieving, because he fears he is not worthy of you."

The thought of Taqtaloq in pain almost swayed me. But I was not yet ready to give in. "I cannot have children," I said defensively. "And even if I could, they would not do him honour."

"And who, when they marry, can make a sure promise of children to a husband or wife?" asked Antoine reasonably. "Children are one of the gifts the Father bestows, according to his will. It is arrogance to believe otherwise."

He leaned in even closer, whispering. "And please explain to me, Marie-Ange, how a fig tree can bear olives, or a grapevine bear figs?" Antoine grasped my face between his hands, forcing me to look into his eyes. "I promise you, dear girl, that any children you and Taqtaloq have will be well and truly human."

Somehow he had discovered my secret fear. And hearing it spoken aloud for the first time revealed it – finally – for what it was: a foolish obsession. We sat looking into each other's eyes for a moment, before he winked and gestured in Taqtaloq's direction. "Go to him. I'll make the tea."

k

*a*mong our people, it is the custom for a young man to offer bride service to the family of his beloved. Taqtaloq had supported Mimikej's mother for two winters before he was able to claim the daughter as his own. In my case, there was no one to serve. I was happy we could be together without the usual period of waiting, but Taqtaloq feared a hasty marriage would dishonour me. It took all our arguments, Antoine's and mine, to convince him.

Antoine married us a week after our return to the main camp.

People were confused by the ritual, and even more so by our refusal to preside over the great feast that tradition demanded. Taqtaloq was too shaken by the experience of burying his first wife, and I was too shy of my new status.

What each of us wanted, above all, was the chance to be alone, in our own wikuom. It was there, finally, that I bore the weight of his body upon me and I welcomed the burden. His hair, that I had once dreamt of pulling out by its roots, now lay thick and shining between my fingers. That first night, I dreamt that I had caught and held a great eagle, its feathers peacefully folded in my arms. And as the sun rose in my dream, my eagle unsheathed its strength, raised its great wings and carried me, unafraid, over a wide country. Seeing with its eyes, I looked down upon the wikuom, gazed curiously at the tiny figures gathering kindling for the fires, then passed beyond the long silver line that separated the land from the sea.

There in my dream, upon the vast, flat ocean, I saw French ships, their lookouts clinging to the masts, eager for their first glimpse of Cibou. And though they looked up and saw us, high above their heads, they had no power to affect the course of our flight. Taqtaloq and I, together, were far beyond their reach.

We spent those first days alone, far from the others. I relished the feel of his hair in my hands, as I plaited and re-plaited it in a hundred new ways. Taqtaloq sat patiently, sometimes wincing at the slight pain of the hair being tugged through my fingers. I was amused that a warrior – trained to withstand great pain – should be so sensitive. But I knew that his skin was as open, as vulnerable to my touch, as mine was to his.

In the way of our people, we used a sharpened awl to trace secret signs on the hidden parts of each other's body, raising the design in drops of blood, then rubbing it with a leaf to ensure it would remain forever. I felt his cool breath on my skin, as he blew on the tiny pinpricks.

"What is it my love?"

Taqtaloq's forehead creased as he gazed at the roughness of his work. "It doesn't seem fair. The designs you traced on my skin are those of a great artist, while these...."

But I gloried in the rough scratchings he had left on my body: an eagle had caught me in his talons, marking me out for his own. Taqtaloq shook his head in wonder at my pride in his work.

Reaching out, I passed my hand over his smooth skin, that bore no designs apart from my own.

"This is the first time you have been marked." I said, choosing my words carefully.

He shared my unwillingness to mention Mimikej's name.

"Not all women are willing to bear the mark of their husband. And as you know, the request must come from the bride." He grazed his fingers over my breast, where a tiny salamander- the totem of his house – lay coiled. "You did me great honour in asking."

I lay my fingers over his, pressing down hard in my need to feel the weight of his hand upon me. "The honour, husband, is mine."

k

*t*hese days alone soon came to an end. Taqtaloq was called to the council fire, to help prepare a response to the enemy's crime of defiling our dead. I remained close by our own fireside, excited by the opportunity to put my skills to the test. No kettle was too heavy, for my back was strong. No sinew could long withstand my nimble fingers.

At night, as we whispered between our furs, Taqtaloq told me all that had passed in the great council, and all that was contained in his heart.

"We cannot attack from here, we are too few. We must return to the coast, where even now the French are waiting, with cannon and muskets. We will strike our enemies with the Frenchmen's arm."

"How do you know the French will help?"

"Marie-Ange! How can you ask that question? You, who were present when we helped the French take the English fort, in a quarrel that was not ours. Among the French, as you know, there is always the question of debts owed and repaid. We will speak to them in a language they can understand."

"What does Antoine think?"

Taqtaloq sighed, then raised himself from my shoulder to look into my eyes.

"He is against it. He argues that such a flame, once lit, cannot easily be put out. Ku'ku'kwes supports him, and she carries much weight in the council."

"And you Taqtaloq, what are your own thoughts?"

His face grew dark, and he tensed in my arms. "Just days ago, I stood beside the grave of my first wife and my son, and vowed that I would avenge them. And now she stands there, Mimikej, watching from the Land of the Ancestors, urging me to fulfill that vow. I will not be free until my enemy lies slain between my hands."

The words that Antoine once said to Muine'j rose, unbidden, to my mind. "When the Son sets you free, you are free indeed." It was only when I saw Taqtaloq's face that I realized I had spoken them aloud. He looked at me for a moment, uncertain, then gathered me even more closely into his grasp. And lying there together, wrapped in the comfort of each other's arms, we slept.

*t*he desecration of our dead was not the only unsettling event that spring. Something else was happening, something frightening. Men did not speak of it in front of their women, for fear of upsetting them. Women did not speak of it in front of their men, for the same reason. But we all knew: the animals were not as giving of themselves as they once were. If they remained aloof, we would have nothing to trade when we arrived on the coast.

"My husband came home with no kill again last night," said Ko'komin as we sat in the women's wikuom.

The men believe we may be under a curse," whispered Eune'k.

"We are indeed cursed," cried another. "But what is its meaning?"

"Let us go to the Elders and ask them to explain it. Surely one of them will know."

There was silence at this. Many of our Elders had died during last winter's sickness. The rest were murdered in the attack. Ku'ku'kwes was one of the very few who remained.

Ko'komin stood. "We must go to Ku'ku'kwes. Let us ask her now."

"It is forbidden to leave while we are bleeding."

"Only if we cross the path of a hunter. We must be careful to remain unseen."

I held back, expecting to be ignored, as usual. But Eune'k stood and stretched out her hand to me.

One by one we crept out of the wikuom. To the men who lounged around their fires, we were no more than flickering shadows as we darted through the village. It was not long before we found ourselves in the clearing in front of Ku'ku'kwes' wikuom. The old woman's son had erected a small dwelling for her just beside his own.

We could not risk rousing him. Ko'komin scampered across the clearing and bent down outside the door, softly whispering, "Grandmother." But it was no good: the old woman's ears were not what they once were. Lifting the flap, Ko'komin ducked inside. A moment later, she was out again, signalling to us. One by one, we ran across the clearing and slipped into the wikuom. Eune'k and I were the last to enter.

The fire was stifling, but Ku'ku'kwes huddled as close to it as possible. There was no surprise in the old eyes as she looked up to see so many women in her dwelling. I sensed she was expecting us.

"We have come to ask you a question, Grandmother."

The old woman nodded, beckoning us closer to the fire. We obeyed, though we looked with longing at the cool wall of the dwelling.

"You have come to ask about our brothers, the animals, and why it is they stay away so long."

No one was surprised. She had often guessed our thoughts.

Ku'ku'kwes poked at the fire with a stick, sending a shower of sparks into the air. We had to bend closer still to grasp the words that followed.

"We do not know why the animals first offered themselves to us in the Long Ago. Nor can they tell us: for their power of speech was taken away on the day Kluskap was called back to the Creator. But before he left, he bound us all – animals and humans – in a sacred pact. In silence, the animals offer themselves so we might live. And as we eat their flesh and wear their skins, we honour that sacrifice, by treating their dead bodies with reverence."

"But now...," Ku'ku'kwes spat onto one of the hot rocks girding the fire, watching it sizzle in response, "now they give their lifeblood ... for what? Metal knives and red cloth."

I remembered the day Antoine and I sat watching the hunters bring their pelts to Charles in exchange for French goods.

As the afternoon wore on, the pile of skins in front of Charles grew higher and higher, until all we could see was the feather of his hat. I remembered, too, the day of the moose hunt, and our chief's concern over a careless word.

"I believe," Ku'ku'kwes went on, "that if the animals could explain to us why Kluskap required such a terrible sacrifice of them, it would not be for the sake of a few scraps of cloth."

The old woman's face grew dark. "I fear there may yet come a time when the animals no longer offer themselves at all."

"But what can be done Grandmother?" cried Ko'komin.

Taking a stick in one hand, the old lady poked the fire even higher.

"It is for the animals themselves to decide."

*

*L*ack of furs for trade delayed our arrival on the coast. Always before, we were waiting when the French arrived, to assign them beach room. Now we arrived to the sound of shouts and hammering, as the workmen strengthened the fort built the preceding season. It seemed as though Cibou were already theirs, and we the strangers. Offshore, two great ships were surrounded by a host of small fishing boats. Mercifully, Charles's ship was not among them.

A young soldier blocked our path to the beach, a lieutenant judging from the embroidery on his coat. He strode up to Antoine.

"Father, please tell these people to move off. We cannot have them milling around the fortress."

Antoine looked surprised, then annoyed. "I cannot tell these people to move. I am not their leader."

The furrows sank even deeper into the skin. "If not you, then who?"

Antoine gestured with his eyes toward the chief, who was, as usual, dressed in the most ragged of robes.

The young man stretched out a rigid finger and said in the high pitch of a child. "Do you mean that ragged old man?"

Antoine gently touched the young man's hand to lower it, for it is not our custom to point in this way.

"He is not old. And among his own people, these ragged garments win him as much respect as ermine and purple do for our own king Louis. The rags are his promise to his people: while he lives, they themselves will never go without a warm cloak."

"That may be, but he can't stay here. You'll have to tell him."

"I would not dare to tell him anything."

The young man looked incredulous. "He's not even armed."

The voice grew condescending. "Well, you don't have to be afraid any longer, Father, now that we're here to protect you. That fortress is filled with soldiers, plenty enough to get these people hopping as soon as Captain Francourt gives the word."

Antoine did not look comforted by this statement. "Where is Captain Francourt now?"

"In the fortress, preparing the trade goods."

Eager for his letters, Antoine went off in search of the French officer. The young man stood fingering his musket and glancing around, as though expecting the rest of us to quake in fear. But everyone had gone off, except for a few children. Though he made a fearsome face, they simply turned, laughing, to their mothers. Lacking even the wit to feel foolish, he continued to scowl at the small pranksters.

We, the people of Cibou, slipped in amongst the crowds of shouting soldiers and fishermen. Strangers, most of them, they too looked at us with suspicion, even hostility.

"Mouse!"

Pierrot, the clown, had sprung up at my back, hoping to startle me. At once, Taqtaloq was between us, bristling and dangerous, looming over the much shorter Pierrot. Among the French, only Charles approached the height of our men.

Pierrot took a step back, then two, appealing to me with his eyes. Seeing the look, Taqtaloq also turned to me, eyebrows raised in a light query. At my nod, he brushed past Pierrot to stroll the few remaining paces to the shore. I knew the merest whisper would bring him to my side.

"Who was that?" asked Pierrot, shaken.

"My husband."

It did not take great wisdom to follow Pierrot's thoughts. He was relieved at no longer having a reason to reproach Captain Daniel, whom he much admired. Pierrot belonged to the cheerful tribe of people who held that, as long as everything came to a good end, no real damage had been done. He was wrong, but I did not tell him so at the time.

Pierrot spoke to me carefully of Charles, without once mentioning his name. "I'm not told what happens in high places – events at court don't reach as far as my cottage in Criel-sur-Mer. But all France was abuzz over the capture of Lord Stewart. They say his captors sit in Richelieu's council, with bigger mouthfuls to chew than the escort of a humble fishing fleet. That's why Captain Francourt led the flotilla this year. Other people are too...."

Taqtaloq had turned and sought my gaze. The journey had been long and he was impatient to reach our own fireside.

"I must go, Pierrot." And taking my leave, I ran to join my husband, who had already turned his back on the activity at the shore. Together, we set off for Taqtaloq's campsite. But before we could reach it, our attention was caught by an unusual sight: Antoine was sitting on a stump, letters in hand, staring at nothing. He looked up startled, as Taqtaloq laid a hand on his shoulders. In his eyes, I thought I saw the glint of tears.

"I must leave," he said, "when the ship departs for Canada."

"But you will return." I was unable now to conceive of a life without him.

"No," said Antoine. "The cardinal wishes to send me to Canada, to work among the people there."

"Why not our people here?"

"I do not know. I only know that I must go. For such is the will of God."

I wondered if he had not confused the will of God with the will of the one he called the cardinal, but I said nothing.

The approach of a sailor in search of Antoine put an end to our conversation. But later, as night was falling, I made my way to his wikuom. I had a question that could not go unasked.

Antoine's face was bleak, bleaker than I had ever seen it. I almost faltered, unwilling to be the cause of more pain. Yet it was Antoine himself who had set my feet upon this path. I had to see where it led.

At my approach, Antoine made an effort to impress a look of welcome on his face. I dropped to my knees beside him and accepted the cup of tea he held out to me. We drank in silence for some moments.

"When will you be leaving?"

"Before the moon is out. Captain Francourt is anxious to sail on to Canada."

I buried my nose in my cup, afraid to go on.

"We are friends, are we not Marie-Ange?"

I nodded – such friends, in fact, that he knew my thoughts before I spoke them. Once an unseeing, unknowing stranger, Antoine had finally become one of us. Why now, I asked myself bitterly, when it was too late?

Caught in his perception, I blurted it out:

"Does it not seem, Antoine, as though your god has abandoned you?"

The quickness of his response suggested it was a question Antoine had asked himself many times before.

"Yes, it does. But that's the nature of our relationship, his and mine. He needs to know that I trust him, when all evidence suggests he has abandoned me. He needs to know that I'll stay faithful, even when I can't see the outcome."

Antoine turned to face me, as though it were important to him that one other person knew and understood the path that lay ahead.

"Sometimes I feel that the Lord is setting his foot on me, as a mason might test a stone in a wall, to see if it will hold. It is vitally important that I do hold, because one day – for his plans to succeed – he may need to rest all his weight on me. And he must know, with complete confidence, that I won't shift."

Antoine's eyes burned into mine. "On that day, I'll be just one of many stones he strides over as he forges ahead to victory. But what if that victory rides on the ability of a single stone to hold fast? And I will hold fast, Mouse, with all my might, as my master's foot passes over. And perhaps as he passes, he'll say, 'Ah, there is the stone that I chose so carefully and laid with my own hands. And it is holding. Well done, faithful servant.' And that will be all. And it will be enough."

I did not know what to say, for his words troubled and confused me. Later that night, I wondered why an all-powerful god would choose to make himself vulnerable, by relying on the strength of a single human soul.

*

*t*aqtaloq's arms wrapped around me as I slipped naked into our furs.

"So he will truly leave," he said when he saw my face.

"Yes, he will leave."

Taqtaloq did not ask what would become of us, but the question lay heavy on our hearts. The path along which Antoine had been guiding us had suddenly come to an abrupt end. And as we lay there, we wondered: could we find the way ourselves?

Antoine himself spoke no more of it. Poised on the edge of some great sacrifice, he seemed determined to enjoy these last days in Cibou. He and Taqtaloq spent the time doing the things friends do. Taqtaloq taught him to balance on the end of a canoe and to throw the spear, bone-tipped with two wooden prongs on each side for grasping the fish. Although it took some time to master, Antoine was finally able to spear the beasts that swarmed in the shadows below. And for the time that he stood there, black robe tucked up into his belt, white feet and knees bare, he seemed to keep the other, larger shadows at bay.

I watched from the beach, fingers flying in an attempt to finish the wampum Antoine had coveted for his king. Too much of my life, and Antoine's, had gone into this wampum. And so I would give it, not to a king, but to a friend. The most valuable shells gleamed as small, silvered flecks on a background of blue water. They would, I hoped, remind him of these last, carefree days, spent on the surface of the sea.

I hid my present as the two approached, laughter in their throats. As Taqtaloq threw himself onto the sand beside me, I saw fish scales glinting in his hair and sparkling on his chest. Antoine, in his exuberance, had simply thrown the fish into the canoe behind him, not knowing or caring where they landed.

Seeing them there reminded me how late it was: they would soon be wanting their meal. Springing up, I caught my foot on a stone, then threw all my weight on the other foot, to keep from falling. I looked down, in horror. Were those my legs straddling those of my warrior husband, cutting off his strength with my woman's magic?

Taqtaloq did not move, but remained leaning back on his palms, legs stretched out between mine. Unable to look into his eyes, I dropped down beside him, my head digging into the sand as I prostrated myself before him.

I felt his light touch on my head before his hand slipped down to my chin, gently but insistently lifting, forcing me to meet his gaze.

"You must know, beloved, that my strength comes from a new source. I cannot be so easily robbed of it."

It was true. For I saw it there, in his eyes, shining from a source somewhere deep in his soul. I sat transfixed, caught in his gaze, until a cough from Antoine reminded us we were not alone. My husband nudged me gently, and once again I rose to my feet, to fetch their evening meal.

*

On the next day, we three borrowed one of the fishermen's chaloupes to sail to the bird islands, just off our coast. Taqtaloq tried out the skin sail I had cured myself. I was anxious to see if it would capture and hold the wind: I need not have worried.

No one lived on these islands: Kluskap had forbidden it. But anyone could travel there in search of food. Bags slung over our shoulders, Taqtaloq and I began scaling the cliffs, seeking the eggs that lay in hidden crevices. Behind us Antoine struggled to keep his footing on the slippery rocks. Book in hand, he wrote down the name of each bird, first in our language, then in his own: egret, heron, cormorant, partridge, goose, puffin.

Niskam was high in the sky when we finally stopped for a drink of tea. Antoine held his cup aloft.

"Let us drink to the success of Marie-Ange's sail. May it be the first of many."

Taqtaloq and I raised our cups to his, as we had seen the French do.

Antoine seemed particularly light-hearted.

"Tell me a story from this land, Marie-Ange."

I was surprised. Antoine rarely asked to hear our stories. And I was no storyteller. Still, I had spent many hours at Bright Eyes's feet, as had we all. One of my favourites was his tale of the giant blue lobster. I closed my eyes, trying to remember the old man's exact words.

"This lobster could not find a wife, being so big and ungainly. And blue. No one wanted to take a chance on a blue husband. What would their children look like? So he was lonely, there in the depths of the sea. And in his loneliness, as he sat rubbing his antenna together, he played the sweetest of songs, that vibrated through the ocean."

"One day, the song was heard by a female of his kind, on the far side of the sea – perhaps in your land, Antoine. And she asked everyone she knew, 'Whose is that wonderful song?' But they could not tell her. Day and night it called to her, penetrating even unto her dreams. Until finally, when she could bear it no longer, she set out, travelling afar in response to the sweet call."

"Sleep had never come easily to the blue lobster, such was his loneliness. And so it was that she came upon him in darkness, still playing his plaintive song. Creeping close, she wrapped her claws around him, amazed at his vast strength."

I glanced at Antoine. Was it fair to speak of such things to him, for whom they were forbidden? But he seemed rapt in the story. I took a breath and plunged ahead.

"There they lay, wrapped in love, rolling over and over in the current. It cushioned and lulled them as it bore them along, their bed a dark, blue sea. When daylight came, the lobster kept his eyes tightly closed, unable to bear the look of disappointment on her face when she saw him. But then a gentle prod urged him to open his eyes. He sighed and obeyed. And there before him, sparkling in the light, was his mate, her shell a vivid, brilliant blue. And he was never lonely again."

Antoine sat up, clapping his hands lightly together, in the manner common to his people. But Taqtaloq sat quietly, chin in hand, gazing at me with love in his eyes. I remembered that he too had taken his chances with an ungainly blue monster. And leaning over, heedless of Antoine, I kissed him full on the mouth.

We sat a few minutes more, watching the sunset and savouring each other's company. It was time to paddle home.

*t*rading began the next day. Captain Francourt had set out his wares in front of the fort, and was seated in Charles's old place, under the white canopy.

As a wife, I no longer had time to sit watching, as I once had. Clam rake in hand, I was heading for the beach when Captain Francourt called to me.

"I do not understand, Marie-Ange. Trading has finished for the day and yet these people will not leave. Please ask them what is wrong."

I glanced at the large crowd, foreboding and silent, gathered in front of Francourt. Quickly, I moved toward Najiktaneket, who was sitting directly in the Frenchman's path, lip thrust out in disapproval.

"What is it, uncle?" I asked, careful to use the accepted term when addressing an Elder.

Najiktaneket planted his eye on the two kettles and two knives stacked in a small pile before him. "I have presented him with three fine pelts, good and thick, and this is all he gives me in return."

The pile was indeed pitifully small. Glancing round, I saw the other piles were no larger. I raised my eyes to Captain Francourt.

"I believe they are waiting for the rest of their goods."

A look of anguish passed over the Frenchman's face and the words poured out, almost too fast for me to grasp.

"Unfortunately, it is all I have been authorized to offer. Prices fluctuate, fashions change. Now that the English and Dutch have entered the game, customers are no longer quite so eager to pay what they once did. And then there's rising insurance costs. Even in peacetime, the English are not above seizing our ships. Our merchants have to dig deep to protect their vessels. And of course, there's the Russian market that is beginning to open up again. Their golden sable is all the rage at court this year."

I put a hand up to stop him. My head could not contain so many new words: fluctuate and insurance – and Russian, whatever kind of prey that might be.

"Help me understand, Captain Francourt. You are saying that a fur that was worth ten knives last year is now worth only two?"

At Francourt's frantic nod, I bent down to confer with the hunters.

"How can that be?" asked Keknu'teluatl. "This fur is even finer than it was last year. Our women vie with each other to produce only the best skins."

We had sacrificed much for this trade. Rather than hunting in autumn, when animals were fat, our men now hunted in the depth of winter, when the meat was tough but furs thick and lustrous. Before the trade, the Elders told us, our people delighted in the richness of the meat, its globes of fat shining on the surface of the soup. Now, not even the new copper kettles could make winter meat more palatable.

Francourt nodded helplessly as I translated the hunters' anger. "All true, but my orders...."

"What is the problem, Captain Francourt?"

The captain seemed relieved to find Antoine at his side. "I was just explaining to Marie-Ange how the value of fur has fallen since last year."

I had never before seen the shrewd look that now passed over Antoine's face.

"That is true. But I hear the value of real estate has risen significantly."

It was Captain Francourt's turn to look confused.

"Real estate?"

"Well, yes. I'm speaking of that fine piece of property out there on the point."

Francourt and I followed Antoine's gaze to the small promontory, where the fort shone in the golden glow of sunset. At this distance, the soldiers were black dots buzzing round it.

Antoine's voice grew patient – a dangerous sign. "I believe the rent is just coming due. It would be terrible, would it not, if the chief chose to foreclose just now?"

"But I have no more goods to trade. This is all I was given."

Antoine smiled again. "Surely a military man like you has something these people can use. A gift to the village, perhaps, to be shared among the people, as is their custom."

Captain Francourt's skin paled, a phenomenon I have always witnessed with interest. "You don't mean muskets, surely, Father Antoine?"

"Well, they certainly would have been useful this past winter. Among their enemies, these warriors now have the reputation of being armed. It is time, I believe, for reputation to become fact. Your soldiers can spare twenty muskets, I am sure. Here, young man, hand me your weapon."

Antoine reached out to the same soldier over whom he had triumphed the day before. Uncertain, the soldier appealed to Francourt, who nodded. As Antoine weighed the instrument of death in his hand, I remembered the night we stood shoulder to shoulder, fighting for the life of our village. I remembered, too, his secret sickness afterwards. And I knew this decision was the result of much anguished thought.

Handing the musket back to the young man, Antoine turned to Captain Francourt. "Shall I tell the chief he can expect twenty such gifts later this evening?"

Francourt's gaze challenged Antoine's for a moment, then fell. My friend then turned to me with a smile. "Marie-Ange. Please explain to the warriors they will receive the remainder of their trade goods from the hands of their chief."

How formidable an ally Antoine could be, as formidable as ever his brother was.

ﾒ

i presented my gift to Antoine on the day before he left. As I drew it slowly from my robe, I remembered the moccasins I had given him so long ago.

Antoine said nothing as he traced the wampum's designs with his fingers: the giant's shadow reflected on the water; the small mouse crouching behind a rock, poised as if to drink; the eagle swooping out of the sunlight to save her; and finally, the great nut tree, its mighty branches spreading along the river bank. Would it speak to him, as it did me, of the father who had travelled such an impossible distance, in search of a lost soul?

That last night, we three lingered around the fire until the sky began to lighten. Although it had grown warmer, we huddled close together around the flames to escape the mosquitoes that swirled in great clouds above our heads.

"They will be worse where you're going," said Taqtaloq to Antoine, as he slapped at the frenzied beasts. Antoine saw my look of shock at my husband's remark and began to laugh, choking and gulping so that Taqtaloq had to thump him on the back. His shoulders continued to shake for so long afterward that Taqtaloq and I grew worried.

We were signalling to each other above his head when Antoine suddenly looked up.

"Do you know why I came here, to Cibou?"

We knew he did not decide these things for himself – someone else determined where he would go, and when. We were wondering how to put this thought into speech when Antoine began to speak again.

"I had a story to tell, an old, old story. And I could not bear to stay any longer in a place where people had heard all the words before, where their eyes clouded over as soon as I began to speak. I wanted to tell it in a new place, using words that fell fresh and vibrant on new ears. I wanted to see, reflected in my listeners' eyes, the same wonder I myself had always felt."

He laid a hand on my shoulder and on Taqtaloq's. "You, both of you, have given me that gift. And I shall never forget it."

There were no words of reply as beautiful as those he had just spoken, so we left them hanging in the air, to consider and admire. After a moment, Antoine rose and with a last look back, faded into the shadows of the trees, his black robe pulling him into the darkness.

It had been our last moment alone with him. When he embarked the next morning, our whole village had gathered to see him off. The smallest children were clambering to be in his arms, while older brothers and sisters stood shyly and sadly by. Ku'ku'kwes, looking suddenly older and even more frail, had grasped a corner of his sleeve, and was rubbing it between her fingers. Her eyes were those of a mother who would not again see a beloved son in this life.

Susan Young de Biagi

Our chief stood with his hand on his son's shoulder. Muine'j's voice rose high and clear, piercing through the chatter. "There will be no more stories, then? I had hoped to hear more."

"Ask Marie-Ange to tell them to you. She knows them all."

Antoine sought my eyes in a long, long look. I remembered that I had shared his first moments on our shores, as I now shared his last. And in that time, I had become someone different: his creation in a way. I raised my head, and smiled my thanks to him. As he smiled back, I felt something valuable – all his hopes for us, and all his fears – pass into my hands for safekeeping.

Chief and council were frustrated by Captain Francourt's early departure for Canada: they had hoped to secure the help of the French warship in a sudden attack on the enemy. What they didn't know was that help was close at hand, running with the sun toward our shores.

My spirit, knowing what lay ahead, grew heavier and heavier with each day that passed, but my mind could not read its message. It was only when I saw the people running toward the beach that I understood what my spirit had been trying to tell me. He was back.

Quickly, I turned and began walking up the beach toward my own wikuom. It was as if I were wading against a strong current; my feelings and the crowds racing toward the ship made walking away difficult. I persisted, determined to be safely away before the red cape made its appearance.

Taqtaloq found me huddled in my furs, my face against the wall. I felt his hand on my shoulder, yet could not turn to face him, so ashamed was I of the rage that still burned within, a rage I had thought conquered. My husband's hand dropped away, even as his breathing grew more and more laboured. After a long moment, I heard him leave. Later, when I had gained control of my thoughts, I went in search of him, but was told he had gone to the council fireside. Worried, I sat down to wait.

It was a long night, one in which Taqtaloq did not appear. I was dozing by the fireside in the early morning light when I was startled to full wakefulness.

"Taqtaloq?"

"No, it is I." The words were French.

"So I see," I responded in my own tongue, determined not to speak that which had been an early bond between us.

"Mouse, where is Antoine?"

"There are many who will tell you what you need to know. There is no need to seek me out."

Charles sat down beside me, clearly frustrated at my refusal to speak his language. At first, I exulted in his frustration. But as time passed and he made no move to leave, I grew embarrassed by my behaviour, that of a sullen child.

"Antoine left with Captain Francourt," I said, in French.

"Surely he knew I was coming?"

I thought for a moment. Would Antoine have kept silent about Charles, to protect me? No, my friend would have prepared me for his brother's sudden appearance.

I shook my head. "I think not."

"But Francourt was to pass on my letters to him. I sent them by courier to the Mother House, asking that they be forwarded to Antoine."

I remained silent as Charles thought his way through the problem.

"The Cardinal has kept my letters from reaching Antoine," he said finally. "He knew I would never permit my brother to voyage to Canada – and a martyr's fate."

I remembered the time when a boil invented for the chief's wife had kept Antoine from sailing into battle. And in spite of my revulsion for Charles, I wished he had arrived in time to invent a similar delay.

"Charles...."

He turned at the sound of his name on my lips.

"What is the meaning of 'martyr's fate'?"

His head snapped up at my words. Then he lied to me.

"It is nothing Mouse: an expression we use when someone leaves suddenly, without telling anyone."

I marked the word to ask Pierrot about later, and was making my escape when Charles spoke again.

"I imagine you want news of your mother."

I sat down abruptly.

"I left her last year in a small cove, in Newfoundland. She herself remembered the landmark, and was able to direct me to it. There was a small village of people there, preparing for their winter trek into the interior. She went with them." He leaned forward to pat me on the knee. "She seemed content enough, Mouse."

I remembered then that someone else had sailed on that voyage.

"And Lord Stewart?"

Charles hooted.

"Shackled on the opposite end of the ship. Do you think I would be so foolish as to let them be together? Stewart had no interest in her in any case; she had outlived her usefulness."

I was grateful for that, at least, and nodded to Charles, rising once more to take my leave.

"So you can imagine how relieved I was to find her there when I returned in the spring."

Again I sat down, then spent the next few moments trying to bring my breathing under control.

"And how ... how did she look?"

"Fat."

"Fat?"

Charles waved a vague hand around his midriff, and looked at me with meaning.

"With a fine young man – much younger than she – standing beside her, looking very pleased with himself. But no more pleased than she. I believe I even heard a giggle."

I could not share his amusement, not yet.

"What colour were his eyes?"

"What?"

"His eyes. What colour were they?"

"Why black of course, like every other young man on this coast."

I sat back, relieved to know my mother was at least released from her dream of Netaoansom.

"Thank you, Charles, for bringing me this news."

"It is not all I have brought you." And reaching into his pocket, Charles drew forth a small, bone whistle. I recognized it at once. Its mouthpiece polished smooth by my mothers' lips, it was the same whistle upon which she used to play small, trilling tunes when I was a child. I could no longer hold back the tears. Feeling a hard shoulder beneath my cheek, I instinctively turned toward its comfort, burrowing my head into Charles's neck. His familiar smell roused me from my stupor, and I straightened, horrified at my weakness. Only then did I see the flicker in the trees.

"Taqtaloq!"

Leaving Charles at the fire, I leapt up and began running toward the shadow. But it was too quick for me and faded away.

I remembered Taqtaloq's deep breathing when I had stupidly kept my head to the wall. As I looked at Charles, I somehow expected to see my own panic reflected in his face. But wrapped in thoughts of his own, he showed no concern for what had just passed between my husband and me. I marvelled that I had once given my love to such a man.

i had not been invited to sit in the council, nor would I be welcome to seek Taqtaloq there. Instead, I remained seated beside my own wikuom, my eye ever on the path that led from the village to the council fire. But Taqtaloq never came. The first day passed, then the second. And through it all, my thoughts chased each other round and round. I knew Charles would sail toward the south in pursuit of our enemy, and that he would take Taqtaloq with him. Charles was in our chief's debt, for our help in the battle against Lord Stewart. And then there were the muskets. Our southern enemy had already come once in search of them. Charles's own fort would never be safe until that enemy was vanquished.

And so Charles promised his aid. This I knew from the scampering that went on around me. But still Taqtaloq did not come. The thought of him sailing without me almost drove me to my feet in panic. Yet I would not shame him by bursting in upon the council, or by searching for him throughout the village.

For myself, I spared no shame. In my panic and desperation, I tore my robes and smeared the red ochre of mourning on my skin. On the fourth day, I cut my hair. I spent the hours making new arrows, against the time when he would need them. But the feathers slid from my shaking fingers.

In the end, it was the chief who sought me out. I stared at him through tufts of short hair.

"You have brought me a message," I said dully. "Taqtaloq has decided to renounce me."

The chief shook his head. "No indeed, I come on my own behalf."

I shook my head to clear it. If Taqtaloq had told no one of what he had witnessed, neither would I open my lips.

The chief kept his voice light as he settled himself at my feet.

"I see you have cut your hair. Well, you are a more submissive wife than that woman of mine. In our first year together, she chose to wield her knife on my new suit of clothing, just because I noted that there were some rather large scraps left over from her sewing."

The chief patted my hand. "How well I remember that first winter with Muine'j's mother: a wild year, glorious and horrible. So it is when two people learn to live together. He will be back. And it will start all over again: the embraces and the fighting. It is the way we are made."

But our chief knew that whatever had caused me to cut my hair was no small quarrel. Nor had Charles's visit gone unnoticed.

"Did you know, Mouse, that Keptin Daniel is sailing tomorrow, with our young men?"

So it had come to pass: I had lost my last chance to see my husband. Our life in ruins at his feet, he would surely seek death, for himself and his enemy. Nor would I linger behind. There, in the Land of the Ancestors, I would take up my post beside yet another path, to wait for him as he passed by on his way to the Great Council.

The thought brought with it a sudden rush of fear. Was there even a place for us in the Land of the Ancestors, now that our spirits belonged to the One who had paid for them with his blood? For the first time, I grasped the enormity of what I had done, in handing over my soul to Antoine's god. Antoine was not here to chase the fears away.

"Mouse!"

I had forgotten the chief. Trying to focus through my hanging hair, I saw concern and shock written on his face.

"You cannot fade from us in this way. Keptin Daniel refuses to ask it of you, so I have come in his place. Will you help us, as you did before?"?"

My mouth, which had been hanging open, snapped shut. Once on board Charles's ship, I would beg my husband's forgiveness. And if he would not relent, I would die – not by my own hand, but honourably, in battle. So that wherever we went, we would go together.

I jumped to my feet so quickly the chief had to struggle to catch up. Grabbing an arm, he said, "No, not like that. First you must wash and put on a clean robe. My wife will help you dress your hair. As for Taqtaloq, you can talk to him tonight, at the dog feast. I myself will escort you, so that he knows you come at my bidding, not that of Keptin Daniel."

ᴋ

*e*ven the most determined scrubbing by the chief's wife could not remove all traces of red paint from my face. She did what she could with my hair, and afterwards I carefully placed my bow and the quiver of new arrows on my back.

It is not lightly that a chief will decide to host a dog feast. Nor is it our custom to eat our dogs, who had no part in the animals' offering of themselves as food. To us, a dog is a friend, a fellow-traveller.

Yet it sometimes happens, in times of war or great hardship, that a dog will be sacrificed. Bright Eyes explained it to me once.

"No animal is more courageous than the dog. Though the courage of men may fail, that of the dog never will. I myself have seen our dogs throw themselves into the jaws of the bear, so that men might live."

So it is that when our hunters require great courage they will eat the flesh of the dog. Of all duties required of a chief, choosing the one to be sacrificed is the heaviest. For it is not the weak or cruel who are chosen, but the dog of great courage, the one who will come willingly when called.

"The wisest among them know," Bright Eyes had said, wiping away my child's tears with a corner of his old robe. "They know and accept the sacrifice demanded of them. And one of their number will agree to come, knowing they will live again in the Land of the Ancestors."

The whole village was silent as the chief set out for the place where the dogs scampered. Some of the other men accompanied him, so he would not carry this burden alone. I myself remained in my wikuom, remembering the wise old man who had been my teacher. He too had chosen to go to the Land of the Ancestors, so that my mother and I might live. Had he, in doing so, left me something of his courage? I would need it for the night ahead.

*M*y preparations had been for nothing: Taqtaloq was not at the feast. Having taken my place at the fireside, I could not leave. I forced myself to sit through the long ritual.

The chief was the first to dip his hand into the pot. I at first looked away, then forced myself to look back as he slowly chewed. At most feasts, the guest of honour is given the first piece of meat, while the chief waits for everyone else to be served. But here, where there are taboos to be faced, our chief eats first.

Charles watched his motions very closely. Then a sigh went up among the crowd as he, too, reached his hand into the pot, coming away with a good-sized piece of meat. Keeping his eyes on the chief, he chewed slowly, not swallowing quickly as some warriors do. Our chief's eyes signalled his approval.

One by one, each of the warriors bent forward to accept his piece of meat from the chief's hand. Each one had a small birch-bark container of oil at his side, into which he dipped the meat before putting it into his mouth.

It was with relief that the men moved on to join the women in their meal of the oysters and mussels. Our women had pre-pared a particularly tasty sauce, to entice the men's appetites. They would need their strength for the days ahead.

The pipes were lit only after the last bite was eaten. Charles and the chief shared the pipe, then passed it to the war chief. After it had made the circle of warriors, the chief rose to his feet.

He did not mention the name of the animal that had given its life for the warriors. For we did not want to know. But he praised its courage. "It is not our custom to spill the lifeblood of our dogs. But sometimes, one will offer it up as a gift, so that our warriors may live and not die."

Then reaching behind him, he grasped the bowl a warrior held ready. One by one, the warriors reached into the bowl, smearing the dog's diluted blood on their face and body. Then quietly, each slipped away to his own wikuom, for one last night among his loved ones. I myself spent a bitter night at my own, cold fireside, thinking of the one warrior who had not called upon the courage of the dog. There was fear in my heart as I asked myself why.

k

*t*he chief himself escorted me to the beach the next day and handed me over to Pierrot, who had volunteered to come on this mission. I guessed Taqtaloq was below, helping to store the sup-plies. I was unwilling to seek him out until we were safely out of the harbour. As my husband, he could still choose to order me ashore, in spite of the chief's wishes. I sought out my old hiding place behind the ship's rail.

As we cleared the harbour, the warriors began drifting onto the open deck. With no need to keep their presence a secret, the drumming began early. From now until the battle began some days hence, there would be no pause in the rhythms. As one man tired, another would take his place.

But where was Taqtaloq? Leaving my hiding place and sidling up to one of the warriors, I posed the question. He shook his head, and nudged the man at his side. Another shake of the head. And so it went down the line. No one had seen him since the day before.

He was not on the ship.

I felt the sickness rise in my throat: he was not on the ship. And I myself was being borne every moment farther away from him, in the company of Charles Daniel. Desperately, I ran to the rail, gauging the distance to shore. If I could not make it, I would die in the attempt. My husband would perhaps know I had been trying to reach him. I was swinging my foot over the rail when I was stopped by a single shouted word: "Taqtaloq!"

The crowd left the drummers and rushed to the rail. Following the pointed fingers I saw, in the distance, a figure running along the crest of the hills, leaping and sliding, then regaining his footing only to leap again over another mighty chasm, heedless of his safety.

At the top of the escarpment he paused, body tensed to spring. As the water foamed over the rocks below, his body arched in a long, long fall.

"He is gone," cried a warrior, "pulled to the bottom by Netaoansom, son of the ocean foam."

I felt my spirit began to slip away.

"He's clear," said another voice, in French. "Drop anchor. And launch the boat. He'll need all his strength just to fight that undertow. He'll never make it this far."

I could not wait while the sailors dallied with chains and pulleys. Once again, I slung my leg over the rail, determined to reach my husband and hold his head above the waves until help arrived. I fought the hands that clasped me around the waist.

"No, Mouse. If he panics, he'll pull you under, never knowing it's you. My men will reach him in time."

Charles held on and would not let go. Wrapped in his arms, I watched as my husband fought the undertow. My eyes, fixed on the black head, were blurred with tears. With no way to free my arms, I shook my head to clear the drops away.

A cheer went up from the deck as Taqtaloq cleared the undertow and began to swim toward the ship. My eye measured the gap between him and the longboat, watching as it grew steadily smaller. Twice he went under, and twice he emerged. I saw the men in the boat cross themselves each time his head dropped under the waves.

"Go in, go in," I hissed, as if those in the boat could hear me, willing them to dive in after my husband.

As if hearing my words, Pierrot suddenly stood up in the small boat and tore off his shirt. Clad only in breeches, and with a rope looped around his chest, he dove in and swam toward Taqtaloq. I watched as my husband leaned into Pierrot's arms. Then slowly, Pierrot moved toward the boat, where many hands reached down to grasp Taqtaloq and haul him over the side. In another moment, Pierrot too was in the boat and the oarsmen were pulling for the ship.

"Let me go, let me go!"

The arms that were holding me fell away.

"Haul it up," said Charles, moving once more toward his place on the bridge.

As the pulleys creaked, I leaned over the rail and gazed at my husband as he lay in the boat, eyes closed, chest heaving. The men gently handed him over the side and laid him upon the deck. I stood uncertainly, hands thrown out at my side, waiting for him to rouse. When he did, his eyes passed over me, then beyond, to range over the crowd. He would not even look at me. I turned, looking for a hole to hide in.

"Marie-Ange!"

He was calling. Turning, I saw him struggling to stand and ran to help. As I dropped to my heels beside him, he reached up and grabbed two fistfuls of hair. "You've cut it. And what have you done to your face? I did not know you."

Leaning his forehead against mine, he whispered. "I'm sorry. I know now that it is I, and not Keptin Daniel, who holds your heart in my hands."

My legs weakened and I fell forward into his arms. His chest was cold, but his grip was firm and solid.

"How did you know?" I asked.

"The Lord told me."

His thumbs gently stroked my eyes, wiping the tears away. "And so I went to seek you out. But they told me you were not to be found."

His forehead touched mine. "I knew I could not leave, could not face death, without seeing you again. By the time I learned you were aboard, the ship had already sailed. And so I ran, one eye ever upon it as it rode on my right shoulder, desperate to think it might turn out to sea at any moment."

As we lay in each others' arms, the drumming rose to a roar, as warriors rejoined the circle and raised their voices in jubilation. Death had been beaten back. For now.

*a*gainst the background of the drums, we huddled together: Charles and the war chief, Taqtaloq and I. In the crowded ship, there had been neither time nor space for Taqtaloq and me to talk of the feelings that had arisen between us. But I could see that Taqtaloq had somehow made his peace with them. There was no rancour in his face as he sat listening to Charles. I could not say the same for myself. The giant was slain, I knew. No longer did he live in my heart; no more did I watch the world through his eyes. And yet I could not look upon Charles without resentment.

I forced myself to concentrate on his words, translating them as best I could. It was a simple plan: a French ship, with French cannon and French muskets, against a village armed with bows. This time, there would be no sparing of enemy blood. It was blood we sought.

Charles showed none of the gaiety he had displayed when we had attacked Lord Stewart's fort. Had he foreseen then it would come to this: a debt owed and claimed? I thought not. Charles did not weigh the costs as Antoine did. A man of action, he fearlessly and without forethought stepped across any line drawn in the sand.

Lines drawn in the sand. Before me rose a vision of Pierrot on the beach, sketching his circles, erasing one, drawing another. Lines endlessly drawn and redrawn.

Understanding came in a flood: endless circles, endless wars. Suddenly I was on my feet, the three staring at me.

"Taqtaloq, I must speak with you."

He was surprised, but stood and came with me.

"This new war, Taqtaloq: it will change the world."

His face was patient but determined as he sought to reassure me. "This is not a new war, Marie-Ange. It is an old, old war, the same war our fathers waged, against the same enemy. Our ancestors would be dishonoured to see us relinquish the fight."

His voice dropped to a whisper, "Our dead would be dishonoured."

I knew of whom he spoke. The shrill-voiced woman was losing her power to control him from the grave. But beyond her stood the small, powerful phantom of a child.

"Taqtaloq, the blow that our enemies struck last winter was the last in a time that is past. This ship, even now, is carrying us into a new time, for which new weapons have been forged."

I laid a hand on the musket at his thigh. "Let us resist it, this future we now sail toward."

He stood there, struggling with the voices that urged him onward. Then, to my joy, he stepped back from the line.

$$\text{\textit{k}}$$

Nose to nose we stood, as Taqtaloq and the war chief watched from the sidelines. Charles was not a man to be easily turned away from his chosen course. His words hammered against the wall of drums.

"We cannot turn back now. For one day they will reappear on your horizon, to finish what was begun in the winter."

"But they will come alone," I insisted.

I paused, struggling to build the words into the construction given to me by Antoine, to use at such times: "Whereas ... whereas if we sail on, they will be defeated. And when they raise their heads again, as they surely will, it will be to seek allies.

I looked squarely at Charles.

And who?" I asked, "Who will they bring with them when they come again?

Neither of us had forgotten the evenings with Lord Stewart, when the two had argued over who was more fit to rule our land.

"It is so like the English," Charles had said, "to believe that all must be resolved at the point of a sword."

Watching Charles, I caught a brief flicker of doubt. While he might welcome a war with the English, he could not promise that he would always be there to support us with his strength. Almost, he wavered.

But Charles was not the man Taqtaloq was. Even as I watched, he succumbed to his own desires. So close to victory, the taste of it in his mouth, he could not relinquish the fight.

"No Mouse, we will go forward. I cannot do otherwise: your chief himself has charged me with this task."

"Our chief's authority rests in the will of the people." I flung a hand out towards the warriors. "We can persuade them against this course." It would not be easy: already the drumming had called forth the spirit of war. But it could be attempted, had Charles the will to do it. I longed for our chief, with his understanding of the subtleties of power. But he had chosen to remain behind, with his people.

"No Mouse, really, I think not."

Charles tried to console me. "It will be a sudden blow, one from which the enemy will not recover. No more will you struggle with this foe. It will be the end."

I knew it would be – not the end – but the beginning.

꙰

Swiftly, the ship carried us into a future we did not want, my husband and I.

The ship pulsated with the music of the drums. The warriors were swept away by its power: covered in dog's blood, they no longer looked human. Charles himself had returned to the bridge.

Taqtaloq and I drew away from the deck, where the beat of the drums trapped thought. The music was welcome to a warrior facing death and the disturbing task of killing. Even for us, the temptation to be swept away was strong, to find a hidden corner of the ship, taste each other's breath, rediscover hidden crevices, then join the battle, giving ourselves over to revenge and the sweet taste of blood. And to die, leaving others to face the future.

Only the thought of those back in Cibou shook us out of our stupor. For their sake, we gathered together the remnants of thought.

"What happens now?"

"I do not know."

So we sat and waited, as the ship carried us ever closer.

We sailed in early on a morning so clear we could see the enemy's smoke spiralling in the distance and smell their cooking fires. Just beyond sight of the enemy, we dropped anchor.

A shout came from the lookout high above our heads. Grabbing his looking glass, Charles began to scale the mast for a better look. His oath rode to us on the crystal air. "She's English," he yelled down to the mate, "a ship of the line. And there's a French ship riding beside her. Prepare the longboat."

The future Taqtaloq and I had hoped to prevent had arrived. Even as we sat considering our choices the day before, vast forces had already been lining up against us.

Charles slipped down the rigging. "Mouse!"

Taqtaloq and I ran to join him.

"Come with me, both of you. Ask the war chief to join us."

Charles sat in the prow of the longboat, his red cape replaced by a dark cloak borrowed from an officer. We three piled in between the sailors.

Charles was tense as we rowed to shore. Leaving the boat in the cove, hidden among the trees, we scrambled up the hill, into the woods, for a better view of the enemy village.

I didn't need the glass to see what was happening. A figure, hands bound and clad in a black robe, was being pushed up the beach.

Antoine.

"The English will string him up from the mast," Charles had once said. There, at his side, I began to shake. I looked at Taqtaloq, who was standing beside me, lips white. Our eyes caught and held.

"An English ship bound for Port Royal, no doubt, then south to the Indies," said Charles. "They must have seized Francourt's ship as soon as he left Cibou. With it, they can make a tidy profit in sugar. Quite a coup for them, especially in light of the trick I played on them last year. My brother would be a grand prize to hand to the English king." The words were light, but the tone carried a deadly intention. He began to slide down the hill, toward the waiting boat.

"Will we attack?" asked Taqtaloq.

Charles shook his head, "This vessel is no match for an English ship of the line. I must think."

We had come to this game holding all the sticks. But with another shake of the waltes bowl, the dice had turned against us. We had lost all advantage save one: the enemy did not know we were here. Charles seized upon that single, remaining stick.

All afternoon, he kept a close eye on the wind, worriedly watching the sails billowing above our heads. Finally satisfied, he called for volunteers. The task? The mining of the French ship: in his zeal to save his brother, Charles was prepared to sacrifice Francourt's vessel.

Taqtaloq was the first to volunteer. French sailors with a knowledge of gunpowder were also selected.

As we waited for night to fall, the volunteers smeared themselves with tar, to protect them from the cold water and ensure they would not be seen. Sitting beside Taqtaloq on the deck, I dipped my fingers in the warm liquid and ran them over his chest, his arms, his thighs. Grabbing my wrist, he pulled me close, seeking my lips. And there, hidden against the rail, surrounded by a ship full of men, we came together. We were still gasping when the shout came. One final, hard kiss, and he was gone to join the others in the longboat.

I jumped at the sound of Charles's voice.

"Come to the bridge Mouse."

Looking down at my clothing, I saw with dismay that I was covered in tar. I swiped at it with the end of my robe, but it could not be removed. Hoping it could not be seen in the falling darkness, I made my way to the bridge.

Charles eyes swept over me, dwelling briefly on the tar. I looked around in confusion. Why was I there? Clearly, there was no need for me to translate: Charles was alone. As I stood there, gripping my arms in the cold, he seized a blanket and tossed it to me. He then turned to gaze out at the sea, where the boat carrying Taqtaloq and his crew had slipped into thick darkness. Other boats, heavily loaded with warriors and sailors, were dispatched to the small, hidden cove that overlooked the village.

There, on the bridge, I went over every detail of the plot in my mind. It was like all Charles's schemes: bold. Taqtaloq and his companions would steal up to the abandoned French ship, and mine it with explosives. Once the anchor cable was cut, the tide would carry it fatally close to the English vessel.

I strained my eyes against the darkness. Not a flicker of light betrayed the large force hidden in the cove where the war chief and his men waited to launch themselves onto the sleeping village.

Charles himself remained on board with his crew: if the plan went awry, a sea battle was still possible. In the meantime we sat, a dark spectre upon the water.

Standing beside the silent Charles on the bridge, I was growing uneasy. But as I turned to go, he seized my arm.

Susan Young de Biagi

"No, Mouse. It is possible we may not survive this night. And there is something you must know...."

My mind fled back to the months I had spent with him, when night after night I had longed for some revelation. But it was too late now. I began to back away.

Charles lunged at me. In the next moment, I knew why he had moved so quickly: my feet were hanging in air, his arms all that had kept me from falling over the stairway to the bridge. I could not see his face, but I knew from the flash of his teeth that he was amused.

"It is no use, Mouse, falling over yourself to get away from me. The words must be said, whether you wish to hear them or no."

And then, lower and closer still, "Why do you think I came back?"

Some words Antoine had once said to me rose unbidden to my mind: "When there's no escape, pray for a miracle."

"Save me," I mouthed silently into the darkness. And in that moment, the sky was lit by a brilliant flash. My teeth rattled from the roar that followed.

Charles was gone, racing to join the lookout on the mast. I remained alone, peering into the darkness and trying to guess what was happening. A second roar jolted across the waves.

They had done it, Taqtaloq and his companions: Francourt's ship had found its target. And now he was somewhere out there, perhaps wounded, perhaps fighting for his life. Sounds came to us across the water, the sound our warriors make to terrify the enemy.

We on the ship could only wait and hope. Not knowing the waters, unable to sound their depth, Charles could not advance until Niskam showed the way.

Anxious to avoid a second encounter with Charles, I stole down the ladder to the deck below. All around me, men lay wrapped in blankets, their heads pillowed on the hard deck

– alert but motionless. Pierrot's head bobbed up from his tightly wound bed roll.

"Come wait with me, Mouse. The hours will pass more quickly if there are two of us."

I caught Pierrot's smile as I dropped down, cross-legged, beside him. I had once asked him why he always seemed so amused by our way of sitting.

"Our women never cross their legs – at least, I don't think they do," he had replied. "It's hard to tell just what's going on under those skirts."

I needed a story to quell the terror rising in my throat. "Tell me about your women, Pierrot."

In the old days, French women were a favourite topic of discussion in the women's wikuom. "They can't satisfy their men," Mimikej had maintained stoutly. "Otherwise, why would so many come here and seek us out? How many have I had to slap away? I don't believe it's the fish they come for."

Now here was Pierrot, who loved women and was more than willing to enlighten me. "What is it you want to know?"

Anything to keep my mind off the battle outside: "Their hair. What does it look like? Do they braid it, as we do?"

"The young ones do, so the men can get a good look at what they're buying. But the married ones keep every strand tucked up in a kerchief. They're mighty particular about that kerchief. My mother keeps a fresh supply of them ironed and starched."

"What colour is her hair, your mother's?"

"Black, like yours. When she let it down, it fell to her thighs. My father used to love to sit by the fire and watch her brush it. But I haven't seen it for years now, not since I became a man."

Pierrot looked startled, as if a new idea had just come to him. "Damn me, it may be white, though I can't say for sure. I once caught her brushing her brows with a sooty stick from the fire."

Susan Young de Biagi

"It may be white," he repeated softly to himself.

"The beauty of women," Pierrot continued. "Whole fleets have been sacrificed to it: lost in the quest of whalebone for their stays."

"Their what?"

"Their stays ... corsets."

Pierrot sat up and squeezed his hands around his ribs. "They wear a garment stiffened with whalebones, to keep their breasts from ... excuse me Mouse ... to stiffen their upper bodies."

He rushed to cover the slip with a flow of words. "The nobility are almost completely encased in whalebone, great cages of it to hang their skirts upon. How many men have died in search of it? Ah, but that is the duty of man: to go willingly to his death for the sake of a woman's smile. I've heard how your traders will travel great distances in search of the tiny beads your women are so fond of."

I tried to imagine the odd garments: bone cages, carried upon the body. Yet the women seemed to accept, even demand, such restrictive attire. It must be a strange place, France. But though I tried to fix my mind on it, nothing could shut out the thought of my husband somewhere out there on the dark water.

*

*A*s we rounded the cove in the first light of dawn, the scene that met our eyes was one of smoking devastation. The two ships, mere skeletons now, lay smouldering in the harbour, a nest of burnt spires and seared canvas. The wikuoms lining the water's edge had been suddenly and brutally denuded: bare poles with a pool of shredded skins at their base. On the beach, people were milling aimlessly, the sound of their cries floating to us over the waves.

Charles was on the bridge, looking through his eyeglass. I raced up the stairs toward him.

"Your warriors tasted victory this night, Mouse. Look, there is your war chief on the beach with Francourt."

Seizing the glass, I glanced at the two men, then quickly scanned the beach, where warriors were guarding small groups of prisoners. Others were carrying the dead down to the shore, laying them out in rows. I quickly handed the glass back to Charles, and forced myself to ask the question.

"Taqtaloq?"

"I have not seen him." Seeing my face, he quickly added, "That does not mean he is not busy elsewhere."

"And Antoine?"

His face grew even more sombre. "Not yet."

There we stood, linked by our fear and our hope, separated by so much else.

"Prepare the longboats."

While the men on the deck below hurried to obey, Charles grabbed my elbow and steered me down the ladder.

As we neared the shore, the longboat nudged its way through charred bodies, floating gently with the tide. I forced myself to look at the gruesome sight bobbing in the water: white skin, tatters of strange uniforms. Not Taqtaloq. Charles jumped onto the sand, then turned to me, extending an arm.

"Stay at my side. It may be dangerous on the beach."

There was no danger now: Charles did not want me to stumble upon Taqtaloq by myself.

His grip firm on my elbow, Charles tried to skirt the line of dead, but I resisted.

"If he lies there, I must know."

Together, we advanced along the long, grim line. We reached the enemy dead first. Most were enemy warriors, bearing the same greased knots upon their heads that had so amused young

Jijiwikate'j in the hours before his death. Here and there among them lay an Englishman. Even his apprehension over Antoine's fate could not crowd out the triumph on Charles's face. Every dead enemy meant one less Englishman to fight for control of this land.

A small space, a body's breadth, marked the end of the enemy dead and the beginning of our own. This second line was much shorter than the first, yet the walk seemed endless. Passing the bodies of men I had known since childhood, I felt only relief at the sight of them: not Taqtaloq, not Taqtaloq.

We had reached the end of the line. Before me there was only sand, stretching cleanly toward the horizon. Falling onto my knees, I let my full store of terror pour out onto the fine golden mantle. I retched and retched again.

As I wiped my mouth and struggled to stand, I saw that a young warrior posted beside Charles had seized his chance to speak.

"The prisoners are being held in the village. Great Heart is there."

Charles turned to me, puzzled. "Of whom does he speak Mouse?"

I shrugged, too concerned for my husband to listen to the wild chatter of a young man in his first battle. They had obviously taken an important prisoner and were eager to show him off.

Ahead lay a small cluster of our warriors. Charles wedged himself between them and stepped into the circle. Over his shoulder, I looked down at the unconscious face of Antoine. And there, cradling his friend in his arms, was Taqtaloq. For the second time that morning, I sank to my knees.

The circle, which had opened briefly to let Charles in, closed around him. Without the strength even to crawl, I lay there, weakly pushing at the wall of legs that separated me from my husband.

A hand on the back of my robe lifted me to my feet. Charles. In a moment, he had dumped me beside Taqtaloq, who reached up a tender hand to my face. I was the only one to see the tears as he gestured toward Antoine.

A vision rose up before me: two men, on the edge of a dark, snowy forest. One resolutely guarding his dead, the other holding out a gourd of soup. Their friendship had been born on a field of death. Would it end, here, on another? Determined that it should not be so, I slipped down beside Antoine and pressed my lips to his ear.

His soul, I knew, wandered far from us. In my spirit, I saw him in a wide meadow of spreading nut trees, the ground below blanketed with their windfall. And in the distance, Antoine drifting among them, stopping from time to time to examine one of the nuts, turning it over and over in his hands. Each one was lovingly dropped into the small brown bag at his waist and then – when that was filled – his pockets. Intent on his search, he did not hear my approach.

"Antoine!"

In spirit, I found myself standing before him, across the meadow, palms held upward in appeal. My voice had reached him, I knew. But like a small boy who refused to be called home, he kept his head down, intent on his task.

"Antoine!"

Reluctantly, he raised his head. I saw the longing, the appeal in his eyes, but I would not, could not, relent. I held out my hand, insisting. With one last, yearning glance at the field, he grasped my fingers.

"He's awake!" The crowd pressed in for an even closer look.

Antoine's blue eyes were clouded, confused. Ranging in frustration over the dark eyes above him, they finally lit on mine, seeking and holding my gaze.

"Maman?"

"No, Antoine. It is I, Marie-Ange. You have been hurt."

He nodded, then lifted his eyes to Taqtaloq.

"Timothé." A whisper.

Taqtaloq forced the words out through tight lips, painfully, his voice harsh. "You had left us, Kitpu, circling far above our heads. I am glad you have come back."

Antoine nodded again, then winced.

"Don't move Antoine. I will call the surgeon."

The words surprised me: I had forgotten Charles was there. Somehow, he had remained outside the circle of Antoine, Taqtaloq and I. Seeking relief – as always – in action, he turned and was gone.

*

*A*ntoine and I spent that day together, he on his boughs, I at his side as he wandered in and out of fever. Everyone else was busy burying the dead and transferring the prisoners to the ship.

Throughout the day, we received puzzling messages. "Great Heart asks that you drink this," said a young warrior, appearing with a gourd of steaming herbs for Antoine. "Great Heart sends word that he will be at your side before Niskam completes his journey."

I was not flattered by the constant interruptions. They had obviously taken an important prisoner, a shaman perhaps. Still, I was beginning to be annoyed at the ease with which this one was ordering our warriors about. At the third such visit, I lost my temper.

"Tell Great Heart that you have more important things to do than to act as his messenger. He is disturbing Father Antoine's sleep."

"I cannot deliver such a message," he stammered.

"Why not? Are you afraid he'll turn you into a toad? If his powers were that great, the battle would have ended much differently."

Not long after, I looked up again to see Taqtaloq himself at my side, a quizzical look on his face.

"Are you angry with me, my love?"

"I? ...Never!"

"Then what is all this talk about toads?"

And then I knew. "Great Heart" was no enemy shaman, but Taqtaloq himself. It sometimes happens that after a battle, warriors will bestow a title on one of their number, to honour an act of great bravery. Some warriors will risk their lives to rid themselves of a childish name bestowed by a doting mother.

I knew Taqtaloq had done nothing so foolish. So something had happened during the battle, something momentous. Whatever it was, Taqtaloq would not be the one to tell me. Among our people, modesty is valued as much as bravery. When once again we gathered round the fire and for many nights afterward – perhaps even after Taqtaloq and I had passed from the Land of the Living – the story would be told of how Taqtaloq came to be known as Great Heart.

As he squatted beside me, stroking my hair, I grabbed his palm and leaned my cheek into it. I remembered the words of old Ku'ku'kwes: "We are watching the men of your generation," she had told him. There arose within me the old feelings of unworthiness to stand at his side. But the love in his eyes banished them.

He was tired, I could see. Moving quickly, I made up a bed for him beside Antoine, then settled myself for a night of guarding the sleep of the two men I loved most: one my husband, the other my friend.

"*i* have failed in my duty."

My heart fell at the sound of Antoine's voice. He had slept badly during the night, and I had hoped the dawn would bring a deeper, more refreshing sleep. But he was wide awake.

I whispered to Taqtaloq to attend to his friend's needs: Antoine would never permit me to help him empty his water. So as Taqtaloq searched for an appropriate vessel, I set off for the beach to gather shellfish for soup. We were just beginning to sip the hot liquid when Antoine spoke again.

"I have failed in my duty toward you, leaving you without protection. But as with Jonah, the Lord stopped my ship and sent me back to you, for you are precious to Him."

As he spoke, he stretched out his hand toward the bag that one of the warriors had rescued when Antoine had fallen. Taqtaloq quickly reached over to hand it to him.

"I am hoping, my friends, you will share a meal with me."

Taqtaloq and I looked at each other over half-eaten bowls of soup. Was he raving?

I had always loved watching Antoine's hands, so frail and white that the light seemed to pass through them. As I watched, these hands busied themselves among the small implements he kept in his bag. As he pulled out the white cloth with the flowers dancing on it, I sat suddenly upright. The time had come to eat with his god. Placing my soup bowl carefully on the ground, I waited, hands folded. Not knowing what lay ahead, Taqtaloq kept on eating, his eyes merely curious.

Antoine pulled out a piece of bread, of the kind the fishermen carried in their pockets. Our people refused to eat this stuff: impossible to crack with the teeth yet not impervious to worms. Did Antoine mean to serve it to his god?

A bottle of wine followed. Carefully pouring some into a small metal cup, Antoine dropped the bread into it. Then exhausted, he lay back upon his boughs, waiting for the bread to soften. Taqtaloq and I stared at the horrid mixture.

Rousing himself, Antoine began to speak in a language I did not understand. I knew who he was calling, and waited to see what form He would assume. The day was bright, yet I was afraid.

By now, the bread had separated into small floating chunks. Antoine reached in and fished one out, offering it to me.

"This is the Lord's body."

It suddenly became clear. We were not expected to eat with Antoine's god, but to feed upon him. I drew back.

Antoine took no notice. Eyes closed, swaying, he held out the cup.

"And this is his blood."

We, the people of Cibou, know that the life is in the blood. To the south, there are some who will eat the heart of an honoured enemy, devouring it even as it beats, in an attempt to acquire something of its character. But our people had never done such a thing.

I knew what Antoine was asking of me. I knew, too, that Taqtaloq's eyes were upon me, waiting to follow my lead. I opened my lips.

The bread was still hard. Crunching it between my teeth, as if crunching on bones, I reflected on Antoine's words to Muine'j. "It is over his broken body that they escape to freedom."

Chewing the bread to powder, I remembered the moment when I turned to Charles in the surf, and all that followed from it. Undressing with my back to my mother, both of us hiding our shame. The sacrifice of Bright Eyes. My mother's banishment. The crime was mine and so was the punishment. I deserved to drink death to its dregs; I drank instead the blood of life. Tilting the cup to my lips, I let the gift trickle down my throat. Then wiping my mouth with my hand, I passed the cup to my husband.

Antoine lay back, exhausted. Taking my hand, Taqtaloq drew me a little way off, gathering me close and pressing his forehead against mine.

"I will return when the sun is high, to take you to the ship. You will be safe until then: a guard has been posted." Yet even as he spoke, Taqtaloq looped his knife onto my belt.

I did not envy him his duty. While Charles and Francourt dealt with the few English prisoners who remained alive, it was Taqlatoq's job to organize the villagers. Already, women were keening for lost husbands and children. Bewildered toddlers, angry adolescents – all were being herded into the hold of Charles's ship.

They would not remain long among us. Among our people it is said, "One cannot keep a snake without being bitten." Most of the prisoners would be sold, dispersed in safe groups of two or three, to villages all along the coast. Some, with ropes bound around their wrists and neck, would make the long trek through the forest, to the land of the broken speakers. A few would be traded to the fishermen. Only the very youngest, healthiest children would remain in our village, to grow up among us.

I was packing up my cups and blankets when Charles stepped out of the forest. Glancing at Antoine, I saw he was asleep and turned to warn Charles not to wake him. But Charles was not looking at his brother.

I knew then that he had waited until Taqtaloq was gone and Antoine asleep before seeking me out. My first thought was to flee, but Charles caught me by the arm.

"You knew I would come for you, Mouse."

"My name is Marie-Ange."

"Antoine's invention! He took you – my child of the forest, my teller of tales – and tried to turn you into … what? A wife!"

The voice became cajoling.

"I meant to marry. I returned to France a hero, wooed by women of rank. But beneath the elaborate costumes, there was only ... emptiness: no smooth-skinned maiden, no hair to trap me in its net, no voice to woo me to sleep with tales of giants rising from a blanket of snow."

The hands that held mine were trembling. This was not the Charles I knew. In his eyes, I saw some of the madness that comes fleetingly to men. I glanced at Antoine, who slept on.

"Come with me, Mouse, into the forest. We were meant to be one. Later, after I return your people to their village, you and I will slip away."

To where, I wondered? To France, where the flowers of Cibou fade before the summer's end? Or the vast ocean, eternally chasing Niskam's shadow?

Charles pressed a hand against my lower back. The sensations came separately: the familiar grasp drawing me close; Taqtaloq's knife at my belt. And then there was nothing but air. Looking up, I saw Antoine standing beside me, breathing heavily.

"Run Marie-Ange, to the ship. Join Taqtaloq."

I ran, but not to the ship. Instead, I circled back through the trees, until I looked upon the brothers once more. Their senses dulled to the life of the forest, they would not suspect my presence.

Antoine was seated on a log, Charles pacing before him.

"By what right? By what right did you take her? She was mine!"

"She was never yours. She belongs to the Lord."

"Then upon my word, Antoine, yours is a greedy God. And you will win this whole continent for him, soul by soul. I once swore to help you. But why, brother, did you have to begin with her? Is there nothing I can keep for myself? Must He have it all?"

There was more at stake, I knew, than a little mouse.

Charles continued to pace back and forth before the shaken Antoine.

"Do you remember, brother, the days when we'd steal away from our tutors and escape to the fair ... when on a dare, we'd twitch the skirts of a pretty peasant? But something happened to you Antoine. 'Come!' I'd say, but more and more, you'd turn back to your books – to Him. And not even the promise of a pretty ankle could lure you away."

"And then one day, they came for you. And I was left alone to carry the burden of our father's ambition. Picture it, he and I alone on that crumbling estate – until the time came for me to leave for the sea. I did not see you again until the day I was assigned to accompany you to this land."

Charles's eyes grew bright with the memory.

"What a pair we made! I sailing for glory, you for souls. I thought this voyage would unite us once more. But once again, you drew away. Now I wonder if even America is big enough for the two of us."

Confusion showed clearly in Antoine's face. "You were not so angry, Charles, when you left in Wikewiku's. What has happened to you since then?"

His brother threw up a hand. "You see! You can barely complete a phrase without using one of their words. What in the name of all that's holy does Wikewiku's mean?"

"Animal fattening moon ... October," said Antoine, barely above a whisper.

"You will never return to France, will you Antoine?"

I saw the terrible pity in Antoine's face as he looked up at his brother, and slowly shook his head.

Charles turned away, shaking. When he finally turned back to Antoine, he stood rigidly, fists clenched at his sides.

"Listen well, brother: the day will come when your God will demand even your life. For He takes all, and gives nothing back."

Charles stalked off. I ran to Antoine, catching him before he fell. "I did not know," he gasped between sobs. "I did not know."

*C*harles spent the voyage in his cabin, leaving Francourt to captain the ship. With prisoners to guard, Taqtaloq spent most of his time in the hold. Antoine and I were squeezed into a corner of the deck. With so many prisoners below, and the crew of two ships – Charles's and Francourt's – above there was barely room for Antoine's pallet.

I could not care for him as I wished, for even the smallest movement brought me waves of dizziness. I spent my days staring at the horizon, a fishermen's trick designed to keep the illness at bay. It did not work. At least once a day, I found myself with my head over the side.

The return voyage proceeded at a much slower pace. All along the coast, in villages inhabited by our people, we stopped to barter for the contents of our hold.

On the first such day, I dragged myself to Antoine's pallet and together we watched the activity on the beach. The war chief had decided to offer five captives to this village: a boy approaching manhood, two women, and two little boys who looked to be between six and eight summers.

"To think that I should find myself on a slave ship."

I turned – surprised – at Antoine's words.

"What do you mean?"

"This buying and selling of people: it is distressing to think of my brother's ship being used for such a purpose."

"But what would you have us do? Left behind, these survivors would quickly seek allies among their own people, then descend upon us once more. Nor can we take so many prisoners to our village, for they would surely overcome us, kill us even as we slept. Our only other choice is to kill them. Surely you would not have us be so cruel?"

Antoine gazed at the youngest child standing taut before his new masters, struggling to keep his dignity.

"Perhaps you are right. At least now they have their mothers."

I hated to disappoint him further. But it had always been my duty to help him understand our ways.

"Those women are not their mothers. Their own mothers would never let them forget how they came to be among us. They would stoke the desire for revenge, igniting a flame that could never be put out. It is better these children be given to new families, first as servants then as sons, if they prove to be adaptable and quick to learn."

"And if not?"

I gestured to the boy on the verge of manhood. "It sometimes happens that they cannot adapt themselves to this new life. They will work, yes, but reject all offers to join in the life of the village. And then one day, when it comes time to take a wife, they will discover that no maiden can attach herself to a man without a family."

"And then?"

"Most of them will leave, stealing some supplies and setting out in the night. At such times, we will make sure there is food scattered about, to help them on their way. It is a long journey through dangerous territory, but the desire for a wife is strong. Perhaps some of them make it."

Antoine closed his eyes, and was silent for so long that I thought him asleep. When he opened them again, the sadness had grown deeper. How could I make him understand?

"Our people are not cruel, Antoine. You will see that our way is best."

He did not agree with me, but could offer no better way.

*A*nd still Charles did not appear. As the number of captives dwindled, Taqtaloq was able to spend more time with me, even sleeping at my side. On the first morning, I was able to slip away and void the contents of my stomach before he awoke. But on the second day, I felt him holding my hair as I leaned over the side.

"I cannot understand it," I said, wiping my mouth on a scrap of cloth I had tucked in my robe. "I am never sick on the ocean."

"It is not ocean sickness." I could hear the amusement in his voice.

My anger rose to see him, so strong and hardy, laughing at me. I felt a slight tug on my braid.

"I remember how it was with Mimikej. I hope you will not be as bad tempered."

My anger fled, to be replaced by confusion. With my own hand, I had lifted the cup that would keep me from bearing. How then did this child survive? Bright Eyes could tell me, but Bright Eyes was dead.

Taqtaloq's child. From that first moment, that's how I thought of it: not as the child of Mouse, the outcast, of the animal blood. But Taqtaloq's child, a small seed of the chiefly line, bearing within it all the strength and wisdom of its father. I swore that this child would not end on a heap of bodies in the snow. And that he who had guarded the lifeless remains of his wife and son would now know the joy of holding his child in his arms. I was determined that it be so. With that determination came a surge of power such as I had never known.

Taqtaloq stood.

"Let us go and tell him."

For one, appalling moment, I thought he was speaking of Charles.

"Tell who?"

"Kitpu, of course."

And so hand in hand, we went to seek out Antoine. As usual, at this time of the morning, he was reading from his book, but he put it down as we approached.

Taqtaloq dropped, legs crossed, to the deck beside his friend, his smile as wide as I had ever seen it.

Antoine raised an amused eyebrow. "It is early, Timothé, for such a dazzling display of teeth. You will blind me."

"We have come to tell you our news. Marie-Ange carries our child."

In that moment, there passed from Antoine to me a series of messages, as clear as if he had spoken them.

"You see, it happened just as I said it would," his eyes smiled.

And then, "What will this do to Charles?"

I could not share Antoine's concern. Instead, I felt a strange sense of triumph. Charles had never accepted my marriage. Here now was proof of it.

That night, I thought of the small one inside me. How hardy, how strong must it be, to have carved out a place for itself in my unwelcoming womb. I thought too, how it restored to me my place in the line of generations, the place sacrificed when I took the cup from Bright Eyes's hands. All my ancestors' hopes for the future had ended in that moment, in the body of small girl: the last step on a path that led nowhere. With this child, however, I would give them back their hopes. I thought of my mother, now an outlaw, yet her grandchild would belong to a chiefly line. I had won that for her, for all of them. I lay back and slept in peace.

"Marie-Ange!"

I awoke to Taqtaloq's hand gently shaking me.

"The chief of this village has asked us to remain, to sit in council. There are strange rumours, he says, rumours of a great war that even now is advancing toward us. They are seeking our help. But Keptin Daniel has refused to remain here another day. You must go to him, and ask him to not to raise the anchor. Our war chief himself asks it of you."

I had never once said "no" to Taqtaloq. But I did so now.

"Let Antoine go. He can plead our cause better than anyone."

"I cannot ask it of him. He was feverish during the night: three times I arose to quiet him."

I could not refuse. It was, after all, the reason our chief had sent me on this journey.

The sailors were preparing to lift anchor. If the thing were to be done, it would have to be done now. I took a moment only to wash my face before setting off for Charles's cabin.

I seized upon the thought of the child to strengthen me. I would not pass on my fear to Taqtaloq's son. Resolutely, I set my foot on the steps to Charles's cabin.

"Come in."

His appearance startled me. The eyes were red-rimmed, the beard– always so carefully trimmed – ragged and unkempt. The smell in the cabin was sour: he had not eaten, for days perhaps.

"What is it? Come to stomp your little foot on my heart? I dare not believe you have changed your mind. And what, no Antoine? I would not have thought you'd advance so far without your protector."

"I have been sent by our war chief."

"Of course: it comes begging for a favour."

"He asks that you remain a day longer in this village. There are dangers that threaten us all."

"Not me."

Susan Young de Biagi

I forced myself to remain calm. "When have you acted solely for your own good? You have ever been a friend to our people."

"A friend.... That is to be my role now, is it? And I am to play it as it is written, by you, by Antoine. Tell me, Marie-Ange – since that is the name under which you are now masquerading: how has my brother managed to dupe you so completely?"

It was an old ploy, one that Bright Eyes had cautioned me against. "Keep your feet on the path," he had warned me. "Do not jump down every false trail at the whim of your foe."

But Charles Daniel was not my foe, though he was driven to use all the tricks of an enemy.

"You are not a man to act dishonourably." That was not true: he had done so – once, and was doing so now. The words hung in the air.

There is a moment, Bright Eyes had said, in which we can turn from our deeds, or cling to them, and let them pull us down. Such a moment had come to Charles. I watched him struggle with the decision.

"Tell the war chief he has one day. We sail at dawn tomorrow."

Relieved at the path he had chosen, I turned to go.

"You will not have the strength to carry this burden."

I froze. How had he learned of the child?

"It is no burden to me."

"Antoine's words exactly. But you are both wrong. Look at Antoine – they meant to take his life. And they will try again. This faith that Antoine is offering ... it will be a burden to you and your people."

I slumped in relief. He did not know of the child.

Charles rose and fixed red-rimmed eyes on mine.

"Why not remain as you are, Mouse?"

I could have asked the same of him. Why not remain in France, he and his fishermen? And yet they came, driven by a force even they did not understand – the same force that drives us all. Did he expect us to be any less courageous, any less adventurous in the face of it? Or were we mere sand to him, meant only to receive the imprint of his boot?

Charles's eyes bore down upon me.

"I thought, in leaving, I could return you to the life you knew."

He sat on the desk, looking out the porthole.

"It was out there, on the ocean."

I waited.

"It was there – heading back to collect the prize, Lord Stewart's damn violin in my ear – that I realized just what I had sacrificed. The wake behind me was the path back to you; in front, lay only my father and his unending expectations. Do you know, Mouse, how impossible it is to turn a ship around when the gales of October threaten?"

He held up a hand. "I know now it is too late for us. I knew it even before Antoine pulled me away. I knew it in the moment that you tried to jump ship to join...," he paused, swallowing "... your husband. And I knew it when I saw you vomiting over the bodies in the sand. But by then, I had simply come too far. It was too late to turn the ship around."

He straightened, hands hanging at his side.

"Forgive me."

There was no ironic bow, no feathered hat sweeping the ground – just a man standing before me.

"Forgive me."

The knock on the door broke the silence of the moment. Charles did not move, but continued staring at me. The knock came again, this time more insistent, then a voice – Pierrot's.

"Captain Daniel. It's Captain Francourt. He's requesting your presence."

Swearing, Charles wrenched open the door. Pierrot stood with his hand raised, ready to knock a third time. I marked his look of surprise at my presence, then ducked below his arm and headed for the staircase.

*

*t*aqtaloq took advantage of Charles's reprieve by spending long hours with the village Elders, discussing the rumours of a great war. That evening, with Antoine safely asleep, he told me all that had passed.

"The peoples to the south, they of the corn, are gathering in a vast alliance, supported by the English. We must do the same, to repel them should they ever dare to advance upon our lands."

Taqtaloq took my hands in his, looking at them so closely for a moment that I grew uneasy.

"An appeal must be made to all peoples along this coast and beyond – a call so compelling that none can resist."

So it was upon us, this thing we had been dreading, and had hoped to avoid. Taqtaloq raised his head, eyes bearing into mine. "Will you do this for us, Marie-Ange?"

Seeing my confusion, Taqtaloq spoke again.

"The beads ... the call must be written in the beads."

It was then I understood. The call for an alliance would be encoded into the wampum, then sent – threads hanging – from village to village. Each council who agreed to help would weave its own promise into the belt, until the circle of allies was complete.

I could not refuse such a request. Taking me by the arm, Taqtaloq propelled me to the village, where the council was already gathering. There, seated around the chief, were the Elders. One by one, they slowly approached, each dropping a small skin sack into my lap. Carefully, I opened the bags and reached in, letting the beads spill through my fingers: bright gold for corn, red for blood, blue-black for the spreading darkness.

Their business finished, the Elders gave the signal to begin the evening meal. Women who had been waiting on the edge of the circle advanced with steaming gourds. Children crept into the Elders' laps, while their parents filled the spaces behind us. For this moment at least, the children's warm presence kept the darkness at bay.

It was a good meal, the best I had had since leaving Cibou: rich stew, so fat it glistened on our lips; marsh rice; long chews of candied fish. At the meal's end, Taqtaloq happily accepted a twist of southern tobacco, sweeter and more fragrant than our own. As he lay there savouring the smoke, one hand on his lean stomach, I smiled to see him so content.

At the exact moment the crowd could eat no more, one of the Elders rose to his feet. From the excited nudges the crowd gave each other, I could see that he was a favoured storyteller.

"What story will you have tonight? That of Apli'kmuj, the lazy rabbit?" A roar arose from the crowd. It was obviously a favourite.

"Or the tale of Beaver, who tried to drown our people with his great dam. But Kluskap tricked him by cutting out a channel with his paddle, so that the water drains out with each tide."

I myself was eager to hear this tale. In Bright Eyes's version, the channel was carved out during a wild chase, as Beaver fled before Kluskap's wrath.

Bright Eyes. How like him this old man was, teasing the crowd in the very same way. My eyes filled with tears.

Already, people were beginning to sing out their favourites. Small arguments broke out, each side drowning out the other. Laughingly, the old man quieted them with a simple gesture of his hands.

"Or perhaps you would like to hear the story of the black seal, who swam through the night with fire in his mouth? It is a tale I will tell for the first time tonight."

The crowd hushed in anticipation. It is a fine thing to be present when a tale is born, for the first in an infinity of tellings. I settled back in delight as the old man began his narrative.

"Ah, the seal. So sleek and black that he slipped through dark waters unseen, creeping up to the very belly of a whale lolling in sleep on the waves."

"For you see, the whale had taken his brother and he vowed revenge. Hidden in the seal's mouth, gripped tightly between his teeth, was a burning ember. But although the heat seared his tongue, he thought of nothing save the moment when he would climb onto the back of the great beast and cast the ember into its lungs."

At this, the old man threw a handful of something into the fire, making it sparkle and dance as a trick for the children. Parents smiled their indulgence. So it is that our storytellers make it easy for a child to remember the twists and turns of a long story. A puff of smoke, a shower of sparks, serve as reminders that the storyteller has turned a corner in the tale.

The old man waited for the excitement to subside before continuing.

"And so the seal swam toward the whale, lying so quietly in the stream that it seemed nothing could wake him. But high above, He Who Travels by Night was treacherous: jumping out from behind the clouds, he shone his torch suddenly on the waters, so that the seal's fur flashed silver on the waves.

"'Come back,' his fellows whispered. 'You will be discovered'.

"But the seal would not be diverted. Turning to his companions, he bid them a silent goodbye from large eyes and swam slowly onward.

"He was already on the back of the sleeping beast when the whale's mate loomed up beside him. A great rumbling emerged from her belly, then fire shot from her eyes. Wild with rage, heedless even of her beloved, the she-whale rained fire upon the seal as he clung to the neck of her mate. As his companions watched, he rode his steed into the very heart of the flames, a dark silhouette against a wall of red. Climbing along his enemy's back, he cast the ember into the blowhole. A great explosion followed, and he fell in the shower of flames."

The children's eyes darted toward the fire, hoping to see a repeat of the explosion. But the old storyteller was too skilled to give them what they expected. Instead, he dropped his voice to a whisper, so that the crowd had to lean close to catch the words.

"The two whales died in that last, fiery embrace, and in the end, only their ribs were left floating on the waters."

"And the seal, Uncle?" piped up one young voice.

"Ah, the seal. Though his companions searched long and hard for their friend, he could not be found. Their tears traced wet paths on wet faces as they swam slowly home to tell his wife.

"That trickster – He Who Travels by Night – had once more slipped behind the clouds, so that they felt rather than saw their fellows beside them: black bodies in black waters. But reaching the shore, they rejoiced to see that their friend had been with them all along, matching stroke for stroke. He had not raised his voice to tell them, for the ember had seared his tongue. But it was indeed he. And though he will never speak of it himself, tales will be told of him as long as there are fires and storytellers."

In that moment, another voice was heard from the crowd.

"Tell us his name, Uncle. What was the seal's name?"

"His name? Why it is Great Heart."

Great Heart. My head whipped round to Taqtaloq, who was doing his best to shrink a tall body into a small package. No use: the old man looked straight at him, grinning, while many hands

Susan Young de Biagi

reached out to pat his back or stroke his hair, that was indeed as dark and sleek as a seal's.

$$k$$

We sailed on the morrow, and spent many more days in villages along the coast, divesting ourselves of the slaves in our hold. In each place, the Elders added their own promise to the wampum. In villages with no artist of their own, I was there to help weave the promise into the beads.

Antoine spent long days asleep in a sheltered corner of the deck, I at his side. Not once did Charles descend from his place at the helm, although I felt his eyes upon us. Antoine's attention strayed just as frequently to his brother, when he thought the other wasn't looking.

It is one thing to sail toward a battle, riding swiftly upon the open ocean, with an empty hold and minds bent upon a single goal. It is another to creep along the coast, the ship's hold laden with prisoners, persuading wary villages of the need for alliance. The return journey took many weeks, but finally we arrived in our own village, chief and council at the shore to greet us. The war chief and his warriors emerged first, to the delight of the crowd. I remained behind with Antoine, who was carried ashore with the rest of the wounded. The few remaining slaves were brought out last. Only the English prisoners and Charles remained on the ship.

I chose not to stay for the festivities. Antoine was tired and I was anxious to see him settled in the fort. I was stirring a stew for his supper when I looked up to see the chief beside me, happily sniffing the pot. Accepting a bowl, he sat at my side with an air of great content.

"Well, Mouse, I had not guessed you would be so useful when I sent you to reunite with your husband on the ship."

It was not like our chief to be so forgetful. I searched for the words to remind him of my true purpose on the ship, without pointing out his mistake.

"I did my best to fulfill my function as translator."

The chief hooted. "You were not required as translator! Keptin Daniel and the war chief understand each other very well. What a job I had to persuade Keptin Daniel to take you on board, so concerned was he for your safety. But I could see that both you and Taqtaloq had already given yourselves over to thoughts of death. The two of you were too valuable to lose over a lovers' quarrel."

He held out his bowl for more stew.

"Imagine my distress at discovering that Taqtaloq had not embarked at all, but had gone in search of you. When I told him where you were, and how you came to be there, he set off running. I could not keep up, but I remained close enough to see his leap from the cliffs, and his rescue."

The chief leaned forward. "I had no hopes beyond keeping you both alive. But once again, Mouse, you have proven yourself useful – very useful. Show me the necklace."

Slowly, I drew it out of my pocket. The chief ran his fingers over the symbols, exulting at the number of new allies.

"Where will you send it now?" I asked.

"To the people of the broken speech, along with the rest of the slaves."

I held my breath, afraid he would send me to their lands, to recruit more allies. It would be unending, this war. I no longer wished to be its instrument.

There was one other very important reason why I did not wish to go.

"Taqtaloq tells me you will welcome a child in the frost fish moon. We both know how important this child is to him. You must not risk another journey."

He had seen my fear, and had moved to soothe it. Was ever a chief so wise? I felt safe knowing our lives were in his hands.

*i*t was the end of Wikumkewiku's, mating call moon, when the fruit was gathered in. It would not be long now before the first of the gales began. The heat was heavy and brooding, the rains held back by an unseen hand. We watched the sea with uneasy eyes. Out there, a great beast lurked just beneath the surface of the waves, ready to whip the ocean to a frenzy with a single lash of its tail.

The wind began in the tops of the trees, lazily at first, then with growing force. No one wished to remain in the wikuoms. Children in one arm and cooking pots in the other, the people converged upon the council fire. Perched on high ground, in the shelter of a great, overhanging rock, it offered sure protection from the coming storm. It was there we huddled, waiting for it to crash over us.

The rain began toward evening. Those who had not sought shelter in time approached with chattering teeth, seeking the warmth of the fire. Beyond the shore, we could hear the ocean roaring. The beast was hungry, eager to have us.

I thought of Charles, who just yesterday had led a small flotilla of chaloupes to the bird islands, in search of meat for the voyage home. Would they know enough to seek shelter, these Frenchmen? Antoine, at least, was safe among us. Across the flames, I saw him wrapping his cloak around two of the smallest children. He gave me a cheerful smile, wide enough to take in the whole crowd.

"It's true the waters are rising," he said, his voice louder than usual. "But never again will they cover the earth, as they once did. The Creator has promised it."

We sat up: a story. Smiling his gratitude, the chief leaned forward. The others followed his lead, as he knew they would.

"It was just after men began to walk upon the earth that daughters were born to them. And so beautiful were they, these daughters of men, that the sons of God took them to wife. Their children became known as the Nephilim."

"What does Nephilim mean, Father Antoine?" asked a voice in the crowd.

Antoine paused for a moment.

"It means 'giants ... warrior giants.' And though no man could equal them in size and strength, their hearts were wicked. This grieved the Creator, who could not bear to see such wickedness upon the earth. So he sought out the one righteous man who remained and ordered him to build a ship. On it, he put two of every animal on the earth. Then on the day the ship was complete and the animals safely inside, the Creator called forth the floodwaters. The seas rose, and the giants...."

"We know, we know," Muine'j broke in. "The Creator turned the evil giants into fish. That part of the story we have heard many times before. But this is the first time we hear of the boat and the animals. Tell us, how did he fit them all in? Did he shrink, make them small, as they did with the boy who shrank to the size of a nut?"

Antoine shook his head, as if to clear it. "Where have you heard this story before, Muine'j? Has a fisherman told it to you?"

The chief broke in. "Forgive my son, Father Antoine. But it is a story we know well, from the Long Ago. Once Kluskap had defeated the giants, he stomped on the ground, so that foaming water rushed down from the mountains. The giants became great fish, who even today bear a great band around their neck, like the wampum collars they once wore as men."

A familiar look, patient but resolute, appeared on Antoine's face. "It is not the same story."

The chief raised an eyebrow.

"Was evil not defeated by the Creator's action?"

"Yes, but...."

"And was the race of giants never more seen upon the land?"

"True again, and yet...."

The chief leaned back. "Then I do not see the difference. True, Bright Eyes never spoke of a boat. But it is equally true that a single tale can have many versions."

The frustration on Antoine's face fled before a dawning idea. "The difference is the choice that lies before us tonight," he said, bending an ear to the roar of rushing waters. For a moment, all of us were alert to the waves pounding against the shore.

Antoine's voice drew us back to the comforting circle around the fire.

"In those days...."

He hesitated, then seemed to come to a decision.

"In the Long Ago, there were many who remained outside, mocking those within the vessel. For as long as the waters remain within bounds, it is foolishness to exchange the freedom of the world for the confines of a small boat. But, when the waters rise, none can match its comfort, for it is a vessel built to withstand even the roughest seas."

That night I slept sitting, my head on Taqtaloq's shoulder, and dreamed that I rode a small vessel through a turbulent ocean. Before me stretched a row of waves, each larger than the one before. An unseen hand kept my boat heading into the waves, rising easily on the crest, then dipping lightly into the trough. When I awoke the next morning, my mind was at peace, though my body was stiff and sore.

Taqtaloq was still asleep, his head bent back against a rock, mouth slightly open. Easing from his side, I walked away from the sleeping crowd, to make my water. As I returned to the fire,

I spotted Antoine at the edge of the cliff. Beyond him, balanced over the waters, stretched the ribbon of colour that so often follows a storm.

Antoine turned to me, his face alight with gladness.

"I forgot to tell you the end of the story, Marie-Ange. The Creator promised that never again would the waves rise to engulf the whole world. And just us your people weave their promises into the wampum, he sent us the rainbow – a treaty written in the sky – as proof of his promise."

Looking down toward the shore, I saw another reason for his joy. There, on the swollen seas, a tiny flotilla of chaloupes was bobbing on the waves. A bright flash of red made me turn to Antoine in relief. He, in turn, gave a single whoop of laughter, then turning his back on the shore, he flapped his hand at me, in the same gesture he used to hurry the children along.

"Go wake your husband, Marie-Ange. I'll make breakfast."

I was turning to obey when a thought made me stop and turn around.

"You have said, Antoine, that our Lord once walked upon the earth. What kind of man was he?"

The smile was back, deeper and more tender.

"Can you not guess? He was a storyteller."

k

*j*ust as it was in the morning of their friendship, Antoine and Ku'ku'kwes spent their days discussing ancient remedies.

"She has a great gift," says Antoine. "From broken skulls to wasting sickness, nothing is beyond her powers. I have been honoured to learn at her side. The cures will be useful to me in Canada."

There it was. He was leaving.

I could barely croak out the question: "When?"

"Charles sails in a week. He plans to spend the winter in Quebec. From there, I can join a party travelling to Huronia."

I sat back relieved: Charles would use every ruse to keep Antoine from travelling on, for this winter at least.

"Charles will not take you to Canada, Antoine."

"It is true that he is angry with me at present, but I can persuade him."

"You cannot."

Antoine leaned closer, fixing my gaze in his.

"Tell me what you know."

And though I wished above all things for Antoine to remain in Cibou, I could not withstand the appeal in his eyes.

"Antoine, what does it mean: a 'martyr's fate'?"

He was too late to hide his laughter. I could see the spark of it, deep in the blue of his eyes, before he firmly snuffed it out and turned to me solemnly.

"It means to die for the Lord." The voice grew soft with awe. "A fine thing is it not?"

My hand flew to my belly.

"But you said He gave his life for us, once for all, so we might live and not die."

This time, his laugh broke all bounds and roared between us.

"Marie-Ange. How do you love Taqtaloq?"

"With my life!"

"You would not count it a mean thing to die for him?"

"I would count it an honour."

"And do you remember what it was like, before Taqtaloq, when there was nothing in your life worth dying for?"

My mind slipped back to the days after Charles had left, taking my mother with him. Bright Eyes was dead, Antoine a bitter draught, and I myself no more than a shadow, as I stood watching the four bodies swinging in the trees.

And then I remembered the time Charles had to clasp me around the waist to keep me from joining my husband in the waves.

"You see, Marie-Ange, it is not my death that Charles cannot bear. It is my love."

And I understood.

k

"*L*et me take that."

Pierrot hefted the kettle I was carrying to the fort.

"What's a little mouse doing, carrying a heavy thing like this? You must save your strength to build your nest."

The young Frenchman cast a sideways look at me, seeking a response. I said nothing. He tried again.

"First time I saw you, you were a little girl. Now look at you, a wife, busy about a woman's business." Again, he looked at me ... expectantly.

"I guess you'll be going out less and less now, what with winter coming on."

I could resist it no more, and bent over at the waist, laughing as I had not laughed in years, perhaps ever. I laughed until the tears came to my eyes. I laughed until I choked. And the more I laughed, the more dignified Pierrot became.

"I can't see why you're laughing. I said naught that's amusing."

My laughter had left me with hiccups, but I managed to sputter out the words.

"Are you asking, Pierrot, if I carry Taqtaloq's child?"

Pierrot grew red, a phenomenon I always witnessed with delight. The sight set me off again.

"I think that French women must hide more than their legs beneath those skirts," I hiccupped. Then a wicked impulse overtook me. Stretching the thin robe tightly against my stomach, I gestured to the small solid, bump. "You see, he is just now beginning to show himself to the world."

Embarrassed, Pierrot quickly turned his head to gaze at the fortress tower, where a French flag hung listless in the dying days of summer. Then, succumbing to the temptation, he stole another look.

"I have been searching for you beloved."

Pierrot grew white at the sound of the male voice, speaking in our language. It was fascinating to watch him change colour in this way.

"I have been showing Pierrot our child."

"Yes, I see. What is it that distresses him so?" Taqtaloq possessed our chief's gift of revealing nothing by his expression. Pierrot grew whiter still as my husband looked him over.

A sudden smile broke Taqtaloq's face. Turning to me, he asked, "It is the one who saved my life, is it not?"

Not waiting for an answer, he clasped Pierrot in his arms, holding him close for a long moment. Then, looking into the Frenchman's eyes, he nodded twice before turning on his heel. I caught a single glimpse of Pierrot's terrified face before turning to follow my husband. I laughed all the way home.

It took courage to stand there, foot upon the gangplank. This, I promised myself, would be the last time I trod these boards. He was there, upon the deck, red cape flapping in the wind. I could hear the sound of it as I climbed. And it brought to mind the other sound I had always associated with Charles: the sound of laughter. It had been months since I had heard that laughter, and I found myself wanting to hear it again, one more time.

The last time I saw him, he had humbled himself before me. Had I not humiliated him by flying from his presence, things might have different between us now. But I could see that his heart had hardened once more. The face was grim as it looked down upon me. Two deep lines had engraved themselves around the mouth, lines that had not been there before.

His eyes flew to my stomach, then just as quickly returned to my face. Someone had told him. Pierrot? No, too kind-hearted. Someone else then. Johann?

I forced myself to begin.

"You have not been to see Antoine."

"I have been occupied here."

"I remember a time when nothing could keep you from your brother."

"That time is over."

"He wishes to join you on the voyage to Canada."

"Then he wishes for too much."

Charles leaned against the rail. "You surprise me, Marie-Ange. You all seemed so happy in your little triumvirate. And now you want Antoine to leave? Our fishermen have a saying: only two will fit comfortably into a crow's nest. Perhaps Antoine's presence is too tight a squeeze."

The face shaped itself into a sneer. "What is it ... three times now that I've seen you trembling before me on these boards? The priest and the husband are careful to keep you from me on most occasions – except of course when there is a favour to ask. Are they not bold enough to ask it for themselves?"

Charles's eyes fixed on mine, seeking a response. I would not give him one.

"Lord, woman, is there nothing that will shake you? You are a pair, you and my brother: no matter how many volleys I shoot across your bow, I still cannot draw your fire. And yet, with you

Susan Young de Biagi

at least, I know the fire is there, buried deep inside. You have forgotten, perhaps, the times I held that flame in my hands."

I had not forgotten.

"As for my brother, he's probably lying on his bed even now, trying to convince himself that the death of his dreams is the will of God."

"You have the power to make those dreams live again."

Charles wiped a hand across his brow.

"What difference does it make if I leave him behind? He can save as many souls here as there. And he's far less likely to end up in the fire. From what I've seen, Marie-Ange, your people don't roast Frenchmen alive, eating their hearts while they yet beat. Except perhaps, for the one small girl who has fed on mine."

It was time, I knew, to end this hostility between us. Reaching out my hand, I seized his fingertips in mine. He was surprised, but did not draw away.

"Do you remember, Charles, when you explained to me about sailing in the shadow of the sun?"

"We two," I said, measuring the distance between us, "are fated to draw never closer, never farther apart. And yet, it is a comfort for me to know there is one who rides upon the ocean, forever tracing a path between the known and the unknown."

Charles looked down at our locked hands. "And what of he who rides the waves? Will you not pity his lonely fate?"

"Does one pity the sun? No, it is too far above us. A little mouse may run in its shadow, but she can never truly go where it goes. You know it is true, Charles."

The black head nodded. I felt, with amazement, the tears upon my hand, then saw him fumbling in his pocket. I guessed he was looking for a handkerchief, until I saw the flash of steel. I had no time to draw back before he reached up and cut off a lock of my hair. I remembered another time, when his sword had lashed out to strike a flower above my head. Our whole history had been lived between those two moments. And now, suddenly, it was over.

Charles looked at me one last time. "Tell my brother to come to me. Go quickly, there isn't much time." As I raced down the gangplank, I heard him calling to a sailor. Together, the two scaled to the very top of the rigging. From where I stood, I could clearly see his red cape ... and hear his laughter boom across the water.

I ran to the fort as fast as I could, breaking in upon a startled Antoine, who just finishing his evening prayers.

"Go to him Antoine. He will take you."

"Sit and compose yourself, Marie-Ange. You will harm the child."

"I have spoken to him," I said, between breaths. "He will take you on the voyage. But you must go quickly. I will help you prepare."

Antoine sat down hard on his bunk. It was all happening too fast for him.

"When does he sail?"

"I know not. But you must be on board, in case he changes his mind."

"What of Timothé? I must bid him farewell."

"I will send him to the ship tomorrow, at sunrise. Come Antoine."

"No, no," he said, shaking his head to clear it. "There were things left unsaid the last time, and the Lord sent me back. This time, I must not be so hasty."

The blue eyes fixed on mine. "Do you wonder, Marie-Ange, why I do not stay here, among you?"

I had never asked him, never asked why he was so willing to leave.

"Long ago, the Lord gave me a vision. I have been given a small, precious store of seeds that must be carefully planted, one by one, over a vast field. One of those seeds was planted in your heart, Marie-Ange. It is only a fragile shoot now, but it will grow."

Antoine turned to me, gripping me by the shoulders. "My life will be short. I will not live to see the harvest. But you will Marie-Ange. You will see: the fields will be white with it. And you will walk among those fields, the pollen clinging to your skirt, your hands dusted with it."

I could not be carried away by the vision, as he was. I knew only that he spoke of his death, and that I was no longer in such a hurry for him to leave.

His fingers tightened their grip.

"Promise me, Marie-Ange, that you will sit at the fireside, telling Muine'j, and all the children who ask, the story about Mali's son and the path to freedom. Promise me you will take my place."

"I cannot Antoine. I have seen you, every day, reading the book, preparing the secret rituals. I know nothing of such things."

Antoine shook his head. "Beyond the cup and the bread and the book, it is the story of the giant, Marie-Ange. I ask only that you tell them the story."

Antoine turned from me and began throwing items into his bag. How small it was, that bag. Yet it had brought him as far as Cibou, and would now carry him far away, to an unknown country.

"You will not return to Cibou."

"No. But know that somewhere out there, I will be sitting at another fireside, telling the same story, perhaps in the same moment as you. Someday, we will walk, you and I, on the banks of a vast, swiftly flowing river, bright as crystal. I promise."

His few possessions packed, Antoine was now anxious to leave. As we stepped from the fort, I turned toward the ship, but he caught my arm. "Go home, Marie-Ange. It is late and Timothé will worry. Pierrot can row me out to the ship. Remember your promise to come in the morning."

Just before dawn, I awoke Taqtaloq and left the wikuom to prepare his tea. As I waited for the hot drink, I peered through the darkness, searching for the green lanterns that always hung on the bow and stern of Charles's ship. Gone! The ship was gone.

"Taqtaloq!"

Together we raced for the shore. Arriving at the water line, we found Pierrot and Johann preparing a chaloupe for the morning catch. Beside a small fire were the remains of their breakfast.

Pierrot's smile was one of relief. "It's good you came. Now I can give you this, and still make it to the banks by dawn."

"This" was a small package, wrapped in skin and handed to Taqtaloq. As my husband turned it over uncertainly in his hands, I turned to Pierrot.

"They left last night, with the tide, the moment Father Antoine was aboard. He was upset, for sure. He made me promise to give this package to your husband as soon as dawn broke. 'Ask Timothé to keep it safe,' he told me, 'for the one who comes after me.' In the meantime, he said, it is yours, to do with what you will."

"For the one who comes after." As I pondered these words, Taqtaloq began unravelling the skins. Inside, he found a thick stack of birchbark, the pieces bound tightly together with sinew. Symbols were scratched onto the bark.

"It's the book of Timothé," said Pierrot, looking over my shoulder. "Father Antoine must have copied it out. You see," he said, finger stabbing toward one cluster of symbols, "there's the word 'Timothé'."

When I translated Pierrot's words to Taqtaloq, he stood for long moments tracing his finger over the symbols.

Pierrot stood behind my shoulder, still staring at the book. "What's this?" he asked, pointing at a second page of markings.

Running his finger beneath the line of symbols, Pierrot spoke the words aloud, in my language: "Grace and peace to you from God the Father and our Lord Jesus Christ." I jumped. Although the words sounded strange in Pierrot's mouth, we could still make them out. Then it was Pierrot's turn to jump, as I repeated the words back to him in French.

"He's translated it! Father Antoine has translated the Holy Scripture."

Taqtaloq and I spent many nights afterward listening as Pierrot read the words from Antoine's book. It was, he explained, a letter written from one friend to another, as the writer embarked on a long and perilous journey.

There were many times when Pierrot stumbled over the sounds in our language, so that we had to guess the word from those around it. Our friend was amazed that we were able to repeat long passages back to him. But so it has always been among our people. It is only the French who have entrusted their memory to books, and lost it in the process.

At night upon our boughs, we helped one another remember the words.

Taqtaloq raised himself on one arm. "These words disturb me, beloved. For it is Kitpu's voice I hear. And I fear for him'."

I wondered: should I tell him of Antoine's eagerness to pour himself out upon the ground, to serve as a resting place for the Creator's foot, to be culled before the harvest?

No, I could not tell him. And so instead, I gave him the comfort of my arms.

*i*t was almost time to move into the forest. Slower and heavier, I knew I would not be able to walk the whole way, and hated the thought of being pulled in the sled. Flakes of snow were already falling on our supplies, tightly bundled in skins. I too was bundled into the sled, feeling just like one of the fat packages. Taqtaloq strapped the harness to his shoulders and we set off.

I thought, as we bumped along, this was the second time Taqtaloq was burdened with a heavily pregnant wife. The memory of Mimikej's complaints made me keep my feelings of frustration to myself. But such gloomy thoughts, I knew, would make me a heavier burden. By lightening my mind, perhaps I could lighten my body as well.

In my mind, I saw myself as a butterfly, but my wings soon became weighted down with snow, and I settled heavily on the sled once more. On my second attempt, I became a merlin, soaring high above the tips of the pines. Far below, Taqtaloq was following the course of the river – a small figure beside a line of tumbling blue. With the merlin's all-seeing eye, I kept scanning the line of the river. But I could see no danger on this fine, white day.

The sled stopped. I fell to earth with a bump. Raising a finger to his lips, Taqtaloq pointed to something in the trees. Looking up, I felt the hairs rise on the back of my neck. The creature's quills also rose, as if in response.

The porcupine, Mateus in our language, is found in every land along this coast, among every people known to us – except the land of Cibou. Our women have long coveted him for his armour, which they fashion into quill boxes. I myself was not adept in the art, but my mother would sit for long hours, patiently threading the quills through the bark. She, like all our women, always yearned for more of the rare quills.

In the Long Ago, said Bright Eyes, hunters would capture a mating pair, and bring them to our island. But always they died, longing for their remembered home. In spite of our best efforts, no kits were ever born in Cibou.

Yet here, in the trajectory of my husband's finger, stood a full grown male. Taqtaloq knew, as I did, that he could not be real. We wondered what his presence signified as he swayed overhead, passing from branch to branch. Quickly, we stepped off the path. It would not do to have him cross in front of us.

We stood watching as he lowered himself to the ground and lumbered into the woods. Nodding to me, Taqtaloq bent his back once more to the burden.

That night, around the common fire, Taqtaloq told the others of the visitation.

"He appeared to our people twice before," said Ku'ku'kwes. "The first time that Matues appeared, a great wave broke upon our village, sweeping many out to sea. The broken sandbar is a shattered reminder of that day."

"He came again once more, during the starving time," she added. "The boy, Me'situkwiek, climbed a tree in pursuit of him, and as he did so, he saw a great herd of elk approaching."

"Ah!" breathed the crowd, in one voice. We had all heard the story of this child, whose race to tell the hunters had saved our people from starvation.

"So it could be a good omen or a bad," the chief pondered.

Ku'ku'kwes nodded. "He appears at times of great import, good or evil."

"Does it matter to whom he appears?" asked Muine'j.

The old woman turned surprised eyes upon the chief's son. Not even she had considered this question. As always, we marvelled at Muine'j's clever mind.

"Let me think," said the old woman. "On the day of the wave, he appeared to E'se'ket. The man and his family spent the whole of that day searching for him, so they were on high ground when the wave hit – the only family to escape death entirely. But the young boy who saw the elk ran so hard to tell the hunters that his heart burst, and he died that night."

All eyes turned to my husband and me. I felt their thoughts. If Ku'ku'kwes's memory was correct, bad news was good for the messenger. But good news could mean death.

Taqtaloq and I looked at each other. Whatever the future held, we would face it together.

*

i sat up in the darkness, convinced I had heard Ku'ku'kwes's voice. Beside me, Taqtaloq reached out a soothing hand.

"Go back to sleep," he whispered drowsily. "It is not yet time to set out."

Relieved it was only a dream, I lay down with my back to him, seeking his dark warmth. He curled his knees into the back of my legs, and laid one hand gently on my belly. I closed my eyes.

"It is for the animals themselves to tell us."

This time, the dream held and I found myself standing in a deep forest. Waddling toward me was Mateus.

"You are the one known as Mouse, of the animal blood." Though male, his voice was that of Ku'ku'kwes.

I nodded.

"Then you know the animals are loathe to offer themselves to your hunters. Each year you will see them dwindle, as will your children, as will your children's children. But while it is true that one pact has been broken, another has been established, this one written in blood."

As he spoke, the quills parted to reveal his tender under-belly. I saw he had been mortally wounded, and that behind him was a trail of blood.

"Go and tell them, 'If you follow me, I will heal your land.' Tell them, too, that they – the people of Cibou – are my first fruits in this vast country."

The light was already fading from the black eyes, but the voice held on.

"They must know that if they follow me, they will pay for it – in blood. Their tears will last a thousand years. But let them know, it is through them that I will heal this land."

The thick body collapsed before me, shrinking before my eyes until there was nothing left but quills. From a great distance, I heard the voice calling, "Tell them, tell them."

As I opened my eyes, I saw above me – in the faint light of dawn – Taqtaloq's concerned face. And as the memory of the dream came back to me, I suddenly knew the import of Matues's visit: tragedy ... and blessing.

k

"**Y**ou must tell them."

"Tell them what? That a porcupine has come to lead them? And that their blood will flow for a thousand years?" Already I was beginning to doubt the dream.

Taqtaloq shoved a gourdfull of soup into my hand. "Eat. You are bad-tempered when you don't eat."

Reaching out a hand to my mouth, he tipped the gourd until I was forced to take a sip. "You have only to continue the task begun by Kitpu. Tell them of the promise, written in blood. Tell them of Ma'li's son."

"Why me?"

"Because you are the storyteller."

"I am not the storyteller."

"But you will be. Kitpu has prophesied it."

"No, Taqtaloq. Do not ask it of me. I do not possess the skill."

"If not you, Marie-Ange, then who? It is time to take your rightful place among us. Bright Eyes would say the same."

And rising, he stepped into the wikuom, leaving me alone with my doubts and my fear.

*h*e was born before the tent poles were raised. As I laboured, Ku'ku'kwes sat rubbing my back, chanting secret words I did not understand, but which I found soothing. Like the voice of the wind or the river, there was no need to find meaning in it.

Most mothers, I am told, examine their son's hands and feet, to ensure they are whole and complete. But I sought out my son's eyes, plunging with relief into their brown depths. The child looked back at me, steady and unblinking. It was as Antoine had said all along: I was indeed gazing into a human soul.

We could not stop looking at him, Taqtaloq and I. That night in our wikuom, I suddenly reminded Taqtaloq of the prophecy surrounding his firstborn. But Taqtaloq did not react as I expected. Stroking the soft, new skin of the baby's earlobe, he turned to me smiling.

"It was a foolish fancy. This child's future is his own, to shape as he chooses."

But watching them sleep, the newborn already tucking his hand under his chin in the same way as his father, I knew his was no ordinary fate.

*M*y son's basket a comforting weight on my back, I set out early the next morning to seek the good moss I needed to fill the spaces between his legs. I smiled as I remembered Antoine's surprise at seeing this custom for the first time.

"Have your women no cloth to wrap between the child's legs, to catch their water?" Antoine had asked.

Not for the first time, I had asked myself why the French would keep a man in such ignorance, by forbidding him a wife. So wise in many ways, in others Antoine knew even less than our children.

As with children, I had found it was sometimes best to lay out a path of questions that Antoine could follow to understanding. It was in this way he came to understand the logic of our ways.

"With French children, how long is it before this cloth is wet again?" I had asked.

"Almost immediately, I expect. They replace it, of course, once it grows sodden."

A vision arose of small legs chafed red by wet cloth. "Why not let the water seep harmlessly into moss? And is there not an abundance of it here?"

In time, of course, Antoine had come to accept our ways. He also grew skilled in the care of even the tiniest babies. Many times I saw him striding through the forest, an orphan on his back, eyes alert to the best sources of moss. And as he walked, he would sing of the little bird who followed the star to the birthplace of his king – the same noel I now sang to my son.

The chief was sitting at my fireside when I returned, drinking some of my good broth. He received my child with the ease of long practice, fitting the small, fine head snugly into his elbow.

"I see he has ordinary eyes."

"There is nothing ordinary about him."

The chief reeled back in shock, then burst into laughter. "So, you are no longer the little mouse I once knew. It was the same with my wife when she bore Muine'j: the circle round our son was prowled by a she-lynx. Even I had to approach with caution." The chief smiled in memory. "A danger I relished."

A rueful look stole over the chief's face. "I was wrong about you, Mouse. When I saw how our people had rejected you, I thought there could never be a place for you in Cibou. So when Father Antoine chose you from among all those on the beach that first morning, I thought.... Ah well, I was mistaken. And I have since come to see that your place is here, among us. This child confirms it."

I was still pondering the chief's words when Taqtaloq returned from the river, droplets shining on his hair and shoulders. He dropped down to my side, watching as I prepared to nurse our child. Taqtaloq laughed at the loud, hungry grunts the baby made as he sucked. So amused was I to see him smacking tiny lips that I did not at first catch his father's words.

"You are not listening, Marie-Ange. I asked you, what shall we name our son."

I looked at him open-mouthed. Among our people, first-born sons were named after their fathers. Already, I thought of mine as Taqtaloqchis.

Still chuckling, Taqtaloq reached up to gently pinch my lips together. "We have not been together long, you and I, but already we have broken many traditions. Let this be another."

I could not wrap my mind around such a thought. Seeing my stupefaction, Taqtaloq prodded me gently with his foot. "Since you seem to have no names to propose, perhaps you would like to hear mine."

I nodded dumbly.

"But first you may want to know the reason," Taqtaloq continued, passionately now. "It is simply this: I want to make sure the sound of his name is never forgotten among our people."

And so it was that our son came to be called Antoine Daniel.

*

"*M*arie-Ange!"

I was already at the door of our wikuom when I awoke to the sound of my own name. Taqtaloq's hands were upon me, but I could see nothing beyond the blanket of my own hair.

Taqtaloq swept the locks from my face, then guided me back toward our boughs. "What is it my love?"

The memory of the dream came back in a flood. "I saw Antoine. It was like the night of the attack, with the enemy brooding in the darkness. I could smell their foul breath, but Antoine was unaware of their presence. He was standing before a group of people, folding the cloth with the flowers – you know the one Taqtaloq – and putting the cup back in its box. When the shrieking began, he ran outside, shouting words of encouragement to those around them, telling them to flee. But some were too old to run. To them, he called out, 'Brothers and sisters, today we shall meet in paradise.' And holding aloft a black cross, he ran toward his attackers. And they cut him down. Oh Taqtaloq. They cut him down."

Taqtaloq did not tell me, as I had hoped, that it was only a dream. Instead, he bowed his head. And in the darkness, I felt his tears splash onto my hands. I could not comfort him, for the worst was yet to come. And somehow, he knew it.

"Tell me the rest, Marie-Ange. I will not let you bear this burden alone."

I was barely able to form the words. "He was eaten, beloved: pieces of flesh cut then and there from his body."

"For his courage," whispered the warrior at my side.

And there we sat, barely able to believe that the one we had so loved was gone. At first we simply held each other. But as the hours passed, the need to speak of him consumed us.

I recalled that first day, when the blue-eyed one had singled me out, throwing me a bag to carry. Taqtaloq's own eyes were tender as I spoke of the hours spent sewing Antoine's moccasins, waiting for an offer that never came.

My husband remembered a night spent leaning on his spear, guarding the frozen bodies: one hand fell across his shoulders, while the other passed him a steaming gourd. We both remembered the nights over the fire, when Antoine told us the stories of his God.

"It is over his broken body that they escape to freedom," I whispered. Like his Master, he too had given his body so that others might live. And I understood why, every morning of his life, Antoine broke the bread and drank the wine. The sacrifice of one life for another is a thing that must never be forgotten.

Later that night, Taqtaloq asleep at my side, I suddenly remembered Charles. The worst had happened: with the loss of his brother, he was now most truly alone. Putting my arm around my sleeping husband and son, I lay awake, wide-eyed, for the rest of that night.

ʞ

*t*here was nothing to do but go on. The nights had grown longer, and the mountains were heavy with snow. It was the time when dreams were woven into tales. But there was one dream, I knew, that could never be told, for old Ku'ku'kwes would not survive the shock of Antoine's death. It was a painful secret to keep: I fussed over our son and Taqtaloq busied himself with his tools whenever people spoke of him. And they spoke of him often, especially Muine'j, who missed his stories. The boy's hard mind needed a tale upon which to sharpen itself.

The drummers did their best to make up for Antoine's absence, often playing long into the night. On one such night, Taqtaloq gathered our son into his arms, leaving me free to polish my beads. As I sat rolling the tiny shells between my hands, I could feel that the people were restless, and Muine'j most restless of all.

It was he who began the chant, soon taken up by the whole crowd. "Ma'li, Ma'li." Raising my head from my beads, I saw that every eye was upon me, waiting. Muine'j had already thought of his first hard question, and could barely wait to pose it. Taqtaloq sat grinning beside him, teeth white in the darkness. And suddenly, I felt the Master's foot upon me, testing, to see if I would hold. Before I could reach for the first line of the story, it was eagerly supplied by Ku'ku'kwes, the old eyes shining with delight.

"Jesus had a grandmother. Her name was Ann."

And in that moment, I found my voice.

References and glossary

Mi'kma'ki is the territory of the Mi'kmaq of Maritime Canada, encompassing what is now Gaspé, New Brunswick, Prince Edward Island, Nova Scotia (including Cape Breton) and much of the State of Maine.

Amassit – silly, foolish

apukji'j – mouse

apjelmit – can't stop laughing

apli'kmuj – rabbit

Beothuk – Aboriginal people of pre-contact Newfoundland, now extinct.

Cibou – from the Mi'kmaq sipu, river. One of the so-called Bird Islands, off Cape Breton's Cape Dauphin, is known as Ciboux. In the novel, Cibou is the name given the territory of a fictitious semi-nomadic Mi'kmaw community.

elmniket – carries a load on his shoulder

e'se'ket – digs for clams

eune'k – foggy

Huronia – central Ontario

jakej – lobster

jijiwikate'j – sandpiper

jipjawej – robin

kalkunawey – hardtack; biscuit

ka'qaquj – crow

kawi – porcupine quill

keknu'teluatl – shoots accurately

Keptin – Captain

kesasek – shiny, luminous, bright

Kisu'lk – the Creator

kitpu – eagle

kloqntiej – seagull

Kluskap – the first human, was created out of a bolt of lightning in the sand and remains a figure that appears in many of the Mi'kmaw legends.

ko'komin – thornberry

ku'ku'kwes – night owl

lentuk – deer

maskwi – white birch tree

matues – porcupine

me'situkwiet – unable to wake up

mimikej – butterfly

muine'j – bear cub

Niskam – the sun

Nukumi – Kluskap's grandmother

sespewo'kwet – talk on and on

siklati – dogfish

sismoqn – sugar

Siwkwewiku's – spawning moon

snaweyey – sugar maple

su'nl – cranberries

taqtaloq – salamander

waltes – an indigenous game of chance consisting of a wooden bowl carved from the burl of a tree. It also has wooden sticks (for counting) and bone (as dice).

Wikewiku's – animal fattening moon

Wikumkewiku's – moose calling moon

wikuoms – family/group shelters

European references

Baleine: King James I encouraged settlement in the colonies. Sir William Alexander, then Royal Secretary for Scotland, was an early promoter of colonization and the first attempts at Scottish settlement included Charles Fort, at Port Royal, on mainland Nova Scotia, and Rosemar, at Baleine, Cape Breton. These settlements were short-lived. French Captain Charles Daniel, of the Compagnie des Cent-Associés, sailed in and attacked the fort. According to the French, they found Sir James Stewart, Lord Ochiltree, on French territory extorting payments from law-abiding fishermen. The French captured Baleine and forced the inhabitants to help build the French fort at St. Ann's, Cape Breton. Later, most of the Scots were returned to Scotland. The area known as Nova Scotia was ceded by treaty to France.

Chaloupe: small single-sail boat used by the French for fishing and transport closer to shore.

de Champlain, Samuel, with the intention of founding a settlement in Acadia, established a settlement at Port Royal, adjacent to the present Annapolis, Nova Scotia.

Daniel, Fr. Antoine, Jesuit missionary, was first stationed in Cape Breton in the first half of the 17th century. Daniel was later posted to Huronia where he met a violent end and martyrdom as Saint Anthony Daniel.

Daniel, Captain Charles, established a French trading post in early 17th-century Cape Breton.

Lescarbot, Marc, based at Port-Royal, travelled widely in 17th-century Acadia. His insights were set down in several published works, most notably his *Histoire de la Nouvelle-France* (1609).

Stewart, Sir James (Lord Ochiltree), along with sixty Scots, established Rosemar, at Baleine, Cape Breton.

de la Tour, Charles de Saint-Étienne, Governor of Acadia.

Sources

Editor's note: Where possible, Mi'kmaw spellings conform to the Smith Francis orthography, which has been adopted officially by Mi'kmaw Kina'matnewey, the Mi'kmaw education authority for Nova Scotia.

- References to the Kluskap traditions, including Kisu'lk, the Creator; Nukumi, Kluskap's grandmother; Netaoansom, his nephew; Kitpu, (eagle) the messenger from the Creator:

  In "Mi'Kmaq Knowledge in the Mi'Kmaq Creation Story: Lasting Words and Deeds," written in 1977, Stephen A. Augustine provides a comprehensive overview of the Kluskap traditions. These traditions were passed down to him from Augustine's grandmother, Agnes (Thomas) Augustine, who heard them from her husband Thomas Theophile Augustine, otherwise known as "Basil Tom." The writer also relied on information provided by his great-grandmother Isabel (Augustine) Simon, in a long-standing family tradition. This is recommended reading for anyone interested in Mi'kmaw spiritual beliefs.

- "He Who Travels by Night"

  In his book, *Maliseet/Micmac. First Nations of the Maritimes*, Robert M. Leavitt discusses how nouns in English will often appear as verbs in the Mi'kmaq and Maliseet languages. In Maliseet, "moon" can be translated as "Walks at Night."

- "Do you ... do you think he saves all his body wastes in this way?"

  Circa 1677, Father Chretien LeClercq wrote, "[The Mi'kmaq] find the use of our handkerchiefs ridiculous; they mock at us and say that it is placing our excrements in our pockets."

- "Do you know how this sweet gift came to us?"

  This tale, known to Algonqian-speaking peoples as the Legend of Glooscap, is well-known in many First Nations communities in Canada and the United States.

Susan Young de Biagi

- "Antoine and I sat and watched each group covet the possessions of the other."

  In his book, *The Mi'kmaq: Resistance, Accommodation, and Cultural Survival*, Harald Prins explains that Europeans and First Nations recognized the value of each other's possessions, even when their original owners did not. To Europeans, beads were simply trinkets, whereas First Nations were astonished that the Europeans wanted their old robes. Seventeenth-century explorer Nicholas Denys spoke of "their old robes of Moose skin, which are greasy and better than new." [Quoted in *The Historical Ethnography of the Micmac of the Sixteenth and Seventeenth Centuries* by Bernard Gilbert Hoffman.]

- "Once," I told him triumphantly, "Kluskap served a whole village from a single birchbark dish. Fifty hunters and their families ate from this dish, and still there was food left over." Antoine seemed startled at this story. He opened his mouth to speak, but another voice forestalled him.

  Related by Robert M. Leavitt in *First Nations of the Maritimes*.

- "Do you know, Mouse, that in our tradition the white lady – a spirit to you – will steal a child away and put a fairy child in its place?"

  The folklore of Normandy and Brittany abounds with tales of a white lady, or *dame blanche*. One of the most famous is the Dame d'Aprigny in Bayeux.

- "Moose are noble creatures, freely offering themselves up to the hunters. They are also proud and touchy, with spirits that linger long after the kill, to ensure their bodies are handled with proper reverence."

  In *The Historical Ethnography of the Micmac of the Sixteenth and Seventeenth Centuries*, Bernard Gilbert Hoffman writes: "According to our historical sources, the bones of moose, beaver, caribou, bear and marten could not be given to the dogs or burned, else the spirits of the animals would report 'to their own kind of the bad treatment they had received among the Indians', and no more would be caught."

  In "Mi'kmaq Knowledge in the Mi'kmaq Creation Story: Lasting Words and Deeds," Stephen A. Augustine states that a hunter will usually place tobacco in the mouth of a moose that has given its life, and the hunter may also burn sweetgrass.

- "Narcissus flower..."

  Quoted from Project Gutenberg's *Ecloges in English*.

- "In one of our tales, a grieving father travels to the Land of the Ancestors to seek his dead son. But when he arrives, he finds that the boy's spirit has shrunken to the size of a nut that the father carries home in a little bag."

  Related by Robert M. Leavitt in *First Nations of the Maritimes*.

- "It came to her in a dream. One night, as she wandered in that other world, she saw a small island floating toward her. On it were tall trees and living beings."

  Legends of the Micmacs by Silas Rand, 1894.

- "Why does a man your size need so tall a house?"
  This sentiment, originally expressed by a Mi'kmaw chief, was recorded by Father Chrétien Le Clercq and cited in *The Mi'kmaq: Resistance, Accommodation, and Cultural Survival*, by Harald Prins.

- "Or the tale of Beaver, who tried to drown our people with his great dam."

  "I myself was eager to hear this tale. In Bright Eyes's version, the channel was carved out during a wild chase, as Beaver fled before Kluskap's wrath."

  This tale has been cited by Robert M. Leavitt in *First Nations of the Maritimes*.

- "The Creator turned the evil giants into fish. That part of the story we have heard many times before. But this is the first time we hear of the boat and the animals."

  This is another famous tale among Algonquin-speaking peoples along the North Atlantic coast. In Howard S. Russel's book, *Indian New England Before the Mayflower*, this tale is called "How Glooscap Fought with the Giant Sorcerers at Saco and Turned Them Into Fish."

Susan Young de Biagi

Acknowledgements

The editors wish to acknowledge the assistance and advice found in the Mi'kmaq Resource Centre and the Mi'kmaq College Institute, at Cape Breton University, and Mi'kmaw Kina'matnewey.

Susan Young de Biagi is originally from Cape Breton and has written and co-written several books as well as writing for multimedia and newspapers. She holds a master's degree in history from the University of New Brunswick. Susan and her family live in Powell River, British Columbia. This is her first novel.